The Barfighter

Also by Ivan G. Goldman

FICTION

Where the Money Is: A Novel of Las Vegas

NON-FICTION

L.A. Secret Police: Inside the LAPD Elite Spy Network
(with Mike Rothmiller)

The
Barfighter

IVAN G. GOLDMAN

THE PERMANENT PRESS
Sag Harbor, NY 11963

For information, address:
The Permanent Press
4170 Noyac Road
Sag Harbor, NY 11963
www.thepermanentpress.com

Library of Congress Cataloging-in-Publication Data

Goldman, Ivan G.
    The barfighter / Ivan G. Goldman.
        p. cm.
    ISBN-13: 978-1-57962-182-7 (alk. paper)
    ISBN-10: 1-57962-182-1 (alk. paper)
        1. Boxers (Sports)—Fiction. 2. Boxing managers—Fiction.
    3. Boxing stories. I. Title.

PS3557.O3686B37 2009
813'.54—dc22   2008041652

Printed in the United States of America.

G

For Connie

Contents

MAY 1984

CHAPTER 1

ANGER CLASS

Barfighters were a minority species in Cheskis's anger management class. Rather than fight each other, most violent men find it safer and more gratifying to assault their wives and children. Class members tiptoed around the facts. Nothing was as serious as the cops made it sound or they were framed altogether. Just now, for example, Muhammad ended his story with another "I swear to you." The phrase ended his sentences like a Canadian "ey." Muhammad was some kind of Pakistani feather merchant, a chubby little man with only a few strands of hair around his head, all of them long and out of place. He'd had a street altercation with a blood enemy that led to the enemy's car windows getting smashed with a club. Muhammad contended the enemy had followed him, broken his own windows, and called police. When he told this sad tale he was terribly convincing. Muhammad could probably borrow money from the most hardened cynic. But Cheskis and doubtless everyone else in the class knew he was a lying sack of shit.

Cheskis often wondered whether the patient Lorraine, their class instructor, had seen the files and knew the precise nature of the deeds that planted pupils in her class. If so, she never gave it away. She never challenged them when they interpreted events like a roomful of verbal cubists. Lorraine was more concerned with their future than their past. Cheskis suspected she was a rare individual, someone truly capable of controlling her own anger. If only she could convey her secret. But few of the class members cared to know it, even though anger had scarred them irretrievably.

Lorraine was in her thirties and slender, like a volleyballer. Slight chest, chin a tad weak, no wedding ring. Her light brown hair was nearly shoulder length and would have looked more attractive, Cheskis concluded, either shorter or longer. She usually wore crisp jeans and blouses and no makeup. Lorraine's voice still had a youthful bell-like quality, which Cheskis found fetching. She smiled most of the time, but not nervously or insincerely. Though inescapably pretty, she still struck him as someone suffering from a mild case of wallfloweritis.

Now the buck passed from Muhammad to Sybil, whose evil mother had stolen Sybil's daughter out of spite. Sybil once mentioned that at some point in their relationship she'd approached her mother's door with an ax but never quite explained what led up to it, where the ax came from, or what happened after she reached the door. Her stories skipped around, creating mysteries. Most of her circular soliloquies evolved back to her mother's scabrous intentions. "She and my aunt (pronounced *ohnt*) turned Chiquita against me. Everybody in the church knew it."

Sybil was Cheskis's only female classmate. Before she started showing up, some of them used to reveal secrets abut themselves, perhaps not the ones that wrenched their hearts in the night, yet digging down far enough to share at least some honest pain with their lost, angry brethren. But Sybil's stream-of-consciousness rants, largely devoid of logical threads, upset the class chemistry and chased away those flashes of candor that might have shed light on the rages that put everyone there. Lorraine hadn't figured out yet how to deal with her. Sybil was fortyish and tubby and dressed as though she were eighteen and slim. Her skin was pure Africa, almost blue. She pronounced English with the precision of Elizabeth Taylor, drove to class in a late-model Mercedes, and was missing two or three upper teeth along the left side of her mouth. Nothing about her made sense. Cheskis was forced to think about Sybil more than he'd like. She was a considerably disordered cog in what was advertised as a mathematically precise universe. Cheskis fought hard to be patient with her. To be angered by a classmate in his anger management class was more irony than he could stand.

Angry people popped in and out of class until they completed thirty-five sessions within the allotted time or met with some misfortune, perhaps getting arrested again for a new angry act that would surely send them to jail this time, or so they'd been warned by the criminal justice system. On some nights enrollees announced it was their thirty-fifth session, but usually when someone disappeared you never knew why. There was an endless stream of replacements, always plenty of fresh doughboys to dump into the trench of their dishonored regiment. Cheskis figured there was enough anger in the world to keep the class going until the end of time.

Usually about a dozen people showed up, meeting every Wednesday night in a seedy, backwater office complex. There was no sign on the door and not a single window in the poorly lighted room, which was no bigger than a one-car garage. The place was about as cheerful as last night's dishes and its hole-in-the-ozone atmosphere was further oppressed by a generalized, palpable shame. Class members were ashamed of their anger, ashamed of getting caught by the cops, or both. And they felt sorry for themselves. Cheskis too. Every night thousands of people all over the world ended up in bar fights, but he was one of the unlucky few arrested for it. Such emotions inspired no camaraderie. Members of the class pushed their chairs back along the wall in a circle to get as far away from the others as possible.

During a fortuitous break in Sybil's monologue, Lorraine, always on the alert for such opportunities, jumped in to steer the discussion back on course. "Is anger," she asked, "ever helpful? Can it have positive benefits?" Sybil, as always, raised her hand. Everyone else, as always, didn't. "What do you think, Marvin?"

Marvin, who wore lots of blue, signifying his status as a Crip gangster in good standing, viewed class proceedings as though he were on a promontory looking down on a distant, inconsequential piece of ground. He projected enormous physical power just sitting there, like an idling diesel. His muscled brown-black arms were crisscrossed with scars and schoolyard tattoos. In response to Lorraine, he shifted his gaze and studied her as though he'd never noticed her presence. After an uncomfortable pause, he said. "Yeah."

"Yes what?" unflummoxed Lorraine said.

13

"Yes, it can be helpful," he said.

"How so?"

"'Cause," interrupted Sybil, "when people are messing with you, you can't just sit there. That's not life." Sybil was ready to pull her oratory train out of the station when Lorraine repeated the question to Marvin.

"Anger can keep you sharp," he replied. "Keep you aware. If you don't get too stupid."

"Martin Luther King didn't get angry," Lorraine said. "He rejected violence. But he won lots of battles." Some class members smiled conspiratorially, silently announcing to the others that this naïve cog in the social-work machine must have her head in Leave It to Beaver-land, but meanwhile they'd just sit there and listen to her fairy tales if that's what it took to stay out of the slammer.

"I don't think anger helps you," volunteered Luis, a neatly dressed young man who in past sessions had made it clear without ever quite saying it that his girlfriend cheated on him in a recurring game that was the focus of both their lives. "It's never helped me. Never." Lorraine nodded compassionately. Cheskis, seeing that the discussion was, for once, bypassing Sybil, said to Lorraine, "May I ask what you think?"

"Of course," she said, "but not if it's a way of bottling up your own thoughts." From Lorraine, this had to be classified as a rebuke.

"I just want to hear your own answer," he said. "Honest."

"I think," Lorraine said, "anger, on rare occasions, can be helpful."

Anger-plagued enrollees cocked their heads to the side like curious spaniels.

"Would you give an example?" Cheskis asked her.

Speaking slowly, she answered, "If your anger is motivated by compassion, it can be a catalyst for positive action. Say when Klansmen murdered four little girls in a church. That made some people angry without making them violent or full of hatred. It created positive energy. But that was an exception. Anger almost always is harmful, particularly to the person experiencing the

14

anger." In every session she found an interval to interject her thesis that anger damages the angry individual more than the target. It even, she sometimes pointed out, contorts people's features, making them resemble beasts. "Losing your temper doubles your punishment," she told them, first with the event that triggered it, "then with the anger itself, eating away at everything that's good in you."

"But when people are doing something to you," Sybil said, "what are you supposed to do?" She'd asked this many times, hoping perhaps, that just once the answer would endorse her right to swing an ax at her mother.

"Alton," Lorraine said, "perhaps you could help us with this one. What's the preferred response when someone is clearly attempting to . . ."

"Mess with us," Sybil said, smiling to herself.

Alton was a tall, stick-figured, Scandinavian-looking fellow in his thirties who clung to the lower rungs of some white-collar enterprise. His clothes always had something just a little wrong. Worn-down heels, a wrinkled jacket, Kmart-looking tie. No one would mistake him for a success. Alton took careful notes and once said vehemently that he just hated it when people lied to him. Cheskis sized him up as a serial wife beater.

Alton picked up his personalized anger folder filled with notes and printed handouts, thumbed through it hastily, then said, "We should count to ten, right?"

"That's what we do when we start to feel angry," Sybil said.

"Right, that's what I said," Alton replied testily.

"Sybil does make a point," Lorraine said congenially. "The question was how best to react when someone is unpleasant to us."

"Isn't that what I just said?" objected the clearly frustrated Alton.

"But someone might not necessarily be angry when someone is unpleasant to them," Lorraine said. "So it's not the same question."

Cheskis, staring at a curve between the buttons in the material of Lorraine's white blouse, spied just a speck of creamy flesh. With a sudden movement she caught his gaze, her smile not wavering as he looked away. "Couldn't there be a difference between reacting to our own anger and reacting to a negative event? Lee, would you care to answer that?"

"I guess if you reacted to a negative event correctly, you wouldn't get angry in the first place," Cheskis said. "So you wouldn't *be* dealing with your anger."

"Precisely," Lorraine said. "Learn to cut your temper off at the pass and you'll actually feel more, not less powerful. Because you'll be in control of your own mind. You don't let some foolish driver or angry partner or inconsiderate boss take over. Your mind belongs to you, and your mind actually works better. Lee, if you don't mind, when you were boxing, did you ever lose your temper in the ring? And if so, were you helped or hurt by it?"

Several sessions ago, when Cheskis had been cornered into talking about the barfight that landed him here, he let it slip that years earlier he'd boxed competitively. Clearly Lorraine, at least, found this information worth retaining. "I don't even remember that far back," he replied.

Lorraine closed her eyes in a long, slow signal of regret. She let Sybil take over again while Cheskis tried to recall how he could have been so stupid as to reveal that piece of his past. But when people are called upon to disclose private thoughts to a group, the discussion wanders into unexpected tributaries. Even dodging questions provides information. At some point someone had asked Cheskis what he hoped for his future, and as he gave a dishonest answer it occurred to him that he hadn't really considered his future in years. His goals were no more insightful than those of the average schmo or schmoe-ette who yearned for a newer automobile, thinner thighs, or some other person, place, or thing to bestow eternal happiness. And it was at that point he mentioned some trivial detail about an opponent he'd faced in college.

After Sybil wasted the remaining minutes, Lorraine took her customary post-session station behind a card table. The students lined up to pay her fifteen dollars each so they could rush to whatever form of freedom awaited them beyond the door.

Cheskis decided this was the night to see Lorraine privately. He'd rehearsed different approaches for weeks, only to walk out defeated. He wanted to speak to her without Sybil or Alton or anyone else around. She always took a little time to assemble all her materials before leaving. Meanwhile, he ducked into the little washroom to check his appearance before the big moment. Not so bad, he decided. But he couldn't pick up even the slightest whiff of that fifty-dollar cologne. The ads for such stuff never mentioned it had to be applied every ten minutes.

When he came out, Lorraine was already gone. So was everyone else except Marvin the Crip. At first Cheskis assumed Marvin was waiting for the toilet and that he might still catch up with Lorraine, but no, Marvin blocked his path. "So you know about fighting," he said. He pronounced the words with a voice as blank as his eyes, bearing down from six foot three at least. Cheskis couldn't recall anyone from the class ever saying anything to him or anyone else before or after a session. No one asked what school you went to or whether you watched the Lakers last night. The avoidance of everyday pleasantries was built into the structure of their fluctuating little group and everyone picked up on it right away. Cheskis was more curious than alarmed, even though your ordinary citizen carefully fashions life in such a way as to never, ever be alone with somebody like Marvin, who was close enough to send off traces of aftershave. Cheskis examined Marvin's precise words. *So you know about fighting.* Was that even a question? "Years and years ago," Cheskis said at last.

"I'm looking for a gym," Marvin said. "For a place to—you know—box."

"You've boxed before?"

"Some."

Marvin had broad, dark-chocolate features. They lacked the sharp lines of an Adonis, but he was a handsome fellow whose blank-nasty eyes were large and intelligent. If he wanted a favor, why didn't he take the edge off his attitude? Besides, what he was asking didn't make sense. Thanks to insurance underwriters and the over-lawyering of America, boxing instruction had been

17

driven from public schools and YMCAs. It survived only in the kind of neighborhood where Marvin must reside—where Police Athletic Leagues and other help-o-crats tried to give indigent, fatherless kids an alternative to streets and gangs. Marvin must know of these gyms, even though he was too old for a kids' program.

"Where did you work out?" Cheskis asked him.

"Gym's not there anymore."

"Looking to turn pro?"

"I just said I wanted to box."

Cheskis could ask Eddie to take a look at him. But an anger classmate would be an embarrassing presence in the gym, *his* gym, soiling it for Cheskis even if no one knew their connection. It took Cheskis a lifetime to find his gym. "I don't know anything about boxing in L.A.," Cheskis said. "I can't help you." He hated Marvin for making him lie and for looking at him like that, making it clear he could see through the lie. Just when Cheskis found the courage to talk to Lorraine, he had to postpone it another whole week because of this classic bully. Cheskis's heart beat faster, his breath came too fast, and he felt it starting. He was pleased he could recall the proper steps. *Assess the situation and examine my beliefs about it.* Well, this person— a threatening person—was probably angry with him. He was probably angry with everyone. *Call a time out.* The formula was failing, but at least he'd managed to roll it out—a small victory. Cheskis surveyed Marvin as he would an opponent—what he might do, what Cheskis might do back—or do first. The game calmed him. *What kind of a dick am I? Fighting makes me calm.*

"That was a nice little story you told, in the class that time," Marvin said.

Cheskis couldn't tell whether Marvin was sincere or playing the dozens—needling him black-man style. He was already weary of trying to interpret the man's vagueness and double meanings. "I'll see you next time," Cheskis said. He stepped forward, forcing Marvin to make a choice. He stepped aside, and Cheskis descended the stairs, making sure not to hurry, which made him even less likely to find Lorraine.

18

Chapter 2

CANNIBALS

The next morning broke windless and overcast. Cheskis stood outside a furniture mover's office with other day laborers while drivers, all Southern white men, made their picks. It was like choosing up sides on a playground, except that the men communicated with nods and barely perceptible murmurs. Several giants and power lifters made the cut first, but Cheskis, looking healthier than most of the competition and younger than his forty-one years, made it onto a crew after about ten minutes. Then he schlepped furniture in and out of buildings for ten hours. It was fast cash—no forms, no deductions, no government. Some economist with a talent for irony had dubbed the arrangement casual labor, which made as much sense as referring to politicians as public servants. Nothing on a moving crew was casual. Everyone limped in with a desperate tale to tell and none of them told it. They were ex-cons, illiterates, IRS or alimony fugitives, men who planned their lives only a few hours or minutes ahead. Most were citizens. Illegals, though prized in other industries for their almost limitless exploitability, were considered poison on a moving crew, where they routinely tracked mud across mattresses, crushed lampshades under book boxes, and committed other acts of mayhem. They had no understanding of the value of American junk.

Cheskis began joining the morning shape-up when he couldn't pay his gas bill. A jolt in county jail the previous winter had made him AWOL from the classroom long enough to cause a problem, and now the department chair at his community college had assigned him to teach only one class. Even so, he no longer entertained, even briefly, the idea of working as a news reporter again. He could no longer bring himself to practice the essence of journalism—asking victims how victimhood felt.

19

Somewhere out there must be an employer who would look past his shredded resume and let him perform an alternate bourgeois undertaking—selling stereos, inventorying toothpaste, entering data. Yet none offered the no-questions-asked existential whimsy of the moving trade, which he didn't have to pretend he liked.

Today it took Cheskis and a wiry African-American with a deep, bronchial cough nearly an hour to finesse a monster hide-a-bed through an impossibly tiny doorway. After only a few minutes Cheskis and his partner decided their task was impossible but knew if they gave up, someone else would come along and figure it out. The demon furniture never gave up trying to spring open and crush their fingers, and when they finally squeezed it into the room they were too drained to feel relief.

Back in his rented patch of Hermosa Beach he turned the TV to a trio of optimists reading news, sports, and weather. Feeling a dozen aches and bruises, he washed down three aspirins with two gulps of scotch to medicate his aching back and his mood. After eating refrigerated odds and ends he threw himself down on the unmade bed, dirty clothes and all. He'd behaved foolishly with both Lorraine and Marvin, succumbing to fear with one and anger with the other. He couldn't trust his mangled instincts. By the time he understood which direction to go, roads washed out from under him.

As he picked at his chicken Caesar salad, surgeon Stu entertained Cheskis and Eddie with tales of his ex-wife, a homely salesclerk he'd married and then, in a series of intricate procedures, carved into a goddess. "Turned out she was screwing one of my partners. And you know what else? The guy's uglier than mud. Next to him I'm fucking Paul Newman. Anyway, when I find out, the rest of us, we buy him out of the partnership. Then when we get a divorce—you'll never guess this—"

"She got alimony," Cheskis said.

"Yeah," said Stu, who studied Cheskis's face as though it were new to him. "Whaddayou do for a living again?"

"I move furniture and teach junior college," Cheskis said.

20

"That's right, a Renaissance man. Anyway, she gets four thousand a month alimony and she and this prick, they have a three-million-dollar house in Beverly Hills. They live next to Burt Reynolds. Can you believe that?"

"What you have to do, mate, is forget her. Go out and build yourself another Sheila," Eddie said.

"Why? I'll never be able to use my johnson again anyway," Stu said. "Not after today."

"It wasn't low," Eddie protested.

"Eddie, you crushed my nuts like they were Ping-Pong balls. If you'd thrown that punch any lower I'd have a broken knee."

"You saw it," Eddie said to Cheskis. "Was it low?"

"It was low, Eddie," Cheskis said. "You hit me low, too. You always hit me low. I'll be singing castrato for weeks." This was a lunch conversation they had every Saturday on the Strand after Eddie closed the gym. Eddie hit low because he was short and because that was Eddie. Near the end of his days in the ring, before he became a trainer, he was known as the dirtiest fighter in the Southern Hemisphere. He was an artist. He could knee you in a nerve that momentarily paralyzed your leg so he could step over and bang you on an ear or an eye or whatever part of your anatomy was tender and vulnerable. He'd been suspended two or three times.

Cheskis, Stu, and a few others formed a special corps of men trained by Eddie who weren't aspiring pros and were too old to compete in the amateurs, though two were cops who competed in police charity tournaments. They all paid gym dues but nothing extra for the personal lessons, compensating Eddie with beers, meals, or whatever special skills they had. They drilled his teeth, handled his legal matters, bought jewelry for his girlfriends. Stu handled the medical needs of Eddie's pros and, like everyone else, made sure Eddie never had to pick up a lunch check.

Eddie had a million stories. Today he told the tale of his last pro bout somewhere in New Guinea. "Same place where the cannibals ate Rockefeller's son," he said. Most of Eddie's stories had this kind of detail, making Cheskis believe they were true, more

21

or less. "For the introductions, a bunch of them, they come into the ring with the bloke I'm fighting. There's this witch doctor with a mask and everything and he's hollering and shaking this spear at me. I grabbed it and broke it over my knee." Eddie demonstrated the act with a phantom spear. "My trainer nearly shit himself, mate. He thought we were going into the soup."

After the officials got everyone calmed down and the fight started, Eddie said, he was already bleeding in the second round. He'd been cut so many times in previous contests that the skin around his eyes was like ancient papyrus. "I'd hurt this bloke a couple times, but I could hardly see and I wasn't going to win on points anyway. They'd have eaten the judges." He earned himself a disqualification for a final low blow in the fourth round, giving his younger opponent something to remember.

Cheskis noticed that many of the customers who paid Eddie for private lessons weren't terribly interested in boxing or working up a sweat. Lonely souls who'd migrated from places like Des Moines and Hong Kong, they wanted to tell Eddie their troubles or perhaps just talk about what they'd seen on TV the night before. How they all found Eddie was a mystery. He was a peculiar choice for the job. No great listener, Eddie invariably steered conversations over to his more interesting self, particularly when his yuppie clients complained about bosses and deadlines. But Eddie had a talent for putting idiosyncratic loners at ease and making them feel privileged to hear his recycled tales of how he'd fought and fornicated across several continents. Eventually he counted out some sit-ups for them and concluded the session by selling them herbs and vitamins that he swore by.

The fees they paid allowed Eddie to keep training his pros, who almost always ended up costing him. Some far-flung acquaintance would send him a fighter from Panama or Ghana or Arkansas. The guy would invariably show up with no proper shoes or gloves, no groin protector, mouthpiece, or handwraps, no *nada*. Eddie supplied their gear, put them up, fed and trained them, washed their dishes, lent them cash, and invariably lost them before he could recoup his investment. They would return to their wives and girlfriends or move on to better-connected handlers, leaving behind enormous phone bills and sometimes walking off with clothes from Eddie's closet. Several years ago one of them borrowed his car for a day in Tijuana and was never seen again.

"What I don't understand is how every one of them shows up without any gear," Eddie said. "They must be using something back home. But they never bring any of it." Friends of Eddie's—other small-time trainers and managers—would come around and tell similar stories. Boxing movies were invariably about managers cheating their fighters. Hollywood never seemed to know about guys like Eddie.

As the cute waitress poured him more coffee on the sun-spattered restaurant patio, Cheskis breathed in the pleasure of that moment. He liked training again after having given it up many years earlier. He liked eating lunch along the ocean with Eddie and Stu. They accepted him as he was, never prying into his past.

Monday morning Cheskis called the generic-sounding Family Counseling Center. He had no idea if Lorraine was there during the day. It was one of the many things he didn't know about her. "I understand you can't give me her number," Cheskis told the woman on the other end of the line. "Just ask her to call me, please." He spelled out his contact information to the person trying so hard to get rid of him. "I'll be here another hour. It's important," he told her, adding, "Please."

All weekend he'd been visualizing how he might proceed, but when the phone rang he felt cornered and clumsy. His voice sounded like someone else's and he couldn't do anything about it. He just raced ahead as though he were reading Lorraine her rights, trying to explain why it was important that he get in touch with Marvin right away, even though he knew it wasn't important to anyone but him because he had an irrational urgency to make things right. She responded pleasantly but with authority. It would be unethical, she explained, to provide personal information on anyone in the class. "I'm sorry, Lee," she said.

"He is coming back, isn't he?" Cheskis said. He thought his voice sounded panicked. "I mean, he hasn't finished up?"

23

"I'm sure you'll see him again," she said. "You shouldn't worry." Cheskis was pleased she didn't want him to worry. He said goodbye fast and slammed down the receiver. But he hadn't steered the conversation away from business. He hadn't asked her out for dinner, or said anything even remotely intelligent or amusing.

He taught his class that afternoon and a student dozed off as Cheskis tried to explain the difference between the active and passive voice. "Don't sleep in my class!" he thundered, startling everyone, including himself. This particular student was a cruel-eyed welfare mom who instinctively reached in her purse for something persuasive as she barked back that she wasn't goddamn sleeping and he ought to stick to goddamn business, goddamn him.

CHAPTER 3

A NATURAL

"Look here, mate," Eddie said. "When you go into a McDonald's and order a hamburger, do you ask if you can pay next week?" He waited for an answer from the husky Latin who stood at Eddie's desk with his gym bag. The desk, situated next to the door, helped Eddie waylay deadbeats before they penetrated his inner sanctum.

The kid mumbled something.

"What was that?"

"No," admitted the kid. Cheskis, who'd just entered the gym with Marvin, tried to move around the spectacle. But Eddie told them to wait and turned back to the kid. "What about the gas station? You pull in and say you'll pay them later?"

"No," said the kid, drooping all over like a teardrop.

"Try the electric company, too. Ask them to carry you. See what happens."

The kid nodded sorrowful agreement. As he turned to go, Eddie held up an index finger. "Last time, mate. Last time. You can train today, but don't come back without those dues."

"Thanks, Eddie."

"And I don't want to see you dropping your right, understand? You look like a faggot on wheels out there."

The kid nodded sorrowfully, winked at Cheskis, and moved toward the rear of the gym. Cheskis had already told Eddie about Marvin. Eddie appraised him, then stuck out his hand. "Eddie Welsh," he said. A trainer would be crazy not to check out a big, lithe kid like Marvin. Heavyweights brought in ten times the money as a featherweight for the same work.

As it turned out, Marvin had guts and plenty of drive, but he also had no balance, technique, or even rudimentary defense, and he punched himself to exhaustion halfway through one round. Meanwhile he was peppered with jabs and light combinations by Tommy Norris, a forty-year-old stringbean stunt man who weighed perhaps 160. When Marvin threw hard, Tommy threw hard, too, but he landed. It was a traditional schooling. Actions, not words. Whoever had trained Marvin, if he'd been trained at all, didn't create a pretty package. Cheskis was embarrassed. At least Marvin kept going until he heard the bell. Under similar circumstances he'd seen others feign injuries and scramble out of the ring.

"Okay, Tommy," Eddie said. "I'll take over." Tommy wasn't even breathing hard, but Marvin panted like an exhausted mule. His angry glare softened into curiosity as the diminutive Eddie stepped inside the ropes. Now what? "Get me my red gloves, please," Eddie told Cheskis.

"The Reyes?" Cheskis asked him. Eddie kept a pair of barely padded competition gloves manufactured by Mexican sadists. With them, he could punch holes in people.

"No, the ones with the Velcro," Eddie said, signifying this would be a lesson, not a murder.

Inside the ring, Eddie told Marvin to assume his stance. "Look at your feet. You're too wide. Get on the balls of your feet, see?" So it began. Eddie sailed straight into the teeth of a job that made breaking rocks look like answering the phone. But to him it was just another day at the office. In three weeks Marvin was hitting the speed bag and shadow boxing as though he'd been at it all his life, astounding Cheskis, but not Eddie. "Mate, I get fighters from another trainer and I spend half my time trying to undo their bad habits. A virgin can be easier." Marvin followed Eddie's orders like a Marine. He not only absorbed instructions quickly, he didn't forget them the next day. One day Cheskis worked with him and got tagged with something serious. Cheskis didn't know if it was a left or a right. "I'm sorry, man," said Marvin, stepping back.

Eddie rushed over. "That's enough for now," he said. Later he told Cheskis, "Don't go in with him anymore. He's too big."

"I just didn't see it coming," Cheskis said.

26

"I know," Eddie said. "He has a gift." Eddie and Marvin never discussed the future. They just mutually assumed that Marvin would turn pro. Already twenty-four, he was middle-aged for a fighter. "There's no time for the amateurs," Eddie told Cheskis. "The judging is all crap, and if nobody knows you, you have to knock the guy out. Might as well get him a little purse. It keeps a bloke interested." Marvin never asked about specifics. He just trained relentlessly, trusting Eddie.

Felix Oliveira, a welterweight who'd done jail time with Cheskis, was training with Eddie for a shot at one of the smaller titles. Felix, who possibly owned the coldest Aztec eyes west of Oklahoma, was a gang leader in the San Fernando Valley and managed by a sheet-metal magnate whose name was Borakovich. Borakovich, in string tie and Stetson, drove down from his mountain castle once to observe Felix train. After ten minutes he congratulated Eddie and Felix on their work and turned to go. Eddie tried to pry some training expenses out of him but secured only a vague promise.

"You know what those vitamins cost me?" Eddie complained later to Cheskis. He had Felix on twenty or thirty pills a day that Eddie obtained from a variety of secret sources. Like Marvin, Felix was doing everything Eddie asked. He'd left his family in the Valley and stayed at Eddie's place, where he kept proper hours and stayed off unsavory substances. His homeys were nowhere to be seen. Eddie did all the cooking, cleaning, and washing up. That's the way he was. He insisted on doing everything.

Felix told Cheskis he'd been stabbed on three occasions after Cheskis left jail for anger class. Evidently these were revenge attacks for deeds on the street. "Did you see a doctor or something?" Cheskis asked him. No, he treated the wounds with toothpaste, he said. He didn't say what happened to his attackers, and Cheskis knew better than to ask.

Cheskis, who hadn't boxed since the Army nearly twenty years ago, first entered Eddie's gym after getting out of jail in February, and worked out three or four times a week with calisthenics, stretching, hitting the bags, shadow boxing, and sometimes sparring. Tommy, his primary sparring partner, was an ex-Marine who, Eddie confided to Cheskis, supplemented his stunt work by providing a specialized service for lawyers or their investigators. For $2,000 he would spring out of the darkness in a black raincoat and ski mask and shoot his prey with a paint gun—pop! Some shit their pants. Tommy never spoke to his targets, who always understood the message anyway—they shouldn't have done whatever it was they did and they better quit doing it.

Marvin and Felix performed a much fuller version of Cheskis's abbreviated routine. Every morning Marvin borrowed his aunt's beat-up car, showed up at Eddie's by 6 A.M., and he and Felix did their roadwork out on the beach. They did four or five hard miles, mixing in sprints and running backwards. Then Marvin took his car back to his aunt in time for her to get to her job. He returned to bed until mid-afternoon, did his gym work, and drove a forklift in a warehouse from 7 P.M. to 4 A.M. He found the job—something he'd never before experienced—because somebody in the gym knew a guy who knew a guy.

Eddie was secretive about his age, but Cheskis, assessing the blur on his tattooed forearms, figured he had to be in his mid-fifties, at least. The training was his Gospel, a sacred text he passed on as it had been passed to him. His other mission was the pursuit of attractive black women. Eddie could follow their ephemerones through a rainforest. When he'd fought in the amateurs, Cheskis knew several white boxers who were suckers for black girls, burrowing in like tics to seek the black magic essence. Occasionally Eddie's hunting disturbed African-American men, but his affable manner combined with his reputation as one of L.A.'s most feared street fighters usually made for peaceful evenings. Blood, broken bones, and scattered teeth trailed him from his hometown of Leicester, England to Sydney, Australia, and ended at the L.A. beach. Along the way he'd been stabbed, shot, and thumped with all manner of blunt objects. "I used to be much harder to get along with," he explained to Cheskis.

28

CHAPTER 4

REYNOLDS

A day came when Eddie told Cheskis, "It's time to get Marvin a fight. I want you to take care of it."

"Eddie, I don't know how to do any of that."

"Neither do I, mate."

"Sure you do. You've done it before."

"I want you to handle this end, mate. So does Marvin. Go down to the commission and get yourself a manager's license."

"I don't want to be responsible, Eddie. Get somebody who knows what he's doing."

"We want you, mate. Please."

"I make only one guarantee, Eddie. That I'll screw it up."

"I'm telling you, it's easy."

"Then why don't you do it?"

"You'll do it better. You'll see, and I can stick to the training. It's better."

They'd be partners. Cheskis never had a partner, but he'd never been in business. He thought about what a friend's father told him once. The three of them were playing catch with a football, and Cheskis kept dropping it, and everyone tried not to notice, making him drop it more. Finally the father told him, "You're treating the ball like it's trouble, Lee. The ball's not trouble. It's an opportunity, see? It's giving you an opportunity to catch it."

It didn't work immediately, but the advice stayed with him. It wasn't until he reached his late teens that he realized maybe he wasn't to blame for his dad being peculiar and not trying to help his son the way other dads did, or that when he did try, it was just a matter of time before one of them stalked off. Usually Cheskis would be in tears and his father would either stay angry or switch to laughter, which was worse.

Cheskis stopped off at the boxing commission's L.A. office, where he filled out a simple form. People took one-year courses to cut hair or service refrigerators, but a license to make life-or-death decisions for prizefighters was no more difficult to obtain than a library card. The commission claimed to do a background check, but it was no more meaningful than a tag on a mattress. Boxing was not baseball. It had no association with freshly mowed grass, red-cheeked youngsters, or lemonade. Ray Powell, the most powerful promoter in the world, had served time for manslaughter and grand larceny, and he was licensed.

The La Brea Auditorium, which used to be called the Serra Auditorium, put on two boxing shows a month. The name was changed after the owner caved in to a boycott by angry Mexican-Americans who pointed out that in his day Father Serra had enslaved, starved, and murdered enough Indians to make General Custer look like Mother Teresa. The La Brea's matchmaker, Cheskis learned from Eddie, was Art Reynolds, a black man from Nicaragua who took kickbacks in two languages. A young woman answered the phone at his faux office at the La Brea, but Cheskis went to see him where Eddie told him he conducted business—his private box at the Hollywood Park race track.

"You say you got a heavyweight? Good, good, I can always use a good heavyweight," he said to Cheskis without offering him a seat. "These local fighters, they're mostly these little Mexicans. People get tired of watching little Mexicans, you hear what I'm saying?"

Reynolds, a portly man in a business suit, was seated with a smiling little Hispanic man and an impeccably dressed redhead. The redhead had large breasts, a tiny purse, and sipped a martini with three olives. She smelled expensive. "You want to look at my fighter?" Cheskis asked Reynolds.

"There's no need, no need. He trains with Eddie Welsh, that's good enough for me. Eddie's a crazy little bastard, but his fighters, they're always in shape. I can put your guy—what's his name?"

"Marvin O'Brien."

"Marvin O'Brien. He wouldn't be Irish by any chance?"

"He's black," Cheskis said.

"Too bad. I love white heavyweights if they can fight a little." The redhead gave his shoulder a cutesy little shove. "Ah-art," she said.

"'Scooze me, girl," he told her. "But true is true." He turned back to Cheskis. "I can use your Marvin O'Brien for a four-rounder August 16." Cheskis soon learned that Reynolds, a crook savant, kept all deals in his head.

"Who've you got for us?" Cheskis said. "My guy's had no amateur fights."

"Don't worry. He won't be no Joe Louis."

"Give me a couple names then," Cheskis insisted.

"Hey, mon, I thought you was new at this." The little man giggled in a way that wasn't terribly flattering to Cheskis.

"I didn't meet your friend," Cheskis said.

"Lopez," Reynolds said. "This is Lopez. You be good to him. He does our Spanish-language publicity." Eventually Cheskis extracted names of two possible opponents and left. Next day he was back at the track. He noticed that every time he needed to see Reynolds he had to put up $20 for clubhouse admission and $8 for the cheapest parking, which was three blocks away. "The one guy was seven and one and the other is fourteen and six," Cheskis complained. "They're way too experienced for my guy."

Reynolds put down his racing form and looked at Cheskis without a smile. "They're cripples, practically," he said. "I don't know how they even got licensed. Their manager probably paid off the doctors. Look, you didn't have to pay me nothing, right?"

"No," Cheskis said. "Was that a mistake?"

"You a funny guy," said Reynolds. He sat with the same redhead sipping another martini and a different little Hispanic. "You don't owe me a thing, mon. Virgins don't gotta pay, right Jenny?" Jenny repeated her affectionate little shove from the day before. "Ah-art!" This time she spilled a little of her martini. A waiter in a bright, white jacket rushed over with a clean towel. He must have been monitoring them like a lab technician.

"Look, my guy is no ordinary fighter," Cheskis said. "The fans will love him. But I can't bring him along too fast."

"Well, he gotta fight somebody," Reynolds said. "You want a free lunch? They give 'em out in Santa Monica."

"What about Louie Storma?" Cheskis said. Prowling gyms around Los Angeles, he'd learned that Storma threw hard, but he was slow and easy to find, an apprentice plumber who fought once in awhile for extra cash.

Reynolds shrugged. "Name don't ring no bell."

"He fought for you three times. I talked to his manager. They want the fight."

"You sure done your homework for a crummy five-hundred-dollar purse," Reynolds said. "You tell Blinky Tamarindo, he wants his fighter at the La Brea, he gotta talk to me, not you." Cheskis chose not to ask Reynolds how he knew the identity of a manager whose fighter he claimed not to remember. Reynolds passed a thin slice of hundred-dollar bills to the redhead. "The five horse, Jenny girl," he told her. "Two to win, two to show."

"Let her enjoy her drink," Cheskis said. "I'll walk over with you."

Reynolds looked him up and down. "Why not?" he said. On the way, Cheskis handed him a C-note. "Get me Storma," he said.

Three minutes later, as Cheskis descended the stairs to the parking lot, he heard the track announcer call the race. The five horse finished out of the money.

Tamarindo kicked over another fifty to Reynolds and Marvin drew Storma for his pro debut. Cheskis and Tommy worked the corner with Eddie. Cheskis was nervous he might make a mistake, but Eddie assured him he'd handle Marvin's instructions and any cuts, should they develop. "Just take a good look where everything is in the bucket, so when I ask for something, you can hand it over."

"Eddie handles everything," Tommy told him. "Don't worry about it."

Storma was a leathery chunk of a man with a serpent tattooed around one big bicep. A couple dozen regulars from the gym cheered wildly as Marvin stopped him in the third round.

It was an all-action fight, compensating the fans for a stinker of a main event between two waltzing welterweights. Storma was too tough to go down, but after meting out a steady pounding, Marvin tagged him with a big hook and had him defenseless on the ropes when the referee jumped in. Sweat-covered Marvin threw up his hands, danced around the ring, and took turns hugging his cornermen, Storma, and Storma's cornermen. He laughed without shame.

SEPTEMBER 1965

Chapter 5

NO PITY

Exactly one week before meeting the soldier with nine fingers, Cheskis stepped on the convict's foot. He hadn't planned it, but when the opportunity presented itself he was running out of options. He felt as though something outside his control had made the decision and he was no more than a spectator. Sometimes there's no time to ponder your choices or ask advice. You just do what has to be done and think about it later. Or you don't, in which case you'll still think about it later.

Minutes before facing off with the convict, Cheskis, just a little scared, waited to be called out of the locker room. He and the other fighters on the team discussed their fear from time to time and the consensus was that a little fear was helpful. Too much was crippling, and none at all could be suicidal. But sometimes just before a fight, if you weren't careful, that little bit of helpful fear could explode into something bigger and shake you like a tambourine, in which case the other guys, though they wouldn't come out and say it, would consider you a pussy. Why this was supposed to be worse than going out there and getting your face and ribs crushed was sometimes difficult for Cheskis to understand. He tried to combat his fear with ferocity. Not anger—ferocity. He imagined himself as a filthy, hairy, crazy Hun riding out on his demon horse to chop opponents' heads with a big hatchet.

Cheskis, his gloves laced and sealed with tape, tried to let the Hun in him take over as he listened to Valaitas's instructions over James Brown's "Papa's Got a Brand New Bag" blasting from the little phonograph player that Stuart, the super middleweight, always brought on road trips. They always played the same song before each fighter's turn. They thought it would be unlucky to turn down the volume, which was why Cheskis had a hard time hearing Valaitas. It would also be unlucky to tie your shoes differently or change mouthpieces or even to wish one of your teammates luck in some incorrect way that might alter events. When a split second of inattention could spell disaster and humiliation, no detail can be overlooked.

"Whatever you do," Valaitas said, "don't smile at this guy, understand? No fraternity handshakes. He's not one a your pals."

No sense denying the fraternity indictment again. Valaitas applied it to college men wherever they might roam. Cheskis leaned close to Valaitas's ear. "Okay if I give him a little kiss on the lips?" he asked him.

"Cut the crap," Valaitas said. "He's all alone in there with a fucking monster. That's what your face shows him, understand? You're a monster with no pity and he's gonna look around and there's no one to help him."

"There *is* no one to help him," said Cheskis the Hun.

"You want to smile at him, wait till after you murder the bastard," Valaitas said. "The shitbird. He's in here for raping children."

"Honest?" Cheskis asked him.

"Rearrange the motherfucker," said Bobby, a sergeant who assisted Valaitas.

"No pity," Valaitas said.

"No pity," Cheskis repeated.

An official out in the hallway cracked open the door and informed them it was time. Cheskis, still perspiring from his warm-up, followed Valaitas and Bobby to the door. The other fighters, most of whom hadn't gone out there yet, raised their fingers in a Number One gesture. It was an accepted form of wishing luck. Caddington, team captain and light heavyweight destroyer, tapped him on top of a glove with the side of his taped fist. "Fuck him up, Stanley," he said. "Stay with him, Doctor Livingston," he said to Sergeant Valaitas. "That's right, tote their shit" he told Bobby, who carried the bucket containing an ice pack, scissors, tape, Vaseline, prayer beads, rabbits' foot, and all the other necessities. "Go fuck yourself," black Bobby said to black Caddington.

Ever since they'd pulled up in front of the prison, jokes emitted nervous laughter at best. The entire team was in a hurry to do the job and get back on the bus, away from the desolation that rose like gray vapor from the concrete floor. For weeks now, everyone had been making quips about competing in a place where they assumed plenty of guys were taking it in the ass. But once they arrived, the subject was no longer mentioned. Cheskis knew he wasn't the only team member guessing which of the convicts did what to whom.

The usual locker room tension had been ratcheted up by news of the previous bout, in which the team's featherweight suffered a shocking first-round knockout from some guy no one had ever heard of. The loser, looking like a lost puppy, sat on a rubbing table talking with one of the two supervising doctors. It's hard to know what to say to a teammate who's just suffered such a devastating calamity, so everyone tried not to look at him, which of course added to the poor kid's desolation. It's bad enough to get your ass kicked, but when it also makes you a leper, it's like barely escaping the flaming wreckage of your brand-new, uninsured car only to be pantsed by an enraged mob. Cheskis had sparred many times with their featherweight, and he was no pushover. But that poor bastard's tragedy had nothing to do with him, Cheskis decided. No matter how much they all pretended otherwise, this was no team sport. It was just him, all on him. He closed his eyes, tried to clear his mind, to find ferocity but none of the anger Valaitas tried to instill. He wanted to be in control yet let his most vicious instincts work for him. A touch of insanity wouldn't hurt either.

The auditorium wasn't as ugly as Cheskis had imagined. The convicts were a noisy circus of denim. They yelled out the name of his opponent, who already waited in the ring. Lawrence, or Horace, or something like that. Valaitas and Bobby behind him, Cheskis paid the opponent no attention as he climbed through the ropes.

"Remember to move your head," Valaitas said, smearing a Vaseline film over his cheeks and nose. In these last moments he would give his fighters one specific instruction, one thing to remember above all others. No more pep talks. No more reminding Cheskis how much rode on this. He'd said that only once, over a pitcher of beer in the PX: "This ain't a kids' summer camp anymore," he'd said. "These guys shipping out, they'll come back missing parts, some of them. That's how it's going to be from now on." Since that one time, Valaitas never discussed Cheskis's fights while he spoke of the Nam, and he never spoke of the Nam while he discussed Cheskis's fights. He was like a politician who always separated conversations about campaign contributions from conversations about the favors they purchased.

A convict announcer stood in the center of the ring with a microphone and a big smile. He was crisp all over, like a high-powered executive, only in a different uniform. His blond hair was thick, wavy, and carefully groomed. He wore a precisely ironed, tailored denim jacket. His watch, possibly solid gold, sparkled under the intense overhead light. Everything about him mocked his situation, announcing to prison authorities that next to him they were little swineherds in Timexes and scuffed shoes. Cheskis, as he was introduced, drew boos and cheers. He caught his opponent sneaking a glance at him. Their eyes darted away.

When Cheskis returned to the corner, Bobby put his lips close to his ear. Bobby. Pink lips, brown, scarred face, sympathetic eyes. "You the prince of fucking darkness," he told Cheskis. "This guy is fucked. Really and truly fucked." Then he kissed him on the cheek.

Cheskis's mind wandered as the referee barked quick instructions. But he heard the last sentence: "God bless you both." Ordered to touch gloves, Cheskis let his opponent's gloves sit out there for a heartbeat before brushing them with his own because, after all, Huns don't go around shaking hands with people they're going to skin and eat. Back in the corner, moments before the bell, Bobby, now behind the ropes, told him: "Just like we do in the gym. That's all you got to do. And remember to feint."

Kill the fear. Remember to feint. And what was it? What did Valaitas tell me?

As they met again in the center of the ring, the other fighter held one glove out in a gesture of sportsmanship. Cheskis touched it with his left and the sonofabitch threw a quick right that Cheskis just barely slipped. Cute. The crowd loved it. Cheskis stepped left, stepped right, and feinted with several punches, all herky-jerky, throwing nothing and watching his opponent's reactions. *What's the matter, man? You jumpy?* This guy looked kind of old, but his skin was so black it could mask any kind of age, up or down. Cheskis stared straight into his eyes, which were fixed on his own. This man had complacent, not particularly scared eyes, just intent, as though he were working on a puzzle. Sometimes Cheskis thought fighters' unrelenting, locked mutual stare was the most unnatural part of boxing—contrary to everything society taught about how to interact with others. Only animals, small children, and truly disturbed sonsofbitches stared at each other like this.

The opponent threw a one-two, though he had no opening. As Cheskis blocked the punches with his gloves, the force of the right hand almost knocked him back. The convict smiled. He could hit, this fucker. *Don't step back. You're faster. You're all speed, a blur, you're nothing but trouble.* These convicts were a question mark. They could be world beaters, stiffs, or anything in between. The opponent threw a right-hand, left-hook combination. A piece of the left sailed past Cheskis's gloves and landed behind his ear. Cheskis still circled, throwing nothing but staying in range. He heard Valaitas screaming above everybody else: "What the fuck are you doing in there?" *Wait. Wait for the next one.* Cheskis saw a jab start and let go one of his own, getting there first. Simultaneously he stepped left, then hooked to the gut hard. He bobbed low to the right and came up with a straight right, which was blocked. Back in his envelope, he feinted another jab. The convict moved early to block the punch that wasn't there and as he puzzled over the outcome, Cheskis let loose a real one to the head, followed by another to the ribcage, everything quick. The convict's body was so tight the glove bounced off his ribs as though he'd smacked an inflated tire. He came forward throwing a volley of lefts and rights, trying to prove his own speed. Something solid landed on the side of Cheskis's neck. He stood his ground and they clinched. The opponent threw several quick punches at his left kidney but couldn't get the leverage to do real damage. Then he drifted one low. *Don't back up.* As the referee broke them, Cheskis shoved the convict, which inspired plenty of shouting from the crowd. The referee cautioned him, gesturing a push with his hands.

The convict came right back at him and Cheskis waited with a left uppercut. As he threw it, a glove from someplace unexpected slammed him in the face like a garbage can lid. Confused, Cheskis retreated to the ropes with the convict all over him. After getting tagged some more, Cheskis tied him up. The cons were really screaming now, probably rising from their seats. Cheskis was pretty sure he felt blood flowing from his nose. The bell rang and he found himself in his own corner, sweating, his face warmed by his own blood. Lots of yelling. He didn't remember getting here. "You got careless," Valaitas said, all the while working on his nose. He stuck an adrenaline-soaked Q-tip into the nostril, swished it around, and squeezed his nose hard with a cloth. "Give him water." Valaitas removed the cloth while Cheskis drank from Bobby's bottle. Somebody in a brown leisure suit stuck his face in Cheskis's and asked him his name.

"Lee Cheskis, PFC, US 16813339," Cheskis said.

"Where are you?"

"What'd he hit me with?"

"A right hand," Valaitas said. "Answer the doc's question. Where are you?"

"Folsom Prison."

The doctor said something Cheskis couldn't hear while Cheskis stared at the doctor's nose. It was a drinker's nose, criss-crossed with colorful, three-dimensional veins.

"What?" Cheskis said.

"Do you want to continue?" asked the doctor.

"I'm going to murder this sonofabitch," Cheskis told him.

"Now let me do my job, okay?" Valaitas said to the doctor. The doctor, giving Cheskis a look pregnant with doubt, climbed out of the ring one cowboy boot at a time. *Thanks for your confidence, hillbilly prick.*

"You're okay," Valaitas said. "Just be careful. You won that round."

"Double jab this guy," Bobby said. "Keep your gloves up. And get those shoulders loose. You're too tight."

"You're not moving your head," Valaitas said.

Shit!

Back out there, Cheskis felt himself retreating from his opponent's power. *Damn! Don't back up!* The convict winged several powerful volleys at his arms. Sharp judges would see they weren't scoring shots. But they made his arms feel like sandbags. Cheskis's jab was working. But at every opportunity the convict came close and pounded him to the body, weakening his legs. As the bell sounded, Cheskis landed a sweet right hook to the body. The convict countered with a late punch to the head and was cautioned by the referee.

Valaitas yelled over at the ref as Cheskis plopped down on the stool. "Take a point from this bastard! What're you waiting for?" Cheskis drank all the air he could. After only two rounds, there wasn't enough oxygen for him in all the world. Bobby poured water over him. It mingled with rivers of Vaseline, adrenaline, mucus, blood, and sweat, some of it the opponent's. Valaitas worked on Cheskis's nose again. "Who won that round?" Cheskis asked.

"You gotta come at this guy," Valaitas said. "He's tired. He can't handle your jab."

"Is this the last round?"

"Combinations. All combinations," Bobby said.

The cons whistled and yelped the opponent's name. The referee told the fighters to touch gloves again. "Last round," he said.

I'm not scared. Understand? I'm not scared.

At first it felt like the convict's punches had less snap to them, but then he hammered a hook to the ribs with sickening force. Cheskis wasn't controlling his man. With maybe a minute to go, he stepped left, and as his opponent followed, slipped back to his right, trapping the man's front foot under his own.

42

Cheskis snapped a double-hook to the head and gut and pushed the convict as he released the trapped foot, making him stumble. Cheskis charged in with quick lefts and rights, driving him to the corner. The convict flung his arms around him and Cheskis pounded him on the inside until the ref separated them. Angry now, his opponent threw stupid roundhouse shots, wasting energy. Cheskis stepped forward snapping sharp jabs, backing him to the ropes as he heard the ten-second warning. Finding strength from somewhere, he punched to the body and head until the bell. Both fighters threw their arms in the air.

Cheskis could hear the crowd again, the cons angry, excited, happy. Pathetic ass-fucking pirates. They just wanted blood. Whose didn't matter so much after all. It occurred to Cheskis that some of them had probably bet on him.

Both fighters' cornermen jumped into the ring celebrating, trying to make it look good for the judges even though the referee was already collecting their scores. The two spent fighters avoided each other awhile, then met up along the ropes and embraced. "Good fight," Cheskis said. Whatever the other guy said, it was muffled, but he said it with a smile.

Chapter 6

NINE FINGERS

Back at Fort Ord, it didn't take long for Cheskis to understand the depth of his error. Already the foul haunted him. Only twenty-two, he was beginning to comprehend the burden of remorse, which could get heavier just from tiny infractions, casual cruelties. He'd neglect to keep a promise, ignore a beggar, hurl an insult—and never be completely sure whether his action or failure to take action would create new regrets—little sore spots of self-loathing that would cause him pain at odd, solitary moments. He was sorry for picking on Jeffrey Goodkind in the fourth grade just because he picked his nose with such inadequate subterfuge. He should have paid attention to that quiet kid whose father was in the nuthouse. He was sorry for backing down from Phil Earth in tenth grade. Quite a few girls he'd stopped calling without explanation. He should make peace with his parents. And now he was sorry for stepping on the convict's foot. How many grievances against himself would he tote around twenty or thirty years from now? They appeared and vanished unpredictably, like Alice's Cheshire cat. Summoning his Hun doppelgänger had no effect on these issues.

Planning and executing the foul took Cheskis no more than a millisecond. He'd fouled other opponents and it didn't much bother him, at least not for long. Maybe this would be the same. It's not easy to draw a neat line of decent behavior around a competition that's basically savage in its intent. Sort of like the Geneva Convention, which says it's perfectly okay to rip apart people's faces and guts with lead projectiles or burn them with fire bombs, but it's not right to choke them with gas.

It was unlikely that winning or losing was linked to anything truly important in the convict's life. All sports created artificial pressures that could seem real if you didn't step outside the box to actually appraise them. Fans troubled by sickness, debt, lost love, deaths of loved ones, fretted over whether someone could advance a puck or plunk a ball into a basket. They admired players for dealing with invented anxieties and were shamed by their own puny sorrows. But other sports were games, and boxing was never a game. For Cheskis in particular, it was bound up with the real world. He was already starting to face opponents with just as much to lose—other soldiers trying to keep their names off the wrong list. At Fort Ord, entire brigades were here today, gone next week. Soldiers trudged around the post looking permanently startled, unable to grasp what was happening to them. They carried telltale sheets of paper from building to building so they could sign off post without being charged for a missing blanket or bayonet. All this was supposed to happen to someone else. Their mamas didn't raise them to be statistics.

Soldiers didn't discuss the war as much as they felt its presence. Back when most of them had arrived on post, only lifers went to Nam. For everyone else, Fort Ord was mostly a playground for late-stage adolescents. They spent weekends debauching territory for a hundred miles in every direction. Even noncoms and field-grade officers who'd been shot at in World War II and Korea looked at military exercises as ends in themselves—not a prelude to life-or-death struggles. Now the place was a staging ground for an actual war that swept through the ranks like a disease with no cure, like some master puppeteer was plucking them one by one out of the box. That was why a week after he stepped on the convict's foot, Cheskis was so aghast to discover the soldier with nine fingers.

The soldier, a lanky Latin who didn't look old enough to be in a real army, was nearly finished wrapping his left hand, the one with four fingers. Flashing the whitest of teeth, he gestured toward a heavy bag and asked, "Okay if I use this?" His brown, adolescent face had the kind of expression you might see on someone who'd just flunked algebra and was trying to make the best of it. Cheskis had no intention of using the bag and was standing not terribly close to it. Evidently the nine-fingered soldier figured that if Cheskis was even thinking about using it, then he must have a superior claim. Helping a guy like this could develop into a full-time job.

Cheskis was doing only a light workout because, though several days had passed since his bout at Folsom, his midsection still felt tenderized. At the University of Wisconsin, where he'd learned to box, he'd once had his ribs cracked like cheap balsa wood. He spent weeks afterward creeping into bed an inch at a time to find the one position that wasn't agony. Like most fighters, he believed body shots hurt the worst. But then an opponent from Northern Michigan University cracked one of his molars right through his mouthpiece. At precisely that moment he changed his mind and decided body shots weren't so bad after all. Now at odd moments the tooth reacted to heat or cold as though it were an electric toaster in a puddle. He'd also graduated with a nose flatter than it was meant to be. And now that he was boxing again, his hands were always sore.

Cheskis told the soldier with nine fingers that the heavy bag was all his, then started shadow boxing. He tried to put on a good show, knowing the kid would be sizing him up, just as Cheskis sneaked glances at him working the bag. The missing finger didn't seem to hamper him. When the bell sounded to end the three minutes, the kid said, "Man, you got an Ali jab. How's anybody get away from that thing?"

"Don't tell Liston," said Cheskis, breathing harder now, pleased with himself.

"Yeah, poor Sonny" the kid said. "Came along at the wrong time. He ran into the perfect fighter."

"A heavyweight who moves like a welter. What can you do?" Cheskis said.

"Patterson, he had no hope."

"He's smaller *and* slower and can't hit as hard," Cheskis agreed. "He brought nothing."

"Yeah, but I still didn't like the way Ali tortured him," the kid said.

"I know," Cheskis said. "It's one thing to beat a guy. But killing his spirit like that, talking to him—I don't like talkers."

"Me neither. But Ali, he's had to put up with a lot of crap."

"Poor guy," Cheskis said. "If he were lucky like us, he could be here making seventy-eight a month." He stuck out his taped, sweaty hand. "I'm Lee Cheskis."

"Manny Roybal," the kid said.

Later Cheskis asked him if he was R.A. or U.S. "U.S.," the kid replied, as was Cheskis. Two letters preceded every enlisted soldier's serial number. R.A. designated a Regular Army volunteer. U.S. was for draftees. As it turned out, Roybal wasn't so timid after all, but Cheskis figured any draftee with nine fingers clearly didn't know how to stand up for himself, to tear through the bureaucratic shroud of paper pushers who made civilization so grievous for anybody who didn't know how to make them screw someone else instead. If he were walking around with nine fingers, Cheskis knew, he wouldn't be doing time here. Which is one reason why armies everywhere love to scoop up kids like Roybal. It's so much easier than dealing with a pain in the ass like Cheskis.

Despite the soreness around his midsection, Cheskis asked the question both of them had on their minds. "Want to do a little work?" Sure, the kid said, but at the same time eyed him like a toy poodle. "We'll just go light," Cheskis assured him. "Look, you do spar, right?"

"'Cause a my finger, you mean? Forget it. Has no effect."

"Shouldn't you get a deferment, though? A soldier with a missing pinky, that's a crime against malingering. You should be out there in civvies. Chasing girls and sleeping late."

Roybal just shrugged, embarrassed by the attention but not, it appeared, by the missing digit.

"Did you say anything about it? When they drafted you, I mean."

"Yeah, but they said it don't make no difference," Roybal said.

"And what'd you say?"

"What're you gonna do?" he said. "Wasn't up to me. It's their rules."

It was always a little scary going in against someone you'd never sparred with, especially if you hadn't seen him against anybody else. Some guys turned psycho in the ring. Without beating him up, Cheskis showed him what was what, controlling him with a smart, quick jab that was good enough to win fights in the amateurs, to keep him off work details, and perhaps, if he played it right, do much more. In less than two minutes Cheskis knew this kid was no threat to him, at least not now. But he moved his gloves and feet with a smooth grace, like a natural swimmer, and his muscles had a wiry strength, acquired, Cheskis would learn later, from generalized farm labor and throwing around boxes of Central Valley crops on a Fresno loading dock. If someone had trained him properly, he'd be better than Cheskis. As it was, he was too predictable, working in an easily decodable rhythm. Lacking subterfuge, he threw no feints. Most of the time he lowered his right when he threw his jab. It was as though he didn't understand the nature of malevolence. Skilled fighters were like muggers. Sneaky, plotting traps. If they decided their opponent was a sucker for a left hook, they might avoid throwing one just long enough to make him forget such a punch existed.

If he kept working with this guy, Cheskis knew Roybal could learn from him while Cheskis had little to learn from Roybal, not at this point, anyway. Sparring with opponents too far beneath you wasn't even as beneficial as hitting a heavy bag. It made you feel safe—a dangerous frame of mind.

The raw mornings at Fort Ord always took newcomers by surprise. Everyone expected California to be as warm and welcoming as it was for Frankie Avalon and Annette Funicello in *Beach Blanket Bingo*. But the post was raked each morning by winds that skipped off the frigid Pacific sitting just beyond the Monterey Peninsula and made ice statues out of anyone forced

48

to stand still, which is exactly what everyone did in morning formation. A huge, green mass of humanity with everybody in place like suffering chess pieces. Squad leaders counting their squads, then yelling results to the platoon sergeants, and on up the line. An unnatural business, all this organized hollering at the break of day in frozen California. They stood 110 miles south of San Francisco, where Samuel Clemens famously said he spent the coldest winter of his life one summer.

Cheskis, freezing along with the other enlisted men of Headquarters Company, swore again to himself that somehow, some way, he would get himself a white sweatshirt. Whenever they turned up at the PX, which was seldom, they'd be sold out in minutes, always too late for Cheskis to get one. Whenever he spotted one on a lucky somebody he gazed at it with tragic longing. The commanding general at Fort Ord wouldn't let soldiers wear their field jackets. No one knew why. But in his compassion for the troops, he decreed it was okay if they slipped white sweatshirts underneath their fatigue shirts. The sweatshirts had to be white so they would be indistinguishable from the T-shirts that peeked from atop the second button of their shirts. The general didn't allow anyone to button the top button. He liked to see white fabric just below the throat. Generals had too much time on their hands. Because of them, aligning objects in your footlocker was treated like brain surgery.

Before they could file into the mess hall, the men of Headquarters Company, as they did every morning, endured twenty minutes of raw-fingered calisthenics on cold asphalt, and then, still in formation, ran three miles around the adjoining gravel field in combat boots. Staff Sergeant Valaitas, well into his thirties, set the pace with boots that barely touched ground. Cheskis, unofficial spokesman for the fighters, all of whom were assigned to Headquarters Company, had once tried to persuade Valaitas to let them out of either the run or the P.T. They were already excused whenever they had a fight that evening, but they'd decided to push for more. "You fucking pansies!" Valaitas thundered. "What else you got to do with your time? Wash your tutus?" Cheskis considered the response a small victory. "He

49

called us pansies," he told the guys later. "If he were really pissed he'd have called us assholes or shitheads."

"You got a point, shithead," Caddington pointed out help-fully. He resented the fighters asking Cheskis to make the request because, after all, Caddy was team captain. The Watts riots less than two months ago were taking a toll. Soldiers pondered small events, casual asides that might have gone unnoticed back in July.

Still sweating from the run, Cheskis, his metal tray piled high with big, American breakfast foods, found a vacant chair next to Monk Pyrzynski. The company executive officer, Pyrzynski, for reasons known only to him, ate from time to time in the enlisted men's section. "Sir, I know this guy with nine fingers," Cheskis said as he sat down at the four-man table covered by a plastic, misleadingly cheerful checkered table cloth. "What're his chances of getting out?" Anyone who knew Monk, regardless of rank, could call him Monk, but Cheskis sirred him for the ben-efit of two privates also seated at the table.

"It's not his trigger finger, right?" asked Monk.

"No."

"Where's he assigned?"

"He's just about done with A.I.T."—Advanced Infantry Training.

"Then he's screwed," Monk said. "He's made it too far. They ain't that stupid. The time to squawk was right away. It's kind of like a property easement. You let someone cross your prop-erty every day, it becomes legal. You have to call them on it in the beginning." Monk, a University of North Carolina grad, had been a starting left tackle for the Tarheels and could probably squeeze enemy skulls into mush with his bare hands. So natu-rally after he finished infantry school the Army assigned him to the post's Headquarters Company, an outfit with a murky mis-sion where basic soldiering was mostly a distant memory. People worked behind desks or were sent out on details that could range from gardening to road maintenance. Only a small core of sol-diers like Monk was permanent cadre. The others were in some kind of military limbo, waiting for papers that would send them somewhere else.

"Anyone he can appeal to?" Cheskis asked Monk.

"Lots of places—his company commander, the chaplain, Inspector General. But he's fried. Hey, how's your boxing scam going?"

"What scam? I did the morning run same as you."

"When's the last time you pulled a detail?"

"You've got an eagle eye, Lieutenant Pyrzynski."

"But summer's lease hath all too short a date."

"What's that?"

"Shakespeare. It means time will screw you."

"Jesus," Cheskis said. "You know something I ought to know?"

"Haven't seen a thing," Monk said. "Take it easy. But you know the deal. Sooner or later you'll be back in the real Army. You got over a year left, and you're stuck with a picket-fence M.O.S. That's two strikes." Cheskis's Military Occupational Specialty was infantry rifleman, coded 111—also known as a picket fence. After basic training, while other soldiers from his old platoon learned how to stack underwear or bake biscuits, he slogged through more mud with other recruits who'd been designated for the tip of the Army spear—the men who trudged forth on the ground and were backed up by corps of fat-assed clerks, cooks, musicians, and morgue attendants who had unlimited access to Coke machines and pool tables. Cheskis longed to be one of them. Any fantasies about the romance of hard-assed soldiering died when a bespectacled trooper marching next to him in infantry school, swaddled like everyone else with impossible amounts of olive green gear, fainted from heat exhaustion. Unconscious before he hit the ground, his face slammed the gravel like a sledgehammer. Why couldn't Cheskis have been a dental assistant or a chaplain's aide?

When he finished college, Cheskis had applied at a few Reserve and National Guard units around Kansas City, but the draft got to him first. At the time, it didn't feel like a catastrophe, because a reserve hitch shot holes in weekends and summers for five and a half years. But it was a different game now. Men of draft age could choose between spoiled weekends or the possibility of a sucking chest wound. LBJ's daffy manpower strategies quickly transformed a slot in the reserves into a winning lottery ticket. Cheskis heard he was the first president ever to go to war without mobilizing. Reservists serving their six months of active duty were as surprised as everybody else when the Army let them go home at the same time it scooped up soldiers from everywhere else and poured them into Vietnam like baskets of minnows.

"Getting stuck between assignments, these days it's dangerous. But they say it's not as bad for guys stationed back East. Maybe the Army figures we're a day closer or something."

"Somebody should take away their maps," Cheskis said.

"It's over in a week," Monk said. "The poor bastards get the call and bam, they go up to Travis and straight into the shit, do not pass go. Next time their families hear from them, they're at a repo depot waiting to be trucked out to the bush. It's hard to even imagine." Very few lifers had actually finished a Vietnam tour. So soldiers with war orders couldn't find anybody who'd even seen the place. It was as though they were all being sent to some unexplored galaxy.

As Monk rose with his tray, Valaitas came over and took his seat. The two other soldiers took off in a hurry. At Headquarters Company, where vacancies for ugly work details drifted around like dangerous microbes, men were particularly eager to get away from a staff sergeant. "I want you to come down some more." Valaitas said. Cheskis had a mouthful of lukewarm bacon and sunny-side-up eggs. In a hurry to answer, he swallowed too soon and suffered a coughing fit.

"Sure, Sarge," he gasped finally, "what do I chop off?"

"I mean it. We're gonna get you down to 32," he said, using boxing parlance for 132 pounds.

"Seven pounds?"

"That guy the other night, he was too strong for you."

"I got careless, but I beat him."

"It was too close. There are 39-pounders out there way better than him."

"Come on, Sarge. That guy was tough. He was probably ten years older, too."

"He was only six years older."

52

"I thought you didn't know anything about him."

"That was Chu Chu Morris. Six and two as a pro. Four knockouts"

"How long have you known that?"

"What's the difference?"

"You knew it all along? You lied to me?"

"I didn't want to rattle you, kid. I knew you could beat him. Anyways, if you lost, we could have challenged it easy. He's not supposed to be fighting amateur."

"Look, Sarge, haven't I always treated you with respect? I mean, I have, haven't I?"

No Answer.

"So why'd you treat me like a jerk?"

Valaitas looked at him as though he were a botanist studying some mushroom that just caught his attention. "I'm an E-6," he said finally. "You'd have to treat me with respect if I wore a beanie with a propeller on it."

"I didn't mean it like that," Cheskis said. "Forget the Army for a minute."

"What I been trying to tell you, kid, is you can't forget the Army. That's what this is all about. You don't make the team at Carson, where you think they'll send you? Listen to what I'm saying. What I hear, their junior welter at Carson is kicking ass. The guy could end up at the Olympics. You don't want any part of him."

Pounded into shape by the Army, Cheskis figured there was no more body fat to squeeze out of him. Coming down seven pounds seemed so impossible that he experienced one of those odd moments when he wasn't immune to the curious lure of war, just as people frightened by heights harbor an urge to jump. Although few soldiers volunteered for the war, those ordered to go weren't always upset. They'd get combat pay, and later, as war veterans with tales to tell, they might get laid easier. But Valaitas, who'd been wounded in Korea, knew how to chase such thoughts from Cheskis's head. "It ain't like a John Wayne movie, kid," he'd say. "It's more like being chased by Frankenstein." Sometimes Valaitas tried to persuade him with ridicule, sometimes graphic horror, sometimes guilt for failing to honor Valaitas's gift. But most of the time he didn't need any ploy at all. Cheskis didn't want to get maimed or killed. And for this too he felt guilty.

"We can keep you just as strong," Valaitas said. "At thirty-two, you'll walk through guys. Carson, they're weak at thirty-two."

"Honest?"

"That's what I hear." Fort Carson was the big boxing enchilada—home of the Army team. Its members were too valuable to sacrifice to combat. Their principal mission was to uphold the Army's honor against teams from the other military branches. Coming down seven more pounds would be ghastly, but so was the alternative. Maybe that's what growing up was about—choosing which rotten choice to make. He decided to forget about his own troubles for now. "I hear Paez is going," he said. "That right?"

"He's got orders for the First Cav." The First Air Cavalry Division, already prowling the Vietnamese boonies, was an outfit whose tactics and methods were so suitable for Vietnam that if there hadn't been a war there, the Army might have requisitioned one. The generals couldn't wait to see the warriors of their indestructible helicopter-borne force show those dinks. Valaitas had the power to intervene for Paez, to keep him out of the storm at least for awhile. But Valaitas, a wise king, used his power selectively, and he wasn't selecting Paez.

"I have somebody who could be a better featherweight, a lot better than Paez anyway," Cheskis said.

"If he's not better already, he's a bum." Valaitas said.

"Just take a look at the guy. You could make him into something. He's got the tools."

"Do I know him?" asked Valaitas, taking the bait.

"His name is Roybal. He's finishing up A.I.T."

"Have I seen him?"

"I don't know. He can't get to the gym as much as he'd like. You gotta give him credit for coming in at all. Those guys get what? Four hours sleep?"

"Bring him around. I'll have a look."

CHAPTER 7

KESEY

Cheskis, waking up thirsty, dodged little piles of detritus to get to the kitchen sink—dirty underwear, half-eaten animal crackers, eggshells. Touch anything and it might stick to you. He moved some dirty dishes aside and drank from the faucet. Before he could retreat back to the bedroom, one of the two little girls came in and asked him, "Got any milk?"

No, he had to tell her.

"I want cereal, but there's no milk." She seated herself at the cluttered kitchen table, evidently waiting for someone or something to help her.

"It's okay, honey. I'll go to the store," he said. He turned around to look for his wallet, hoping it hadn't been carried off by vermin.

Samantha called out from the bedroom: "Annie, there's powdered milk in the cabinet. You know where."

"Where?" Annie said.

Samantha came out dressed only in Cheskis's T-shirt, which revealed a hint of her bare butt when she reached to get the package off a shelf. She prepared sugary children's cereal and powdered milk for Annie, who looked about seven. Cheskis followed Samantha back into the bedroom, and she slipped out of the T-shirt. "Close the door," she said.

Cheskis didn't feel particularly at ease screwing Samantha while her daughter ate breakfast in the next room and Roybal might be awake on the couch. But he was reluctant to express these thoughts. He tried to be perceived as a man of the world, but to him, Samantha, probably several years older than he was, at times seemed like a member of another species. "How come you're always so damned cheerful?" he asked, licking her nipple. She stroked his hair.

"Because I've got Jesus with me," she said. When he didn't reply, she added, "Especially today, 'cause Sundays. I go to my tight-assed little church and pray for Robert McNamara." Still no reply. "I was kidding, you dope."

"I know," he said.

"You're such a liar," she said, trailing delicate fingers along the seam of his jeans inside his thigh. "Wait," she said. She got up, rummaged through drawers, found half a joint, came back to bed, and lit up. Cheskis asked for a hit.

"You told me not to."

"I'm such a liar," he said, reaching for the joint.

"No you don't," she said, holding it away from him. "You want some of this doobie you've gotta pay."

"Anything," he said.

"Dope fiend," she said.

"Sex fiend," he said.

"You see right through my plan."

He leaned forward and kissed her on the mouth. She brought out her tongue just enough—warm, sweet—then, pulling back, handed him the joint. He took a deep drag, handed it back to her, and, holding the smoke in his lungs, managed to say, "But don't give any to Roybal." Exhale.

"Why not?"

"You know. He's in training."

"I thought you both were."

A squealing came from the living room along with grown-up male voices and some kind of banging sounds. Cheskis jumped up and put on the T-shirt while naked Samantha matter-of-factly stretched across the bed and peered underneath for some kind of garment. In the living room Cheskis found Roybal and a large balding, blondish man Cheskis had never seen before. They'd cleared floor debris and were racing across the room on all fours, each with a squealing little girl on his back. The stranger reached the wall first and turned to race back. But Annie, his passenger, swayed toward the floor, yelling, "Oh, oh, oh—" The man flipped over quickly, saving her fall, but they ended up in a pile. Meanwhile, Roybal, with Annie's sister squealing in delight, negotiated the turn successfully. The stranger lunged forward and grabbed Roybal by the ankle. "No fair, no fair," Annie's sister yelled. He let go, and the sister tagged the wall. "Two out of three!" the stranger hollered out.

By this time Samantha emerged wearing a bright, flowered robe. "Kenny," she said, looking pleased.

"Hi, sweetheart." He rose quickly and they fell into a hug that might or might not be sexual. Smiling, the man let her go and stuck his hand out toward Cheskis. "I'm Ken," he said. The thick, muscled fingers could have been a carpenter's. Cheskis prepared for a dumbass squeeze contest but got only a manly shake.

Samantha placed her arm around Cheskis and kissed him on the cheek. "Isn't he a sweet bundle of love?" she said to Ken.

"Unequivocally," he said.

"Use littler words, okay?" Roybal said. "I'm just a poor Mexican."

"And you already met Roybal," she said. Roybal was still on all fours with Annie's sister straddling his back and hanging onto his ears. Cheskis couldn't remember her name. She and Annie were about a year apart.

"We didn't just meet him. We murdered him," Roybal said. "We're the champs."

"Right," the sister said.

It turned out that sometime during the night Ken had stumbled in and curled up on the floor near Roybal. Cheskis, suspecting the visitor had planned to sleep with Samantha, was unsure who was the cuckold—him or the other guy. For a man who'd evidently had a hard night before ending up on Samantha's floor, Ken was remarkably chipper. He decided everybody should join him somewhere for a giant breakfast. He was buying. "No arguments," he said.

"Who's arguing, Gringo?" Roybal said. "You stole California, you buy breakfast."

"Roybal, I especially want you to come—in case they're short of busboys," Ken said.

"You're such a white bastard," Samantha said.

"I'm a polka dot bastard," he said. "Right, girls?"

"Yeah, he's polka dots," Annie's sister squealed, and the two little girls giggled.

In minutes everyone was dressed and tooling down the road in Ken's VW van, the little girls chirping about things they saw along the way. The vehicle, of indeterminate age, was painted a bright blue that didn't come out of any factory and the front doors had "INTREPID TRIPS, INC." etched on them in big, orange, quirky letters. Roybal sat up front with Ken, who somehow had managed to put everyone into a contagiously fine humor. Cheskis felt like a student who'd landed in just the right class for once.

"So what're you guys? Colonels or something?" Ken said. The haircuts always gave them away. The Defense Department apparently feared if military personnel wore their hair like everyone else they might mingle too much with the populace they were supposed to defend with their last drops of blood.

"They're secret police," Samantha said.

"Yeah? What're you working on these days?" Ken said.

"It's a secret," Cheskis, Roybal, and Samantha answered almost simultaneously. Samantha's girls whooped and giggled.

"I'm gonna get French toast!" said Annie's sister, who, Cheskis learned again, was named Delyte and answered to Delly.

"Me too," Ken said. "Stacks and stacks of French toast. They'll have to send out a truck for them."

"Where's the truck get 'em?" Delly asked.

"From the French toast factory. Listen, children," Ken said. "I must apologize, but I need to take a little detour of approximately—"

"What's a detour?" Annie said.

"I have to go a little out of our way."

"Awww!" the sisters half-yelled.

"Less than a mile. A minor, minor delay to pick up a friend. Then it's on to the French toast dispensary. Okay?"

"Okay!" the little girls whooped.

"You're Kesey!" Roybal declared, spitting out the words as if to say, "Ah ha!"

58

"You are secret police, aren't you," Ken said. "Disguised as a Mexican, I see. Clever. But not clever enough, hombre. I'm on to you."

It took Cheskis a half-beat to put the Ken and the Kesey into a single context. He was in a van with a celebrated novelist whose output was being compared to the work of Thomas Wolfe and J. D. Salinger. Kesey pulled up at an old yellow house on a street with no sidewalks. It had a beat-up, faded exterior much like Samantha's place. "Be right back," he said.

"Where'd you meet Kesey?" Cheskis asked Samantha.

"Same place I met you, sweetheart." Two weekends earlier she'd waited on Cheskis inside the Catalyst, a loose, cavernous joint that offered music, food, and booze in several rooms thrown together in dissimilar, slapdash décor that somehow managed to be relaxing and noisy at the same time. Her waitressing was only slightly better than her housekeeping.

Cheskis had never met a celebrity before, although last year he shook Vice President Humphrey's hand when he'd campaigned on campus. In a filled auditorium, students cheered as Humphrey took humorous slaps at hapless Barry Goldwater and his dark, nuclear image. Cheskis was already sorry he knew Kesey's identity. Fame changed everything, every glance, every aside. If he tried to ignore it, that would be an act too.

Kesey came out the door accompanied by a disheveled, sandy-haired man who looked even older than Kesey. He had a lined, distinctively handsome, Mount Rushmore kind of face. Later Cheskis and Roybal would learn that this was the legendary Neal Cassady—model for Kerouac's whirling Dervish Dean Moriarty in *On the Road*. Cassady and Kesey had bumped into each other somewhere inside the small galaxy of whatever was hip. Trailing behind Cassady were two skinny, sexy girls in frilly white blouses and tight cutoffs who looked slightly Japanese, slightly Mexican, and were no doubt Filipino. They playfully tried to drag Cassady back into the house while he kept talking:

"No, no my darlings, it's imperative that we make a pancake journey," he said in double-time. "We'll follow Kenny in your

59

sturdy, Michigan-made Studebaker and enjoy a splendid American breakfast in the company of illustrious, fascinating companions. I shall personally take the wheel so we don't wind up taking a tragically wrong turn. Keys, please."

Ken left the threesome standing on the scraggly lawn, popped back into the driver's seat, and took off while Cassady kept talking. Their destination was Arthur's, a café with a worn stucco exterior surrounded by wildflowers. There was no sign out front—not unusual in this part of Northern California, where locals tried to prevent tourists from finding their hangouts. Inside, diners sat at rough-hewn benches where they smoked, talked, and ate in cheerful bunches. This is not the America that's going to war, Cheskis realized. That must be on another floor. But he was starting to feel comfortable in Santa Cruz, a place unlike any he'd ever been. Residents lived among winterless, green hills that overlooked the sea, and the easy life just washed over them, giving them time to sit over bongs and argue the nature of the universe. He couldn't understand how all these people made a living without factories or steel mills, without navigable waterways or railroad yards—none of the things that brought people to crude, powerful cities like Kansas City and Chicago.

Residents here gathered in tribes—surfers, bikers, poets, all coexisting, sometimes commingling. Over in Monterey, Cheskis had found coffee houses along Cannery Row where a smug crowd played chess and passed around mimeographed poetry. Cheskis's G.I. haircut made him a rube at their carnival. But they'd all love Kesey even if he wasn't *the* Kesey. Put Kesey in the infantry and in two days everyone in the squad would be copying his every gesture.

Neal, seated at the other end of the table, never stopped his marathon monologue while his two ladies played their roles as adoring bookends with exquisite tenacity. Samantha's daughters gobbled their breakfasts, quickly tired of the restaurant's crayons, and went outside to play. Cheskis, having only black coffee and yogurt, had been terribly tempted by the mounds of bacon, ham, scrambled eggs, French toast, and all the other steaming, fragrant items that would prevent him from getting down to 132. He forced himself to eat his yogurt, one of the sour, white foods he could barely keep down. Kesey, who'd been a high school and college wrestler, understood his suffering. "How far are you from your weight?" he asked Cheskis.

"Less than five pounds, but the closer I get the harder it gets."

"You use diuretics before the weigh-in?"

"Yeah."

"Which ones?"

"Whatever the coach gives me."

Kesey advised celery, daffodil, or alfalfa, which he said could be purchased in tablets at health food stores. He also told him about senna leaves, a natural, heavy-duty laxative. "It scoops out whatever's in your intestines, which is more than you think. I bet it's worth three or four pounds. You're home, man. Eat something."

"Our coach knows all the tricks," said Roybal. At times Roybal treated advice from outsiders as though it were an attack on Valaitas. But Valaitas himself was uncomfortable when people deified him. He preferred to merge into his surroundings. Name a kick-ass Army school that shredded and reassembled trainees into deadlier assassins and Valaitas had been through it— Rangers, airborne, Special Forces, all of it, even jungle school in Panama. But his fatigues were bare. He didn't wear the tabs he was entitled to. Cheskis once heard the battalion commander chew him out for it. Soldiers risked life and limb to earn some of those patches. "I washed out of Ranger School," the colonel had said. "Did you know that?"

"No sir," Valaitas answered.

"And it gripes my ass that you show so little respect for your accomplishments."

"I respect Ranger School," Valaitas said. "And I respect you, sir. You probably got screwed by chicken shit."

"We could stand here all day and blow smoke up each other's ass," the colonel said, "but I wish to hell you'd get those tabs sewed on."

61

"I know sir," Valaitas answered, leaving a pregnant void where a promise ought to be.

"Ask them what they do all day," Samantha said.

"What do you do all day?" Kesey said.

"We beat each other up," Roybal said.

"Look what they make friends do to each other," she said, suddenly serious. She must have been storing this resentment.

"They don't make us, Sam," Cheskis said. "I know it looks loony, but we enjoy it." He wouldn't even try to explain how they both cherished the everyday "work"—the sparring, the adrenaline rush of facing down another man, whoever he is, to take a shot and still be there.

"Getting slapped around is just what Ches needs," Roybal said.

Kesey studied them both as though he had something on his mind. Finally, he said, "Can you guys sit out your hitch doing what you're doing?"

"Maybe," Cheskis said. "But not here. We'd have to make the Army team. In Colorado."

"And if you don't?"

"You get maybe three months to show your stuff here," Cheskis explained. "Then maybe you get a tryout. If you're not picked, you get orders for somewhere else."

"Like Vietnam?" Samantha said.

"Maybe," Cheskis said.

"Ches is gonna make it for sure," Roybal said.

"He's the one I'd bet on," Cheskis said of Roybal. "He's got the talent. I've just got the tricks."

Without any warning, Samantha started sobbing softly. Seriously sizable tears flowed down her tanned, lustrous skin. It made her look a little like Ingrid Bergman in *Casablanca*. Cheskis didn't know what to do. "It's okay, sweetheart," Kesey said, placing a hand on her shoulder. Now that Kesey got there first, Cheskis felt even clumsier. But he put his arm around this woman, suddenly painfully aware that he didn't really know her very well. "What's wrong, Samantha?" he said. He squeezed her tighter against him, and, sobbing even harder, she threw both arms around him. He thought she might lose her breath, like a small child who'd cried too hard and too long. Cheskis walked her outside to the makeshift parking lot. He realized then she must be his girlfriend. Samantha's daughters, playing some kind of game in the dirt, immediately ran over and hugged her, pulling at her long skirt. "Don't cry, Mommy," they said repeatedly but not together. "Don't cry, Mommy." And bam, they started crying too.

That's when Neal and his bookends shot out the door, not stopping for pleasantries. The girlfriends looked back uncertainly but kept up with him. In moments all three were in their dirty green Studebaker, shooting down the road into the Santa Cruz greenery.

"It's just so damn ugly, so sad," Samantha said. Her voice trembled like Billy Holiday's, as though it might not get to where it was headed. "Fighting each other so you don't have to go off and fight? It's like *Spartacus*. Remember when Kirk Douglas killed Tony Curtis? To save him from being crucified? We haven't progressed at all. What the hell is wrong with us? You turn around for just a minute and they start another war."

"We don't go all-out," Cheskis said. "We don't really hurt each other."

"I'm okay, kids," Samantha told her daughters. "I love you. Now scram, all right?" The girls ran to Kesey and Roybal, just coming out the door.

"You're such a kid, Lee," Samantha said. "All of you, you're all just kids. You're a smart one, but they're screwing you and you don't even know it. You should never have let them take you."

"Good advice, Sam. Next time they draft me, I'll just mention your name." Cheskis was ashamed to tell her he could have stayed out had he really wanted to. The loopholes were closing fast, but only a few months earlier you could get a deferment just for getting married or enrolling as a grad student. Cheskis had considered law school, but he was broke. He should have made a more spirited effort to join a Guard or Reserve unit. Anyway, he was lucky to be stationed at Fort Ord, situated among a string of palmed resorts, with Santa Cruz and San Francisco to its north and the Big Sur mountains to the south. Most of the other guys from his Basic Training unit were sent for further training at famously dreary posts such as Fort Leonard Wood, Missouri or Fort Polk, Louisiana, hundreds of miles from anyplace civilized. Cheskis had boxed in a tournament at Leonard Wood. The nearby town was a sad, scheming cluster of pawn shops, used car lots, beery juke joints and trailers used by bitter, ten-dollar whores whose soldier customers lined up outside as though waiting for diphtheria shots. Thinking about it, he took Samantha by the hand. "Why don't we go back to your place?" he told her. "I'll lend Roybal the car for an hour."

"Make it two hours," she said.

FEBRUARY 1984

CHAPTER 8

COUNTY

Cheskis found a dark man in a dark suit waiting for him—a man very much at home, not troubled by the sinister tumult just outside the room. Looking up from the cigarette-scarred Formica table, he told Cheskis he was Paul Castro, his court-assigned attorney. It was a spare, nearly bare room about the size of a classroom, bigger than it needed to be. It reeked of stupid deeds and dead ends. The teeming jail beyond the door didn't hold master criminals who cracked safes filled with gold ingots. Typical inmates broke into a gas station that had seventy bucks in the register, shot someone for no good reason, or were ratted out by a friend in a small-time dope deal. Cheskis, suddenly embarrassed by his orange jumpsuit, closed the door behind him as he limped over and took one of two available beat-up blonde-wood seats across from the lawyer, who had a briefcase and a file folder on the table in front of him. "I'm Lee Cheskis," he said.

"The guy who hits cops."

"Did I miss the trial?"

"Listen, you hit a cop. They've got a rule around here. Hit a cop, go to jail."

"What if a cop is strangling somebody's mother?"

"Then you call another cop. I don't make the rules, but anyway, the cop wasn't strangling a mother."

"How do you know? You haven't even interviewed me yet."

"Good point," Castro said. "So what happened? Before you hit the cop."

"A four-hundred-pound Mexican with a giant head was trying to turn me into pancake batter. So when another Mexican came at me, I sort of figured he was up to no good."

"Yeah, those damn Mexicans."

"May I assume you're Mexican-American?"

66

Castro nodded affirmatively.

"I'll use whatever words you prefer," Cheskis said. "Latin, Hispanic, Mexican, Mexican-American, though he could have been Guatemalan or something. I didn't check his papers. Nationality wasn't the issue. You want to marry my sister, you won't hear a peep out of me."

"No offense," the lawyer said, "But your sister might be a little old for me. Or dumpy, dull, too cheerful, psychotic, addicted to who-knows-what substances or up to her eyes in credit card debt. How's her cellulite situation? I just hate cellulite, don't you?"

"Men are such pigs," Cheskis said. "Now may I be frank?"

"Of course."

"If I were some rich bastard, what would that get me lawyer-wise? As opposed to you."

"Let's see, you might have made bail by now because it goes through a longer process when the lawyer's appointed by the court. Also, your attorney would have a nice embossed business card, but actually, I do too." He handed Cheskis his card, embossed gold and black on white.

"Nice card."

"Thanks. My cousin down in Santa Ana prints them. A rich-folks attorney might have a more expensive tie, he wouldn't be wearing an off-the-rack suit, but you'd still be screwed because you broke the nose of—" He flipped through the file on the table—"Martin Marquez. Off-duty LAPD officer."

"Look, when I found out he was a cop, I stopped."

"It says that here," the lawyer said.

"You kidding? The cop told the truth?"

"Sure, he's a Mexican. Now let's start from the beginning."

"It was all very stupid," Cheskis interjected.

"Mr. Cheskis? I see these situations all the time. That's the one thing they have in common. They're all very stupid. What looks really stupid, at least from my point of view, is hanging around a sleazy joint in East Hollywood in the first place. You don't run into Rhodes Scholars down there."

"They had a fight on TV I wanted to see. Look, you want to find out what happened or not?"

"Okay, go on."

"During the fight—"

"The one on TV."

"Yes. I was having a civilized conversation with the guy next to me and—"

"Not the man with the giant head."

"No, another guy."

"He have a name?"

"I didn't catch it."

Castro read down the police report. "Could he be Mr. Daklondo Moore of 4815 Melrose Avenue?"

"Could be. This guy's black, right?"

"Let's face it, he sounds black."

"What'd he say?" Cheskis said.

"Let's just get your version first."

"I'm not giving you a version," Cheskis said. "I'm telling you what happened. The subject of Duran came up."

"When?"

"During my conversation with the black guy."

"Roberto Duran?"

"Yes. And I pointed out that Duran is old and fat so he's fighting guys who are too big for him. He should get down in weight or retire."

"You said that with Mexicans around?" the lawyer said.

"Duran's from Panama," Cheskis said.

The lawyer shook his head to signal the extent of Cheskis's hopeless naiveté. Castro's thick black hair was combed stylishly over his ears. He took care with his appearance, even to the point of wearing a pressed handkerchief in the breast pocket of his suit jacket. Except for his mannerisms, he could easily pass for gay. He might even be gay, Cheskis decided.

"Excuse me, what's your name again?"

"Castro."

"Okay, Mr. Castro, I wasn't even talking to this guy."

"The man with the giant head."

68

"Right. And he started yelling at me and threatening me."

"Mr. Hector Torres?"

"If Hector Torres has a giant fat head. *Una cabeza grande.*"

"Lay off the Spanglish, Mr. Cheskis. Or do you want to do this in Spanish?"

"What if I said yes? You speak Spanish?" Cheskis asked him.

"No, actually."

Under other circumstances, Cheskis might have enjoyed this little victory. "The fool with the big head—"

"Mr. Torres."

"Torres. While he's yelling in my face he removes his watch and hands it to his girlfriend."

"Where'd she come from?"

"I don't know. She came from wherever four-hundred-pound shitheads with enormous heads find their girlfriends."

"Then what?"

"I hit him."

"So you struck first," Castro said.

"Look, this guy already promised to kill me. Was I supposed to wait?"

"You were supposed to get the hell out of there."

"You're right. You're absolutely right. It's what I should have done. He asked me outside. I should have gone out there and then run like hell."

"Just when did he ask you outside?"

"While he was shouting."

"Before or after he removed his watch?"

Cheskis searched his memory. "Before, I think."

"We'll get back to that. So why didn't you try to leave?"

"Lots of reasons. I was watching a good fight. The place was crowded, and I didn't want to turn my back on him. You never go outside with these creeps anyway. Out there he might pull a razor, a gun, he might have friends. You're always safer in the bar."

"I'll remember that next time I insult Roberto Duran in front of drunk Mexicans. Tell me. You do this often?"

"No."

"You've been arrested before, though. For fighting. It says so right here."

"Not convicted," Cheskis said.

"I see some disturbing the peaces down here. I think we know what they mean. You're too old for this crap, Cheskis. It says here you teach college. Is that right?"

"Part time," Cheskis said. "At Palos Blancas."

"What do you teach?"

"Journalism. Or at least I used to. I've missed two classes."

"I'll try to get your bail reduced. Did you see a bail bondsman?"

"I never got the chance."

"Everybody gets the chance. I've seen people I wouldn't touch with a leaf blower make bail through a bondsman."

"Believe me, I tried. Nobody would listen," Cheskis said.

"They're playing games with you," Castro said. "Do you know you're on level eight? That's for psychos and murderers. Probably some jailer's idea of a joke. Throw the white professor to the barracuda, watch the fun. Cheskis. I never heard that name. Are you Jewish?"

"Does that make a difference?"

"This is idle chatter, Cheskis. Stop looking for street fights."

"Sorry. My father was Jewish."

"How'd you get busted up?" Castro asked him. In addition to the bad ankle, Cheskis had a discolored eye, a generically bruised face, and a nasty scab running all the way down one forearm.

"I fell."

"You've seen too many movies, Cheskis. Half the guys in here would rat out their mamas for a Quaalude. I'll try to get you into a safer section. I'll do it right away, but things move slowly around here. I'm surprised you're not in the hospital already. People get carried out of here all the time."

"I know. Just when everything's calm, all of a sudden somebody's trying to gouge somebody's eye out. Most of the time you don't know why, either."

"There's always a reason," Castro said. "Even though it may not look reasonable to most of us. Sometimes it started out on the street, or maybe a deal went wrong. A gambling debt, bio-rhythms. Something. Okay, let's back up and start at the beginning. Take me through it."

Castro took occasional notes as Cheskis related the whole sorry tale of his fight with the man with the giant head. The man was thick everywhere—his arms, his chest, his gut, probably his eyelashes. But the size of his head was startling. He could have walked out of a Picasso. Only his eyes were small. Dullish crystals that peeked above his fleshy cheeks. A beast with so great a trunk that Cheskis knew he'd have to get very close just to reach the extraterrestrial head that looked impervious to injury anyway. Cheskis, reminding himself it wasn't good to think too much in these situations, stepped inside and threw two lefts—a straight shot to the body, which felt like encased mucus, then an uppercut that missed the jaw but caught lips, teeth, and some nose. Cheskis stepped away as he ducked beneath any possible counterpunches, keeping his right pinned to his cheek. He quickly assessed the damage, like a submarine skipper peering into a periscope. Fathead, bleeding from nose and mouth, showed more rage than shock, no fear.

Cheskis stepped back in and hooked to the body with a right as fathead charged in throwing wild punches, winding up his fat arms. Cheskis got slammed with an elbow and felt his right eye close immediately. He slipped underneath again and landed a straight left and right to nuts so encased with fat he thought he might have missed them altogether. But then fathead howled and doubled over. He threw his whale weight over Cheskis, who didn't slip out in time and thumped to the floor as though crushed beneath an elevator. Cheskis heard a crack as fathead's elbow broke his fall. The tissue-paper carpet stank from decades of spilled beer. As the monster yowled, clutching at Cheskis, Cheskis worked to scramble out. Wrestling, he was a fish out of water. Oh, Jesus, fathead had a handful of his shirt. Somebody kicked him in an armpit. The girlfriend. As fathead, using his good arm, tried to encase Cheskis in a headlock, a voice in his head whispered that dying here and now might not be so terrible. Screw that, he grabbed the monster's hair in his right fist and slammed him with repeated lefts to the head. Still on the floor, Cheskis felt a kick to his chest and grabbed the girlfriend's leg. He got hold of her belt, pulling himself up as she twisted and clawed at him. She was one of those young Mexican-American women who carefully smeared their naturally brown complexion with a powdery gray paste that Cheskis would find on himself later.

Another Mexican came at Cheskis, who smashed the man's nose with a left, then tripped the gray-skinned girlfriend down on her fatheaded lover. The Mexican with the smashed nose pulled a semiautomatic the size of a boot and with both hands thrust it in the face of Cheskis, who, expecting a bullet, involuntarily closed his eyes. As he opened them again the gunman grabbed him by the shirt with one hand and held the pistol inches from his nose. "Hit the floor!" he yelled through the blood, trying to force Cheskis to his knees. He slapped the barrel against Cheskis's ear. "Get down, I said." When Cheskis sank to his knees, the gunman ordered him to put his hands behind his back. No bullet yet. Could this be a cop? Cheskis was ready to kiss him. Again, "Hands behind your back!" this time accompanied by a kick to a kidney. Cheskis, feeling a blend of nausea and pain, complied, and the gunman-cop handcuffed him. But bless him, the cop, blood all over his face, now trained his pistol on fathead, who was rubbing his elbow. He and the gray-skinned girlfriend had made it to their feet. Seeing the pistol, they froze in place, suddenly placid—comfortable with the routine. The cuffs, the ride down to the station where they would describe all the outrageous, unjust misdeeds that had been committed by some crazy person they'd tried to ignore. Among a chorus of pains, Cheskis began noticing that the tendons around his right ankle felt like they'd been stretched over a loom.

"Well, it looks to me like self-defense against the bar patrons and extenuating circumstances on the cop," Castro told him. "We'll see if everybody's had a chance to cool down. Torres and his girlfriend were also charged, but the D.A.'s trying to stick you with assaulting a police officer. That's the one to worry about. I told you, hit a cop, go to jail."

"Meanwhile, can I get out of here? I may still have a job to save."

"We'll ask if anybody tested the cop for alcohol. They almost certainly didn't. Start in on that and they might back off. Did you see him drinking? This Marquez."

"I never noticed him until he came at me, but hey, when do I get out?"

"What I'll be trying to do is plead you down to disturbing the peace. They'll say they want aggravated assault, but I think I can get them down to the disturbance charge or maybe we'll have to settle for common assault. They're both misdemeanors."

"Can we beat the charges?" Cheskis asked him.

"You don't understand. We're pleading *nolo contendre* to either disturbing the peace or common assault. If we go to trial, they'll charge you with everything. I guarantee it." A trial, he explained, wouldn't start for at least six weeks, and if Cheskis failed to make bail, the time would be spent here. "Lose the trial and you could go to the penitentiary," he said. "We're talking about a felony. You assaulted two customers and then hit a cop. That's what everybody saw."

"But can't we win if there's a trial?"

"Taking this to a judge is suicide. He knows the rule, and you hit a cop. So maybe he dismisses the felony, finds you guilty of common assault and sentences you to time served, which, as I said, would be several more weeks. What have you gained?"

"What about a jury trial?"

"Don't take the chance of going to prison."

"You don't believe in the legal system?"

"Of course I do, if it's used properly. I advise you to use it properly."

"If we make the deal? What happens then?"

"You could be out in a couple days."

"Make the deal," Cheskis said.

"If I can, I will."

"You think you can?"

"I think I can. Now let me ask you something, okay?"

73

"Sure," Cheskis said. But he felt numb between his ears watching this fool who was himself extend his rap sheet.

"Cheskis."

Cheskis blinked his eyes and looked to Castro.

"You okay?"

"Just peachy," Cheskis said.

Castro studied him now as though he were some mysterious object. "What're you doing to yourself, man? I mean what're you doing here?"

"You sure I don't belong here?" He barely got those words out. Unbelievable. He was tearing up. He stood, turning away. Castro offered to call the college. Cheskis shook his head no and was out the door.

Cheskis ate at a table with other unconnected misfits who weren't crazy enough to be locked up with the schizophrenics or harmless enough for the wing reserved for white-collar types and pretty youths. He tried not to think about the saliva and who knows what else some of the kitchen goofballs were probably sneaking into the food. Finished with his bologna, white bread, and canned green beans, he left the pink pudding untouched as he prepared for the lonely walk back to his cell. "Know why we keep you alive, *jefe*?" Cheskis looked up into a brown face across the table that hadn't been there moments ago. A good-looking Latino with short, slicked-back hair, a droopy mustache, and a kind of hangdog look until he opened his mouth and shot off his voice like a hot rod. Cheskis had seen him before but never at this table. He was heavily tattooed and moved around the jail as though strolling his private grounds. "It's an experiment," the man continued. "We want to watch what happens to a rich Jew in here who don't pay his rent."

"I'm not rich," said Cheskis. He'd been in two fistfights before lunch. Each night he slept with his feet toward the bars so he wouldn't get stabbed in the head by someone passing down the corridor. Just three cells away a sleeping man had been knifed in the foot.

"You're famous here, *jefe*—a professor. We never got a professor before. That's good money you're making, right?"

"Nice to know you care," Cheskis told him, "but if I had any money I'd be out on bail, right?"

"Maybe. Or maybe you got an older brother or somebody who inherited the family business so you had to be a rabbi or a professor or something and you couldn't get word to them on the sailboat."

"How'd you know where I work?" Cheskis asked him.

"I'll ask the questions, *jefe*. You got what? Another week inside?"

"Wish I knew," Cheskis said.

"Six hundred fifty, man. That's what it takes to keep one dumb *guayaba* healthy for a week. You get your friends to call this number." He pulled out a chewed pencil. "Give me something to write on," he said to the African-American inmate next to him. The man scrambled through his pockets and came up with a dead Lotto ticket. The Latin man took it without comment, wrote a number on it, and handed it to Cheskis.

"I don't know who to call," Cheskis told him. Sadly true. No one to call on in a pinch, to put a little cash in his jail account so he could skip the unspeakable cafeteria swill in favor of the vending-machine fare that was the jail's version of haute cuisine.

"Where you from?"

"Kansas City, New York, lots of places."

"You got to find a home, *jefe*. Everybody needs a home, okay? Now listen, guy like you, you'll think of somebody. They gotta get the money to one a my homeys inside a two days. By this time Thursday or the deal's off. You should be happy, *jefe*. There's no shame in buying your life in this place. You showed you got balls, but balls, they take you only so far. Say you get a knife. Say you kill me, no easy thing."

"Who's talking about killing you?"

"Just saying. You wanna do twenty years to save a lousy six hundred and fifty smackers?"

This gangster, Cheskis realized, had arrived at exactly the right figure to make the deal worth doing for all parties. Cheskis smiled at him and said, "Four fifty."

"I can see you're one a those depressed, moody whiteboys whose mommy didn't love him enough. So I threw you a bone. But we ain't really friends, *jefe*. Six fifty's the price." Cheskis nodded his understanding, then carried his tray and its remnants to the waste area, where trays were piled all over the counter in various balancing acts and the leftover food didn't smell quite like food.

Cheskis was in a cell with three other men. All of them mostly just grunted at each other, but Cheskis felt less tension in his cell, where an unspoken truce prevailed. The cellblock's principal drawback consisted of a mad regiment of tinny radios that assaulted the air with competing rap, R&B, salsa, and country-western, creating auditory hell on earth. As Cheskis sat on his bunk leafing through a three-year old *Popular Mechanics*, the cellmate across from him said, "You know who that guy was? The one talking to you in the cafeteria?"

Cheskis looked up to see he wasn't the same cellmate who'd been there for three days. Somebody made a switch. He told the man, whom he guessed was Iranian but turned out later to be Armenian, "I don't even know who *you* are."

"Mike. I'm Mike."

"Okay, Mike. So who was that guy?"

"Felix Oliveira, man, from the East Valley. A very dangerous cat."

"Funny. He told me he was a Certified Public Accountant."

"I'm trying to help you, man. Don't disrespect me." Mike was on the thin side, and looked to be nearly as old as Cheskis, which around here made him a geezer. He squinted when he talked. His teeth were movie star white and now he looked agitated, at the edge of anger, a reminder of why it was a bad idea to talk to anyone. The prevailing mood was sickly rage.

"I was just making a little joke, okay? A joke." Cheskis was tired of making concessions to the prevailing psychosis and felt himself speaking in a higher pitch, breathing faster, preparing to explode for his own safety.

"Okay, man, okay. I'm just not used to jokes, is all. Not in here."

Cheskis took a deep breath and stuck out his hand. "I'm Ches." Mike had paid six packs of cigarettes to be transferred out of a cell with a cracked toilet and a geek who talked to himself. Also from the East Valley, Mike said Oliveira was an enforcer on the streets and in the slammer. "You better believe he's wasted people. He's also a fighter, a boxer, you know?"

"What's his weight division?"

"Don't know. But he's got a good record. Lotta wins. What'd he want from you?"

Cheskis thought a moment. "It's best not to tell you."

"Just pay 'em. No offense, but white guys, a lot of times they have to pay in this section, except for Italians, guys like that. The Aryan Brotherhood."

"Aren't you a white guy?"

"Yeah, but I'm Armenian. I got friends. Let me tell you, when these guys choose you for a target, fighting 'em don't help. Beating 'em don't help. They'll jump you four or five at a time if they have to. What got you in here anyway?"

"Petty crap."

"I don't know, man. Around here you can fall between the cracks. I been here since before Christmas. Waiting for the wheels to grind, you know? At least in the pen you can move around. They got a library, weights, somethin'. You know guys cop a plea just to get to a penitentiary?" Cheskis believed it. Another week in here and he'd confess he'd been on the grassy knoll with a hunting rifle. Which wouldn't surprise Mike. Cheskis learned his new friend believed in a cartoon world of ubiquitous conspiracies in which nothing was as it seemed. "They never tell you the truth," he said repeatedly. JFK was murdered by Nixon, LBJ, the FBI, CIA, and the Mafia, which was run by Sinatra. His singing was just a front. Oswald and Sirhan Sirhan were both pathetic patsies. Extraterrestrials had kidnapped and released who knows how many Earthlings, and Mike wasn't fooled by the Trilateral Commission or the Bilderbergers, a secretive group of capitalist chieftains and their government vassals who met annually to run around naked in the forest in the dead of night. They were at the bottom of every damn thing wrong in America.

"Wait a minute," Cheskis said. "Isn't it the Bohemian Grove conspirators who run naked in the forest? The Bilderbergers meet at golf resorts."

"How come you know so much about them?" asked Mike. Cheskis couldn't help noticing he'd pulled a gleaming eight-inch shiv from inside a metal bunk post, waving it in front of Cheskis's nose like a cobra.

"I read a story about them. In the *Berkeley Barb,* I think." His back to the wall, Cheskis looked around for something he could use to shield him or perhaps bash Mike's head in. The other occupants of the cell were quarreling over Cheskis's toilet articles.

"Oh yeah, I read that," said Mike, putting down the blade. "Sorry, man."

"You can't be too careful," said Cheskis, steering Mike to less troublesome discourse. In jail, this was pretty easy. All you had to do was ask someone what the authorities were doing to screw him. But Mike, though he considered himself a victim, also freely admitted his crime, which was atypical. No matter what grievous acts they'd perpetrated to get themselves in here, the inmates, almost to a man, felt unjustly singled out. "Got laid off from the battery factory and I had all a these child support people on my ass," Mike explained. So he turned to till-tapping. He'd find a store that felt right, then wait like a tiger in the grass for the cash register to open, grabbing bills and tearing out of the place. "I met some dudes I knew from the street who were doing pretty good so I thought I'd try it too. Where you go is one a these outdoor shopping centers where they can't close off the corridors? Then you pick your spot and map out a getaway."

But he had a trick knee from The Nam "and the V.A. won't do shit about it." After he was cornered and captured at the Old Town Mall in Torrance, he realized at last that his disability made him unfit for nonviolent felonies. Cheskis nodded his head compassionately.

"Were you in the service?" Mike asked him—a casual question, just part of the conversational flow. No, lied Cheskis. Mike, a little younger than Cheskis, faced conscription during the lottery years, when the government organized everybody's luck. "I came up Number Fourteen," Mike said. "Story a my life. Lemme tell you, you didn't miss a thing. I got drafted into the fucken Marines, too. Can you believe that? There were two of us in boot camp, draftees. The other one banged his head against a tree till they let him out. When he first started doing it, we told 'em, 'Cut off an ear instead. Let 'em know you're serious.' But then he got out. We couldn't believe it. I shoulda banged my head against a tree. But he got there first."

"Sometimes," Cheskis said, "the simplest strategy is the best strategy."

"Ain't it the truth?" said Mike, who'd served in an artillery battery around Da Nang. This duty was only moderately dangerous, he said. "The generals, they didn't want the NVA to get any of our guns. Make 'em look bad, you know. So we always had plenty of grunts between us and the bad guys. Those grunts, though, they were expendable, and a whole lot of 'em got expended, let me tell you. What I didn't like was when we moved the guns. Then you had to worry about mines, snipers. Anything could happen on those roads."

Had Cheskis risked Vietnam he might be looking back at it almost fondly, as Mike did. Instead, it reminded him of a stink on his soul.

At dinner Mike led Cheskis to a table of Armenians from Glendale. Cheskis wasn't introduced to anybody, but he felt no particular hostility from them. He spotted Oliveira at his regular table, and after finishing his lukewarm spaghetti, picked up his tray and made his way over there, careful not to bump anyone.

"Sit down, whitey," Oliveira said. "Tell us about your golf game." Men at the table chuckled. They all looked like they'd kill a man for his shoes and then go out for a hamburger.

"I thought about it," Cheskis said. "There's no one to give me the money. I mean no disrespect. I'm just telling you how it is."

Oliveira showed no expression. "Take a walk with me, *jefe*. Leave the tray."

Cheskis followed him past the pile of dirty trays and garbage down a corridor to the TV room. Filling up after dinner, it was already standing room only. Oliveira approached two Latinos who'd scored chairs. They rose wordlessly, and Cheskis sat down with Oliveira. A gorgeous local anchorwoman was reading a news story on the overhead TV and all around the room men debated the intensity and frequency of her sexual activities.

"I'm thinking, hey, maybe this dude wants to die or something. That it, *jefe?*"

Cheskis didn't answer immediately. "No," he said finally.

"I hear you take care of yourself pretty good. You been in the ring?"

"Just the amateurs."

"I got a silver medal. You know that? From the '76 Olympics."

"No, but I heard you're a pro."

"When they had the U.S. tryouts I had two broken fingers. So I went down to the Mexican trials—see, I was born in Jalisco. I knocked out their two best guys. I woulda won the gold, but by then the whole hand was fucked up and I lost to the Russian." Oliveira's expression suddenly changed from friendly to blank. "Us both being fighters, that don't buy you nothing, *jefe.* Life is hard."

Cheskis, as he'd done so often since entering the jail, felt a kind of nausea as he visualized his own death, not as a distant reality, but as an imminent event he could almost taste.

"This don't add up," Oliveira said. You're not one a those, you know, uncomfortable whiteys? The nervous ones? Don't know what to say? Guys like you, they got friends. How long you been in L.A.?"

"Five years."

"What about the people you work with? Professors."

"I don't much like them."

"Okay, but do they like you?"

As Cheskis shook his head it occurred to him that he had a stronger bond with this tattooed sociopath putting the squeeze on him than anyone in his department. Their communication, bolstered by its immediacy, had texture, even if it would end with Oliveira killing him.

There might be people who'd give him the six fifty if he could find them—Maggie, for instance. Nice way to touch base with an ex-wife. *I'm in jail, I need protection money.* But he couldn't fling himself at the ankles of friends or lovers he'd jettisoned, from the Army, work, college, high school. It had made sense to leave them behind because they didn't know him anyway, not the core of him. A sister would be a logical place to go, but Judith, even if he found her commune, even if it had a telephone, would offer him, at best, advice from the *I Ching*.

"Listen, you're getting out of here, *jefe*. Real soon. You got a car, right? You can sell it, give me the money." Oliveira's blank expression was rooted deeply in the Earth, a thousand years before Cortez. The eyes were incapable of mercy or remorse. They were terrifying. This man must be terrifying in the ring. Cheskis didn't trust himself to speak, but he spoke. "What goes on in here, stays here. Isn't that right?"

Oliveira nodded only slightly. It was barely perceptible. Then he let out a suppressed laugh. The murder behind his eyes was already just a memory, but one that wouldn't go away soon. Which was no doubt how he intended it. Had Cheskis been standing, his legs might have quivered. In spite of himself, he laughed a little because that's what Oliveira wanted. "Hey, let me ask you a favor, okay?" Oliveira said. "Fighter to fighter." Cheskis nodded weakly.

"Go see my manager. Tell him I want a fight in May, got that? His name is Ted Borakovich. He lives with all those rich, fat-ass *guayabas* in Upland. Tell him to fix it with my trainer, okay? Eddie. He's all pissed off at me. Won't come to see me or nothing, the flakey bastard. Tell Borakovich I'll be outta here in March. I want a fight in May, and I wanna train with Eddie. Got that?"

"Borakovich, Upland, Eddie," Cheskis said. "Out in March, fight in May. M and M."

"Good. Now look, after Borakovich, you talk to Eddie for me. Eddie Welsh. At the Blackjack Gym in Redondo Beach. He won't listen to Borakovich, understand? He'll say fuck it, he's through with me, shit like that. It's bullshit. Tell both of 'em I want a fight in May. Anybody. I'll be ready for anybody, I don't care who it is. I'll go to Argentina, Australia, I don't give a shit, long as it's a good purse, okay?"

"Where's Upland?" Cheskis said.

"Near San Bernardino. Borakovich, he owns a business, but he's never there. You gotta catch him at home."

"One more thing. What's a *guayaba*?"

"Can't tell you. They wouldn't let me be a Mexican no more."

Mike knew. "A white flower," he explained.

Cheskis never did get moved to another sector in the jail, but the next morning lawyer Castro visited him again and the day after that he was in front of a judge who changed the deal.

"Anger management class? What the hell is that?" Cheskis said out in the hallway.

"It's a good deal," Castro explained. "Nothing to it. You go to some classes and when you're done everything disappears. Like it never happened." Cheskis remained dubious. "Look," Castro said, "if you're not happy when you win, when *do* you get happy? So be happy. 'Cause we won."

CHAPTER 9

BEST FRIENDS

Cheskis stayed home just long enough to scrub off the jail dirt and headed out for the Dead Mackerel. He lived in Hermosa Beach, one of those rare Southern California neighborhoods where people actually walked to their destinations. His little place had been illegally converted from a garage several landlords ago and provided plenty of clues that it was never intended for human habitation. Angles were imprecise, nails bent, doors like cardboard. Sometimes at night he could swear he smelled brake fluid. Women who returned brought plants. But few returned. Bringing them here made relationships short.

His three-block walk took Cheskis past a honeycomb of tiny apartments carved out of little beach houses—a patchwork, affordable dormitory for burned-out hippies, surfers, and others left off Hollywood and aerospace payrolls. Endless, temperate sunshine bleached buildings and cars into creamy hues. Everyone said that someday real estate here would skyrocket. Yet someday never seemed to come. Neither did tourists, who frequented the better-known Venice and Santa Monica beaches up the coast, or Newport and Laguna to the south. Most retail businesses barely clung to life. A generous sprinkle of vacant storefronts always waited for the next optimistic loser.

The Dead Mackerel had originally been called the *Ded* Mackerel, but Bert the owner's wife conventionalized the spelling after she concluded irony was finished. Inside, a few scattered afternoon drinkers watched an NBA game. Without asking, young, cap-teethed Steve set a scotch in front of Cheskis, looked down, and asked him, "Where you find a watch like that?"

"Target. I got it on layaway," answered Cheskis, once again roped into a juvenile exchange with Steve, who ridiculed not just jewelry, but clothes, cars, net worth, and haircuts of regular customers, pretending always that he was kidding. But the act fooled no one, because he was an actual—not figurative—bad actor whose career consisted of a few non-talking seconds in a barely seen lawn mower commercial.

"You cut that kid too much slack," said Ronald, coming down the long bar toward Cheskis. Just about everything Ronald said was as loud as anybody can say things and still be considered sane. Steve probably heard him, but that disturbed neither Ronald nor Cheskis. Ronald was probably Cheskis's best friend in L.A., but Cheskis wasn't terribly fond of him. Ronald probably wasn't terribly fond of Cheskis either. They'd never even traded phone numbers. Their relationship worked because Ronald mostly just wanted to talk about himself, allowing Cheskis to steer clear of his own life. "You should put that little fucker in his place," Ronald said, although Steve wasn't actually a little fucker. He was a big fucker. You can't go around assaulting bartenders, Cheskis explained. You'd wind up thirsty. "Besides, it's not my job to punish the wicked." Cheskis had already been involved in one fight inside the Mackerel. Not long before that he'd been barred from a joint down the street. Getting his name on a second list on the same beach would cross a line he didn't want to cross.

"Bert's wife won't let Bert fire him. He's gotta be shtupping her," Ronald said. Bert's wife was at least twenty years older than Steve and even resembled Anne Bancroft in *The Graduate,* which probably contributed to the general supposition that she took up with younger men. Steve, whose father was some kind of auto industry captain back in Michigan, lived in a white palace on the water, had a Corvette in the garage, and took home an endless stream of young women after weakening their deductive dexterity with free shots of tequila.

Cheskis prepared to dummy up about his time in jail, but Ronald wasn't curious about his absence anyway. He immediately launched the story of his latest fistfight. "I'm in this restaurant way up in Van Nuys, and I'm paying the cashier when a guy behind me with this skanky girlfriend, he asks me to change a hundred for him. I said, 'Look, man, I can't make that kind of change for somebody I don't know.' Right away he gets ugly, like 'Listen motherfucker.' A big white dude. He's ready to go, gets nose to nose. Fuck this, I hook to his gut and throw a straight right, kick him a couple times while he goes down. He caught one in the throat, starts making these weird gurgling noises? Everybody's going nuts. My money, like a couple hundred bucks, it goes flying, the manager's already on the phone."

"What'd you do?"

"Man, I boogied." Ronald was a big-boned kick boxer—part white, part Asian—with bleached hair and lots of tattoos peeking from his clothing—dragons, flames, serpents, and precisely wrought Asian characters. He sweated hour after hour, week after week in a gym, pounding bags, sparring, practicing, dreaming each night that someone would pop the boil on his rage, let him feel that adrenaline rush. Yet Ronald was a bleeding-heart humanitarian compared to followers of the world-famous Brazilian Ju Jitsu guru who'd set up headquarters in nearby El Segundo: thick as head lice around these parts; their principal tactics were to choke people unconscious and bend their joints in the wrong direction. Crossing one of these sadistic zombies was what got Cheskis eighty-sixed from the other bar.

It was Cheskis's battle in the Mackerel with a husky, red-bearded yuppie that had strained his relationship with Ronald, who felt vaguely dishonored because red-beard belonged to the same kick-boxing gym. Showing off for his friends, the yuppie had pushed Cheskis in the chest over some imagined slight. Cheskis, according to ritual, was supposed to push back. Instead he snapped off a left jab, right cross, left hook—the most basic combination. The right was deflected by a piece of shoulder, but the other two shots landed clean, and red-beard slipped to the floor like a dropped phone while his friends melted away. Because Cheskis was so successful it made his opponent look like some harmless creature he'd assaulted for no good reason. Now Cheskis half-believed it too. The only thing dumber than getting in bar fights is feeling guilty about them later.

Unable to sleep, Cheskis sat up in bed trying to move past page fifteen of *Remembrance of Things Past*, but his mind wandered every couple of lines. His gaze shifted to his only wall hanging—a black and white photo of him and his family at Lake of the Ozarks. He, his parents, and his older sister sat on a photographer's crescent moon inside a carnival tent. Everybody smiled for the camera, but the lake was home to clouds of mosquitoes, and when they'd rented a rowboat, they spotted snakes in the lake. Moments after they left the carnival, a stone from the gravel road flipped up and cracked their windshield. Cheskis's dad instantly cried to the heavens that if he'd added the cost of a new windshield to the cottage rental they could have vacationed someplace decent. Cheskis soon learned it was all his fault. They'd skimped on the vacation to pay for braces he didn't need anyway. The trip turned out like all the rest. Cheskis's father wore that freeze-dried smirk as he let everyone know the braces made his son look like a space creature, that he swam like a *schvartze*, played chess like a four-year-old, appreciated nothing his parents did for him. Didn't he throw like a girl?

Palos Blancos Community College played a game of catch-up—trying to teach working-class kids what they should have learned in high school. Cheskis's students were a duskier bunch than America at large, yet the whites tended to be too white, afflicted with see-through, trailer-park skin. Most of his students had been hypnotized since infancy by electronic media and found reading uncomfortable. Yet they expected to find work as writers. It was hard to be angry with them.

As always, Cheskis had a hard time not staring at McMasters's skull. Why he shaved it was a mystery. The top of his head, an unhealthy shade of pink, was streaked with protruding veins and cratered with ghastly little bumps and indentations. He should wear a hat. Two hats, maybe. "But I only taught the class to do the department a favor," Cheskis explained, trying to look anywhere but at McMasters's hideous pate. Cheskis had in fact consented to teach the class only to please the hierarchy. Squeezed between the fall and spring sessions, the brief winter session attracted few students and paid only a pittance.

McMasters had no doubt been personally inconvenienced when he had to take over for jailed Cheskis. But the man lived for his job anyway. Expanding his duties was a reward, not an inconvenience. A walking bundle of neuroses, he was unfit for routine social discourse and went home to a practically mute Japanese wife who rarely left the house. When she spoke it was like trying to hear a robin's heartbeat.

Repulsive as it was, Cheskis knew groveling to McMasters was preferable to scattering his resumes around the local community college circuit and launching a new round of job interviews with professors whose hands-on experience was mostly limited to trade publications or gray little weeklies. They generally responded to Cheskis's four years on *The New York Times* with the fear and loathing Hunter Thompson exposed in so many corners of the cosmos.

"I don't understand what you mean by personal reasons," said McMasters, closing his eyes. Cheskis had on occasion run into people who bugged their eyes out to accentuate a point. These people were invariably nuts. McMasters did them one better. He closed his eyes at the end of each sentence and didn't reopen them until he was at least a few words into a new one.

"I'm sorry," said Cheskis. He peered off in the distance, pretending to recall some tragedy he couldn't bear to relate, hoping to appear sympathetic and vulnerable, to awaken some dormant humanity concealed in McMasters's pitiless pathology. A journalistic Typhoid Mary, he focused lesson plans on the rules of the *Associated Press Stylebook,* which dealt with questions such as whether "Avenue" should or should not be abbreviated in an address (it should). If he were pressed to write an actual news story he'd probably burst into flames. McMasters chaired the department because no one else would. Once they achieved tenure, most of the faculty loaded all their classes into two days a week and were rarely seen, whereas department chairs had to suit up every day.

Like tenured professors everywhere, McMasters and his colleagues were so immune to consequences, so insulated from disaster, that they took on dispositions of spoiled children.

McMasters was free to skip classes, cluck like a chicken, or show up in a dress. A male professor in the Geography Department did in fact wear a dress. The provost dressed in all purple all the time—purple suits, purple shirts, even purple shoes he must have had specially dyed. Cheskis once ran into McMasters at a vegetarian restaurant off-campus. His back was turned so Cheskis touched him on the shoulder in greeting. McMasters let out a piercing yelp and jerked as though he'd touched a live wire. Apparently believing Beelzebub had summoned him for his final errand, he turned toward Cheskis a face congealed into a mask of desperate terror. The poor schnook went through life expecting to be murdered in vegetarian restaurants at noon. How would McMasters react if confronted by an angry four-hundred-pounder? Though hatred curdled out of him like sour milk, somehow he'd find a way to avoid a fight. He'd beg if he had to, and he wouldn't be arrested. His life would go on as piteously as before, but no worse than before, either.

McMasters hadn't gone so far as to say Cheskis was fired. But he refused to hand back the class he'd inherited during Cheskis's week in the cooler. Worse, he was vague about what classes he might offer in the spring. As a part-timer, Cheskis had no rights. To fire him, all McMasters had to do was take him off the schedule.

As Cheskis stepped past the department secretary she informed him he must turn in his keys at campus security. "Why?" he asked, sounding weaker than he'd hoped.

"You're not on the schedule." Another ugly turn.

He passed through a maze of outdoor passageways lined with bulletin boards that had nothing to declare during the sparsely attended winter session.

The key-keeper was an attractive, slightly buxom young black woman who grimaced when he stepped up to the counter. A radio set on very low volume played Diana Ross. Rooms in the college were either dim and basement-like or bombarded with mega-beams of fluorescent light. This one was dim and basement-like. After taking his name and key, the key-keeper said matter-of-factly, "I heard about you."

"Maybe I heard about you, too," he said.

"Oh yeah? What was that?"

"It was all good," he said, flashing a smile that didn't help.

"Here's your receipt," she said, business-like.

"You really did hear something?" Cheskis asked her.

"Forget it," she said.

"It looks like I'm outta here, kid," he said. "So if you have news, now's the time to tell me."

"Just heard you were some kind of dangerous dude, that's all." Christ, if she knew about his jolt in the can, it must be all over campus. "I don't even know why I said anything," she added.

"I don't either, if you won't tell me all of it."

"People, they say all kinds of things," she said.

"What did they say this time?"

She leaned closer across the counter. "Somebody said you killed somebody," she said.

He felt his eyes grow wide and his lips open as he stopped breathing. "When? When do they mean?"

"You don't know? How many people you kill anyway?"

"That's not—I don't know what I meant. Come on, what'd you hear? I won't tell anyone where it came from. Promise."

She bit her lower lip. "This friend of mine, she's Chicana? She said the Mexican Mafia's protecting you so nobody did nothing about it. And that's all I know, okay?" She returned to her desk and pretended to read a file as the radio played another song. No sense correcting her. Let them believe the story. If he was in fact fired, it would be a good thing to leave behind.

CHAPTER 10

EDDIE

Borakovich wore a salesman's smile, cowboy boots, and a Rolex. You could ride a camel across his living room. When he learned Oliveira was getting out, the smile changed to a look of concern. "I can get him the right fight," he said. "I know I can, but if he screws up again. . . ." His voice trailed off. A slender brunette with slightly too much tan entered the room and introduced herself as Stormy. She carried with her the scent of a woman who'd always had money, though Cheskis would later find out she'd learned to imitate the leisure class during her short career as a soap actress.

As Oliveira predicted, Borakovich wanted Cheskis to talk to Eddie Welsh in person. "He'll want to ask you about how Felix looks and everything."

"He's not fat, is he?" Eddie Welsh asked Cheskis.

"He looked okay," Cheskis said.

Welsh nodded thoughtfully. "You a friend of Borakovich?"

"Not really," Cheskis said.

"Good. I can't stand the sonofabitch. You know what he's gonna do? Make one phone call to Ray Powell. For that he gets a third of the purse." The phone rang. Welsh picked it up without excusing himself. His flat nose, scarred eyebrows, and expanded, sagging eyelids told the tale of a man who'd paid his dues in the fight game. He was wiry and on the short side but didn't act like it, speaking double-time in a Commonwealth accent Cheskis couldn't isolate. A New Zealander, perhaps, or South African. After listening to his caller a few moments, he said, "You know how many times I gave you that number?" Pause. "No, more than that. It must be twice a week. Now listen, mate. I'll give it to you one last time, but do something for me, okay? Tattoo it on your arse. Promise now. You promise?—lying bastard." He leafed through a Rolodex, barked a number into the phone, then hung up. "That bloke's got no life," he told Cheskis. "But he's too dumb to know it." He returned to telling Cheskis what miserable bastards Borakovich and Felix Oliveira were and how cruelly Oliveira broke his heart. "I thought the title shot would mean something to him. I got him in the best shape of his life. He could have given Sugar Ray a fight—the real Sugar Ray. He lived at my house, ate my food, borrowed my money."

Welsh never inquired just what circumstance had placed Cheskis inside the jail with Felix Oliveira. Oliveira's name popped the cork on Welsh's emotions, which poured out with few pauses. "Walk over here a minute," he said. Cheskis followed him across the gym to a panting, red-faced, middle-aged woman who lay on her back, attempting with little success to do leg lifts. She was built like a top—tiny shoulders, spindly calves, and an enormous roll of flesh all around her midsection. Welsh, still telling Cheskis his troubles, placed his hands on her shins, holding them down as she performed agonized sit-ups in turtle time. He paid her no attention as he continued his tale of woe, repeating himself often. It was a strangely one-sided conversation, spoken as though Welsh knew Cheskis well even though he'd first laid eyes on him five minutes ago. "That's enough, Marlene," he finally told the woman. "See you Tuesday. Take those pills." She nodded, unable to speak or stand. Welsh, unconcerned, beckoned Cheskis to follow him as he left the poor woman to fend for herself, reseated himself behind the desk just inside the entrance, and took a swig from an open bottle of Guinness.

"You know how much work it took to get him in shape like that? Then he goes to jail over more of his silly bullshit and the fight's off. The bloke never learns. You can't tell him anything." He pleaded his case as though Cheskis could grant him justice.

Welsh's gym sat in a gentrifying section of Pacific Coast Highway a mile south of Hermosa Beach. Cheskis had spotted a few serious fighters, but most customers looked like they owned

Saabs or BMWs and spent their day in cubicles. Perhaps a third were women, most of them young. With doors open front and back, the gym was caressed by an ocean breeze that on this part of the beach didn't come cheap. Cheskis had never seen a boxing gym like this. They tended to be in neighborhoods where white drivers drove through fast, doors locked.

"He was driving drunk again," Welsh said.

"Who was?" Cheskis asked him.

"Felix, Felix. We're talking about Felix Oliveira. Driving drunk in the Valley where the cops all know him and know his car. When they pull him over, he starts giving them shit. I'm telling you, I had him ready. I mean ready. We could of had that title." Cheskis nodded, as if to say he felt Welsh's pain.

"Borakovich will try to get him Byrd in May," Welsh said. "Powell's putting together a show. At least I hope he can still get Byrd, the lying bastard. You tell Felix he's gotta come down here and live with me. I need to watch him, make sure he eats right, takes vitamins. It's no good when he lives in his neighborhood. Tell him that's the only way I'll do it."

"I won't see him," Cheskis said. "He just wanted you to know he's coming."

A young attractive Asian woman walked over and asked to use the phone.

"Use the pay phone." Welsh said.

"I don't have any change," she said, standing her ground.

Welsh reached down and pulled a receiver from behind the counter. "You got one minute."

"Thank you."

He punched out the number she gave him. "Next time bring change." He looked out on the gym floor as though he'd spotted a puddle of slop. "Your feet!" he shouted. "You! You! What's his name? Tony! Your feet!"

A skinny kid shadowboxing in front of a remarkably clean, full-length mirror looked down at his feet and brought them closer together. He looked about fourteen.

"That's it, mate! You can't punch when you're spread all over like that. You look like a faggot on wheels."

Cheskis was relieved to see the top-shaped woman had made it to her feet. The young woman using the phone smelled distinctly nice and her shorts flattered a wonderfully pleasing butt. It was, he decided, a Samantha-class butt. In his mind, Samantha was still a young mother in Santa Cruz, frozen in time, as was everyone else he'd discarded like socks in a Laundromat. Welsh caught Cheskis appraising the young woman, smiled, then grimaced. "This is a business phone, understand?" he told her.

She looked over at Welsh as though *he* were the errant puddle of slop. "Gotta go," she said into the phone, then handed it to Welsh, who hung it up with surprising gentleness. He asked Cheskis his name and Cheskis introduced himself again. "Where you live?"

"Hermosa," Cheskis said.

"How come I never seen you?"

Cheskis felt like he hadn't turned in his homework. "I don't know," he said.

"You ever fought?"

A long time ago, Cheskis told him, in the amateurs.

Welsh nodded, then launched a search behind the counter. He came up with a pair of yellow Mexican handwraps, still in the package. "Put these on," he said, handing them to Cheskis. He found himself obeying. Perhaps some deeply embedded string of Cheskis chromosomes obeyed fight trainers. Probably a year ago he'd have declined the wraps. But at this moment it felt curiously okay.

Wrapping his hands was no longer so automatic. He had to undo some of his work and start again. The phone rang and Welsh, ignoring it, came out from behind the counter with two pairs of gloves and headed toward the rear of the gym. "Come on," he said. They ended up next to a small, sun-baked ring that sat behind the building. A dozen or so customers filled the space around it, skipping rope, hitting bags and socializing. Cheskis's gloves had Velcro fasteners, which he'd never seen before. "Here, stick out your hand," Welsh said. He slipped the gloves over Cheskis's wraps and fastened them quickly, then did the same for himself. Cheskis kicked off his shoes and followed him through the ropes, feeling awkward in jeans and a T-shirt. They had no headgear or mouthpieces, and Welsh's hands weren't wrapped. Neither had warmed up.

"Throw a jab," Welsh said. Cheskis just looked at him. "Go ahead!" Cheskis aimed a light jab at one of Welsh's gloves. "Throw a real one. Try to hit me. Right here." He touched his chin. "Come on."

"Okay. You ready?"

"Go ahead." Cheskis threw a better one, this time remembering to snap it back. But Welsh picked it off with his right glove and swatted Cheskis across the ear with a left. "Hands up!" Humbled Cheskis raised his gloves back into position and locked eyes with Welsh. "We got a lot a work to do, mate," Eddie Welsh said.

AUGUST 1984

CHAPTER 11

LORRAINE'S EARS

It didn't take anger rookies long to wonder about Cyril. Old and bent like a buzzard, he couldn't have weighed more than ninety pounds. His clothes hung around him like a shower curtain. When he had to move from place to place it was an involved process, like kick-starting ancient machinery. If Cyril decided to attack anyone across the room, it would probably take him five minutes just to get there. So why in the world did the court system stick him in an anger management class?

"My wife called the police," he would explain to newcomers in a gray, country voice that was slow and caked with tremors. His wife kept calling 911 on him for beatings that apparently happened only in the veiled recesses of her mind. But Cyril and the responding cops were trapped by the justice system's zero-tolerance policy for spousal abuse. Cyril, who refused to place his deluded wife in a nursing home, was rewarded by trips to criminal court. The wife would call, the cops would remove Cyril from the house, pack him off to a cheap motel because he had nowhere else to go, and file a report. When the case reached court, judges always feared to drop it because one day Cyril's crazy wife might actually spin him into the red zone and reporters would feast on a doltish judge who'd let off a wife-beater. To be on the safe side, they placed Cyril in anger management. He'd completed the course so many times that despite his pockmarked memory, he had much of the material memorized. Because he had no temper, getting stuck in an anger management class didn't impose much of a hardship. It was more interesting and less troublesome than watching TV with his wife.

"What's the deal on Cyril?" Cheskis asked Lorraine as she put the key in the door of her little truck after class. "Think he'll ever control his rage?"

"Don't be a jerk," she said. But she said it with a mischievous smile. This was encouraging. Earlier she'd informed him unambiguously that counselors were forbidden social contact with clients. "If you even speak of this again, you'll have to transfer into someone else's class," she said, sounding like some alien Lorraine he'd never encountered. But now he had only three classes left.

"I don't care if you transfer me out," he said. "I want to see you. Just for coffee. We're not exchanging rings or bodily fluids."

She opened the truck door, looked at him with an unreadable expression, looked down at the sidewalk, looked up again, and said, "Tea. I don't drink much coffee."

"Wonderful, I'll buy you a cup of tea."

"No you won't. But in the interest of accuracy, what I'm turning down isn't coffee. It's tea."

"Look, you know that little restaurant, Terry's Place? A few blocks south on PCH?"

"Finish your last class and I'll think about it."

"They give another class Thursdays in Huntington Beach. They already told me I can get in. I'll go there next week. Give me half an hour before you go home," he pleaded.

"Who said I'm going home? I'm going for a cup of tea." She named a diner near the Marina. "If I were to run into someone I know, I'd probably say hi."

"You won't regret this," he shouted back as he headed for his car. In his rush to back out of the parking lot he nearly flattened two rollerbladers. They shook their fists at him as he swung onto the street. Fifteen minutes later he seated himself across from Lorraine, who was already sipping tea. By this time he couldn't imagine why he'd been so stupid as to arrange his own demise. He felt powerless against an attack of relapsed adolescence. His brain was mud. "You've never asked me what I do for a living," he said, to kill silence. "All you know about me is my police report." *Dumb thing to say.*

"I don't pry into official documents. But I have wondered about you, Lee. You don't have that—I don't know—somber look you had. Like your dog got run over."

"Somber. Thanks."

97

"You're more relaxed now."

"Not this minute."

"But every once in a while you come in with a bruise on your face. Like that one." Cheskis touched the hint of a mouse under his right eye. "I don't mean to—Yes, I do. I mean to pry. What gives?"

"I haven't been in a fight in a while," he said. "Not since the one that put me in your class."

"Excellent," she said. Was she wearing a touch of eyeliner? He didn't notice it in class. She may have dolled herself up just for him—a confidence-building thought. She wore her usual crisp jeans, no heels. The blouse was pink tonight. Silk, probably. She had small hands and small earrings. He studied her delicate ears. *Now I know I'm crazy. I'm falling in love with her ears.*

The waiter finally showed up. He looked at least sixty and apparently soaked his hair in India ink. When he learned Cheskis wanted only coffee, he seemed hurt. He brought it and got away before Cheskis could request a spoon.

Cheskis explained the welt. "It sounds a little silly, but I've been working out in a boxing gym."

"Working out? I don't—What's that mean? Are you fighting?"

"I spar sometimes, but mostly it's just hitting bags, shadow boxing, that kind of thing."

"Well, you're wrong. It's not silly," she said. "It's way beyond that. It's crazy. But if it helps you—"

"You helped me."

"That's . . . fine, possibly. I don't know, exactly. Haven't you exchanged fighting for . . . fighting?"

"Sometimes things that sound stupid work. Boxing is one of those things. For a lot of guys—it levels you out."

"That's a good thing to know, Cheskis. I could use some of that myself."

He liked her calling him by his last name. "I'm thinking that fight that put me into the class was my last. Even if I were looking for a fight, just finding one would be—difficult, I think.

You reach a certain age and the psychos see you as a civilian. You're an old fart—not you, I mean—"

"Just what do you mean?"

"You've got a mean streak, kid."

"Not really. Kid. Is that a term of endearment?"

"It's not Toots, Honey, Sweetie. But Lorraine's good. And what I wanted to tell you, Lorraine, is that I've really—I enjoy your classes, even the ones with Sybil."

"That solves that puzzle. You brought me over here to tell me you enjoy the class."

"I thought you were stopping for tea anyway," he said.

"Don't be silly. I wouldn't go to a diner all by myself at ten o'clock at night for a lousy cup of tea. I can do that at home."

"Then I guess things are looking up for both of us," he said.

"Don't get overconfident. I haven't made up my mind about you yet. Do you really like the classes?"

"I like *you*," he said. "You're smart, you're nice. You're pretty. Never boring. I like listening to you talk."

"It's not me. It's the teachings, the dharma."

"Did you just say what I thought you said?"

"Why? You going to report me to the anti-dharma police?"

"Dharma as in Buddhist dharma."

"Sure. Once you understand that suffering is inevitable," she said, "you can deal with it. Anger makes us suffer. That's a big, big concept in Buddhism. Things like conceit and jealousy do too. But anger and hatred are the most destructive negative emotions. It's what I try to pass on, in a kind of left-handed way."

"That's fantastic," Cheskis said. "You're a Buddhist secret agent."

"The best way to avoid anger is through patience and tolerance. It's what I try to get across. Is that subversive?"

"Don't get mad," he said. "You're supposed to be a role model."

She placed her chin on her fist, studying him, nothing behind her eyes hidden or calculated. He felt he'd been traveling along a street with no signs, taken wrong steps, aimless steps, no steps. Cheskis wanted more coffee as well as a spoon, something to do with his hands. But the waiter must have disappeared for good. Patience and tolerance, he said to himself.

99

Lorraine, it turned out, wasn't a full-fledged counselor, but a barely paid intern finishing up her Master's. He got the feeling she wasn't destitute, though. She told him she'd been a real estate agent, that she used to broker high-rise and shopping mall deals and drink booze and snort cocaine. She'd lived with men twice, but not for long. In all those sessions in that ugly, claustrophobic room, he'd been staring at a portrait without seeing it. Cheskis had assumed Buddhism was a belief system for narcissists who ignored the world beyond their own little lotus position. But that didn't describe Lorraine, who was clearly concerned for all the difficult, fuming souls in the class. "I can't speak for everybody," she said, "but when I meditate, I'm hunkering down to maintain my sanity—so maybe I can be of help to somebody instead of the pretty much useless bitch I used to be."

Not much later he found himself revealing he'd once been a news reporter, that he grew up in Kansas City. He even told her the tale about his folkloric great-grandfather, who, in his seventies, had departed Tsarist Lithuania with a knapsack on his back, bound for Palestine, and that no one ever heard from him again. Cheskis hadn't thought of him for years. "I like to think he made it, that he walked through all the deserts and bandits and maybe even had a new batch of kids over there," he said, "like some kind of pasha." Words poured out of him. He needed to contain himself, but reveled in the luxury of candor. He told her he used to miss his wife, but not so much anymore.

"And how's Marvin doing?" she said. Marvin had finished his anger classes with another instructor whose class fit into his no-frills schedule.

"I'd guess Marvin's doing better than he's ever done in his life," Cheskis said. "But it's just a guess. He doesn't say much about himself. I know a lot about what he's doing, but not what he used to do, where he went to high school, none of that. Just the here and now."

"Does he know all those things about you? The things you used to do?"

He shrugged.

"That's what I thought."

Cheskis explained that three months earlier he'd blundered into a job as Marvin's fight manager. "I don't know what I'm doing. I just learn while I do it. Sometimes it's fun, but sometimes it's like bargaining with reptiles."

"Can you two actually make a living doing this?"

"Not likely," Cheskis said. "Somebody explained to me there's no middle class in boxing. Either you're Sugar Ray Leonard and Angelo Dundee making millions or you're waiting tables and dodging the landlord." Recently, he explained, he'd given up moving furniture for delivering pizza, which was less demeaning than he'd expected. "Everybody's happy when the pizza guy shows up. People love us even more than firemen." The waiter came back with a refill and a spoon.

"Let me ask you something," Cheskis said.

"Shoot."

"What do you know about rumination?"

"Dwelling on a memory and playing it back into perpetuity."

"Right."

"Usually what we're talking about is a disturbing memory, a mistake, something we wish hadn't happened."

He poured himself another cup. "Yeah," he said. "There's a German word I can't think of that says it better. It means 'paralyzing burden of memories.'"

"Sometimes a mistake seems irreparable," she said. "But all things lack the ability to remain the same. You, me, this table, everything. What was wrong, what was right, none of it will endure. That's called the suffering of change. Remorse is a Western affliction. There's no word for it in Tibetan. There's a word for guilt, but it's not a guilt that sits out there and grinds you up. It's a guilt you do something about."

"Like going to anger management classes?"

"Sure. If it helps you to be patient and tolerant, to be kind."

"Is that supposed to absolve you?" he asked her.

"Possibly," she said. "I can't prove it with calculus, but most of us evolve, we adapt. We keep screwing up anyway, but if we're smart, we change some more. Whatever you did or think you

101

did that was wrong, you use the memory of it to behave better in the future. You overwhelm the negative karma from here on out. Look, I don't know everything. It's why I study. It's probably all right to dislike what you've done or even who you were. This is not a confessional. I don't need to know any of that. But you can't be at war with yourself. That's poison. Just another form of anger."

"Sybil says you can't just let people mess with you."

"If someone is cruel or rude to me," she said, "my concern is for the person because they're hurting themselves."

"With bad karma."

"You can call it that."

"So you believe there's always justice," he said.

"Eventually, yes. It might take awhile. I suppose you think that's naïve."

"Not naïve, exactly. Just mistaken—in a nice way. And if remorse is a Western thing, why do Japanese commit suicide to say they're sorry?"

"Because they're deluded," she said. "Vietnam, that was a delusion. Thinking we could make people like us by bombing and killing them."

"I guess there's some kind of balance to the universe," he said, "but a very smart guy once told me that the balance is a result of chaos. There's an awful lot of blind luck, good luck, bad luck. That's not much like karma."

"I'm not sure they're mutually exclusive ideas. I'll have to think about it. Who was this very smart guy?"

"I don't like to drop names."

"Drop one," she said.

"Someone I knew a long time ago. Ken Kesey."

"Wow. Now I can drop the name. I know someone who knows Ken Kesey. How'd you meet him? When you were reporting?"

He nodded. It was more or less true. When Cheskis was a reporter he found Kesey again and conducted mini-interviews. Ask him the right questions and he was master of all quotes.

"It's got to be fun, meeting with famous people, talking with them."

"I'm not upset I'm the pizza guy," he said, "if that's what you mean."

"It's not what I meant at all, Cheskis. Not everybody's duplicitous, you know. I'm not *in* your boxing business."

"Sorry."

"You don't hear much about Kesey any more. Or at least I don't."

"The newspapers are leaving him out of their running freak show. That's not a bad thing. What they call news doesn't represent life. It only pretends to. Which reminds me, you think Cyril saws up women in his basement?"

"Cut the crap, Cheskis. Don't try to joke your way out."

"I'm just happy to be here."

"Me too," she said. "I don't like newspapers either. I read them before I go to bed so I don't have to start my day with that stuff. But here's the problem—"

"What?"

"I can't drink any more tea." She looked up and the runaway waiter magically appeared. "Check please?" She asked him.

"What about dinner and a movie?" Cheskis said. "Tomorrow, I mean."

"You have three more classes," she said. "Then we'll see."

"But—"

"Let's see how you feel after you finish your course in Huntington Beach. Otherwise it'll be awkward. I don't want that." She leaned forward and kissed him on the mouth. "Let that hold you."

MAY 1985

CHAPTER 12

VEGAS

Nine months after turning pro, Marvin was still undefeated, with eight of his eleven victories coming by knockout. He developed tricks as he went along, learning to blend offense and defense into a seamless cycle of destruction, but there were perilous moments—in the third bout, for example. The opponent, who'd played football for Stanford and looked like he could tear open a Volkswagen with his teeth, went down from a sneaky uppercut inside of a minute. He made the count, but still looked wobbly. Moments later the opponent struck Marvin so low and with such force, they must have heard it in the balcony. The enraged fans let out such a roar Cheskis couldn't even hear Eddie, who was screaming right next to him. The ref took a point and gave Marvin time to recover, providing the opponent the break he needed to clear his head. Marvin knocked him out in the next round anyway.

One minute into Marvin's most recent bout, his snapping right hand opened an ugly gash in the corner of his opponent's left eye. Within seconds the guy looked like Poe's "Masque of the Red Death." The referee took one look and waved the fight over. Marvin should have earned a technical knockout. But a judge at ringside claimed the cut was caused by a nonexistent clash of heads, so the fight was ruled a technical draw instead. Cheskis saw the punch that opened the cut. Plenty of fans saw it too. They booed and yelled "Bullshit, bullshit" with growing volume. Then it died down as it always did. It was a traditional but pitiable weapon against corruption and incompetence. Cheskis paced around the ring yelling at all the officials, promising an investigation, until the chief inspector leaned between the ropes and threatened him with suspension. It was one more inevitable injustice in the endless cycle of what Lorraine called *samsara*, which his grandmother called *tsouris*. Marvin's opponent, upon hearing he'd escaped with a draw, lit up like a pinball machine. He ran over and hugged a stunned Marvin.

Only a few blocks from the La Brea, as Cheskis drove with Eddie and Tommy to take Marvin back to the crappy neighborhood where he shared a crappy apartment with his aunt, Marvin started crying. "They robbed me," he sobbed. "Why'd they do that? What the fuck I ever do to them?" Cheskis, recalling all the hours and perspiration Marvin and Eddie had put into training for the fight, could have cried himself.

"That fucken judge was probably a mate of the other bloke's manager," Eddie said. "Did you see which one it was?"

"No," Cheskis said. "I guess they don't even have to tell you."

"It works that way sometimes. Don't worry about it," Eddie said to Marvin. "We'll handle the bullshit. Just keep training. You'll get there, mate."

"*How*'re you gonna handle it?" Marvin spat out. Cheskis had never seen Marvin angry at Eddie before.

"Just keep winning," Eddie said. "The rest takes care of itself."

"You're still undefeated," Cheskis said. "When they introduce you, they can still call you an undefeated fighter."

"It's not the same, though," Marvin said. "When the ref was giving us instructions? The guy never even looked me in the face. He's a punk for doing that. Look at your man when you're going to fight him. Let me see the bitch in your eyes, because I'm not afraid of anything. The only thing I fear is God. Let's fight again, see what's really in his heart."

"He'll be on the next stage outta town," Tommy said.

"Forget him," Eddie told Marvin. "Anyway, it's better to get robbed than knocked out. Schmeling knocked out Louis. He just got caught. It could happen to anybody. He learned to live with it."

"Yeah, but Joe Louis didn't lose till he got old," Marvin said.

"No, Schmeling knocked him out when he was only twenty-two," Eddie said. "Fair and square. Caught him right on the button."

"He learned from that loss," Cheskis said. "It made him stronger. What fails to kill me makes me stronger. Nietzsche."

"Who the hell's Nietzsche?" asked Marvin.

"Wasn't he a kraut?" Tommy said. "A friend of Hitler's or something?"

"He was a raving maniac," Cheskis said.

"Man, here I lost a fight and you're telling me about maniacs."

"You didn't lose. It was a draw," Eddie said.

"Maniacs can be good teachers," Cheskis said. "Look at Eddie."

"Stop the car," Eddie said. "I gotta teach this bloke a lesson. Look, he's smiling," he said to Cheskis. "We got Marvin smiling back here."

"Fuck you guys. You're all maniacs," Marvin said.

"Yeah, but we're *your* maniacs," Cheskis said.

Marvin's little place was in one of those California apartment buildings that look like motels. An exterior staircase led to open walkways on each floor. The building probably looked pleasant in its first few years, but the contractor took shortcuts, and walls were lampshade-thin. Now everything was peeling, threadbare, and unattended, including the starved remnants of what was once a tropical garden.

Down in the car, as Marvin climbed the stairs, Eddie said, "Let's surprise him next fight. Let's get us real cornermen shirts, inscribed."

"We have to find him a nickname first," Cheskis said, "so we can put it on the shirts. But I like the way we do it now, everybody different. It makes us look hungry, like we're from the street."

"I just want to cheer the kid up," Eddie said.

"Then find us a nickname."

"That's your department, mate."

Cheskis soon learned he'd been swindled by Reynolds in the first fight. There were plenty of fight opportunities around as long as they were willing to travel up and down the coast. Opponents were mostly out-of-shape club fighters like Storma who trained only sporadically. These guys were much more plentiful than Cheskis had realized. Because they didn't have to make weight like fighters in other divisions, there was an endless supply of heavyweights who picked up extra cash taking an occasional match and sometimes working as sparring partners for top-rung contenders.

Ferreting out palooka opponents was a standard method of managing a prospect. They called it bringing a fighter along. Most fighters were not brought along. They didn't have managers or promoters trying to build their careers. Instead they were thrown into the wrong fights at the wrong time, dumped into last-minute contests with ill-fitting foul-protectors, unhealed cuts, and borrowed shoes. Their cornermen might be and often were tipsy, vapid oafs who forgot to bring ice and offered no useful instructions beyond the standard "Get this guy" or words to that effect. Some of these no-hope fighters had talent, but it was never developed properly. They looked across the ring at rising dauphins wearing fancy trunks and shoes, trailed by squads of nutritionists, marketing specialists, and concubines. Those at the very top rung—Muhammad Ali among them—were paid salaries by investors during the early years, when purses were lean.

"Kid, when it's all over, the same people are always left holding the bag: anyone who trusts anyone else," Eugene Philyaw, plumbing supplies wholesaler and part-time fight manager, told Cheskis. Philyaw had only one fighter these days—Boris Svoboda, a giant Czech immigrant with a shaved head who was old and slow but dangerous as hell. Like most big punchers, Svoboda, nicknamed Boris the Bohemian, was loved by fans. He would never beat a world-class fighter, but if Philyaw made the right plays at the right times, Svoboda might advance to the rank of stepping-stone—a journeyman whom budding stars would have to deal with before advancing to the upper reaches of the division.

"You want to know why our two guys won't ever fight?" Philyaw posed his question in the sturdy, leathery bar adjoining the La Brea. "'Cause they'd both have plenty to lose and nothing to gain," he said, answering his own question. Cheskis knew this already, but if he wanted Philyaw to tutor him in the nuts and bolts of the fight biz, he had to be patient and let the man talk to him like a twelve-year-old once in a while. All around them cornermen, photographers, writers, ex-fighters, and hangers-on talked fights. The business was full of guys who made their real living elsewhere. Many had dabbled as managers or silent partners to managers at one time or another before surrendering to the hard realities of fight finance. If Marvin managed to move up, the right fights would get harder to find, deals would be more complex, and Philyaw's mentoring might make a difference. Besides, Cheskis rather liked him. The hardest part about being tutored by Philyaw was not staring at him. That's because he looked like Humphrey Bogart.

Philyaw looked so much like Bogey that no one would believe it without actually seeing it, and even then they had a hard time believing it. It was said he'd caused fender-benders just walking down a sidewalk. Cheskis marveled that Philyaw, rather than trying to alter his looks, embraced them, smoking old-fashioned, no-filter cigarettes and *dressing* like Bogey—in an old-fashioned hat and rumpled trench coat. In 1985 this apparel would be rare anywhere, but in Southern California it was rarer than bar mitzvah bacon.

"What could he possibly do to look *less* like Humphrey Bogart?" Lorraine said to Cheskis after she'd consented once and only once to accompany Cheskis to the fights.

"He could wear an iron mask," Cheskis responded. "Then he'd look like the Man in the Iron Mask instead of Humphrey Bogart. But I guess that wouldn't improve things much, would it?"

Philyaw had once managed the most promising middleweight on the West Coast. But the kid's bright future was irreparably harmed the night he carelessly stopped a hail of police bullets with most of his vital organs while running out of a liquor store he'd just held up in the Crenshaw District. It was rumored around the neighborhood that a secret room of a doughnut shop on Pico had photographs on the wall that showed the cops taking turns posing with their ski-masked middleweight corpse as though he were a prize elk. Some even claimed the head was mounted in the basement of the 77th Street Station.

They said Philyaw took the death harder than the kid's mother. Maybe because she didn't have to pick up the funeral tab. He'd been shelling out cash for years to build the kid's career. The liquor store misadventure landed on Philyaw just as he was poised to pull the lever on a middleweight jackpot. Philyaw, who'd heretofore denied any resemblance to Bogart, disappeared after the funeral and eventually came back in his Sam Spade get-up with a Camel dangling from the corner of his lips. No one understood the meaning of this turnaround and no one confronted Philyaw about it directly. It was too easy to envision him grabbing the gat in his trench coat and casually plugging his inquisitor like Bogey did to Major Strasser at the end of *Casablanca*.

"In this business, kid," Philyaw said, "you can't avoid getting screwed at least once in a while." Even the shrewdest of the shrewd got taken. Felix's promoter Ray Powell, possibly the smartest man in the business, once flew in a Samoan fighter from New Zealand who signed a long-term contract, pocketed a $10,000 signing bonus, and returned home where he joined a professional rugby team and never fought again.

"You watch. Powell will deal with that dumb bastard. But nothing will happen till he stops looking over his shoulder," Philyaw said.

Philyaw knew a Chicago trainer who, it was believed, had been advising one of Powell's fighters to get a lawyer to rescue him from his standard kleptomaniacal contract with Powell. "They broke both the guy's arms," Philyaw said. "The poor bastard couldn't wipe his own ass."

"Whose arms? The trainer's or the fighter's?"

"The trainer's. And you know what? It turned out it was all bullshit."

"The guy didn't get his arms broken?"

"No, they broke his arms all right. It was bullshit that he was saying this stuff about Powell. It was just one of those rumors that get passed around. But it was still a good message. Maybe even a better message. 'This is what happens to you if there's even a *rumor* you're trying to fuck me.'"

Most fighters had never even owned checking accounts. Even as they found success they lacked the know-how to get hold of the tantalizing clouds of currency floating around them like feathers in a breeze. Rocky Marciano signed a contract that gave his manager half his earnings of any kind into perpetuity. His owners hounded his intake unto death. In retirement the beloved champion accepted cash-only speakers' fees in an effort to elude them. Fighters' principal business weapon was their instinct for delinquency, which might make a difference against small-time managers. But it was mostly ineffective in the higher echelons of the sport. By the time they learned the score, they were out of the game.

Though still a prelim fighter, Marvin was becoming a draw at the La Brea, making it more difficult for Reynolds to extract kickbacks from Cheskis. But Reynolds had a negotiating advantage other matchmakers didn't. The La Brea's owner was a Cleveland real estate billionaire who also held title to an NFL franchise that over the years had evolved into a license to print money. He rarely visited the La Brea and evidently viewed the building and everything that went on inside it as a tax write-off, leaving Reynolds free to wet his beak with ruthless efficiency. His kickbacks weren't the only ongoing La Brea swindles. In virtually every event there—whether it was a rock concert or a basketball game—embezzled tickets leaked out and went to the highest bidder. Bigshots paid *mordida* for better-situated skyboxes. Cartons of booze disappeared out the back door, and suppliers of all kinds rained kickbacks on their benefactors. It was said that the management team split the untaxed, under-the-table profits as methodically as an NYPD station house. Everyone got a piece but the schmuck from Cleveland.

Lorraine offered him a glass of red wine when she opened the door. "Put it down," he said. She gave him a quizzical look. "Please," he added. She set it down on a small table and he took her in his arms. "I just wanted to kiss you properly," he explained.

"Then shut up and kiss me properly." She wore shorts and a T-shirt, no bra. Nothing purposefully sexy, as far as he could tell. It just turned out that way.

They pulled their lips away but hung on to each other. He felt himself getting aroused. "Hang onto that thought," she said, "but you had a couple phone calls. Sounded like one of your boxing pals." Cheskis didn't live with Lorraine officially. She'd invited him to move in, but he couldn't stomach her aristocratic neighborhood on the Palos Verdes Peninsula. Residents lived in distant reaches of circular driveways that led to imitation Spanish missions sprawled across the palmy, flowered hills. Lorraine's nonconforming home cast a more modern, modest shadow. She'd scooped it up from a Hollywood gaffer before the For Sale sign went up.

Lorraine knew none of her neighbors. From time to time they could be spotted going by in walking costumes. The closest stores were quarantined two miles away, and residents never walked anywhere except for exercise. They had nothing they actually wished to accomplish at the end of their pedestrian journeys—no dry cleaning or quarts of milk to pick up, but looked quite purposeful as they walked around in circles.

The phone messages were from Lester Duddles, who identified himself as a matchmaker for Ray Powell. "Your guy ready for an eight-rounder in four weeks?" he asked Cheskis.

"Who's the opponent?"

"I won't lie to you," Duddles said. "It's a real fight. The guy is Carlos Garcia. He's 9 and 0. The fight's in Vegas and it pays four thousand. I saw your kid at the La Brea Friday and he can punch. He presses the fight. The guy Garcia was supposed to fight tore a muscle in the gym." Duddles sounded like a white East Coaster, partly relaxed, partly weary, as though this conversation needed only a fraction of his attention and the rest of him could dream about Bermuda.

"What'd Garcia do in the amateurs?" Cheskis said.

"I think your guy can beat him," Duddles said. "That's fine with me and it's fine with Ray. The guy's a pain in the ass and we're sick of him. Also, if the co-event doesn't go the distance, your kid could be on TV. Look, I got a lot of guys on my Rolodex who'd grab this in a second. If your kid wants to fight, let him fight, you know?"

Duddles said Garcia was a Cuban defector who fought out of Las Vegas, that he'd scored eight kayos in his nine wins and was "a big fucker." It was only after Cheskis hung up that he realized he never did get Garcia's amateur record. It might not have helped anyway. Amateur records were difficult to check and routinely exaggerated or invented in both directions. But clearly Garcia was no standard palooka. Cuba sifted through all its toddlers to find the best potential boxers, and its team routinely kicked butt. Those who defected to go pro in the States invariably left behind wives, children, and anyone who'd ever helped them succeed. They weren't generally the sweetest of people.

Cheskis traced Philyaw to the bar at the La Brea, where he was no doubt drinking bourbon and soda. "I've never seen this Garcia," he said, "but I heard about him. Let me do some checking and I'll call you back."

"I've got less than an hour," Cheskis said.

Eddie never heard of Garcia. He said he'd call Borakovich, a Powell insider. "I don't know if he'll tell us the truth, though." Carlos Garcia, it turned out, was a six-foot-five behemoth with a fine amateur record but was also a borderline lunatic whose towering lack of trust sabotaged his innate abilities. He'd refused to take on a manager, had fired three successive trainers, and was training himself for his next fight. "Powell wanted his son to manage him," Eddie said, "but you can't talk to this bloke. He's supposed to have a good punch, but you know in the amateurs, they train to do just three or four rounds. That's it." Eddie had worked Marvin up to forty-five intense minutes with no breaks except for water. "This Cuban will get tired, mate. This would be a good win."

"He's got thirty pounds on our guy," Cheskis said.

"They won't do him any good," Eddie said.

Taking care of Felix was eating up Eddie's gym profits, and prying training expenses out of Borakovich was like digging for coins in the Arctic Circle. Cheskis also knew there was no sense asking Marvin his opinion. He'd fight anyone. It was Cheskis's responsibility to put the right people in front of him at the right time.

Philyaw's information jibed with Eddie's. "He's big, he's strong, but not that slick. Comes right at you. I think they may really be ready to kiss this guy off, but it doesn't mean you'll win. These Cubans, they're schooled, pal. Really schooled."

"If you were me, would you take the fight?"

"How old is your kid?"

"Twenty-five."

"I don't know, Ches. It's a tough one. The other guy's been fighting since he was a little kid. There's nothing he hasn't seen."

"If we lose, what do we lose? If we win, what do we win?"

Philyaw paused. "You're right. But even if you lose, you can't afford to look bad."

Cheskis tried to get an extra thousand out of Duddles.

"Look, man," Duddles replied, "you're already going from five hundred a fight to four thou. I ain't selling rugs here, okay?" No sense telling him Marvin's last fight paid a thousand. No sense negotiating at all, it looked like.

"What about travel expenses?"

"Standard. Expenses for three days, two people."

"Plus the fighter?"

"C'mon, man. Including the fighter."

Cheskis knew Eddie would want to go to Vegas early to burn off Marvin's travel fatigue. They'd barely clear expenses.

"Look, Cheskis, what do they call you?"

"Call me Ches."

"Ches, you don't know me, I don't know you, but let me tell you, this is a good deal. And I'm tired of having to sell it to you."

"I want to do the best for my kid."

"Like I said, you want to be in the fight business, you take fights. These things don't fall out of trees. Stay in the game awhile, you'll see."

After making the deal, Cheskis explained it all to Lorraine, who, although she despised boxing, always enjoyed the business details. After all, in another life she'd worked in sales.

One night at a little Italian joint in Culver City she told him about one of her old deals. "It was the biggest I'd ever worked on. By far. I represented this character from Japan who had ultimate authority. It was a trade, actually. Complicated. I'd worked on it off and on over a year, talking to accountants and lawyers on three continents. This man I represented was decent in some ways, but he had no scruples. I know that doesn't sound possible, but that's the way he was. You can guess the rest."

"Don't make me."

"I had to fuck him, so I did. One time. He kept his word on that. It was a Motel 6 in Riverside. He liked it cheap and dirty." Her face was totally blank.

"Why'd you tell me?"

"I didn't plan to, but I thought I might someday."

"Is that when you became a Buddhist? After the Japanese guy?"

"I was already a Buddhist. At least I thought I was. I wasn't the first Buddhist whore. Thailand has—I don't know—a million? . . . Now I have to blow my nose. Can you believe that?" She also wiped little tears from the corners of both eyes.

"It's bad, but I pushed Mel Pritikin off a swing when I was eight. Kiss me."

"No."

"Why not?"

"Because you think it's kind of a sexy story," she said. "That's not fair."

"Look around any singles bar and you'll find plenty of people doing much creepier things. I don't feel bad about what you did because I know you'll never do it again. I only feel bad you feel bad about it."

"Kiss me." It was only later that Cheskis realized Lorraine had confessed her deepest regret while he'd skated away once again.

Cheskis cashed in Duddles's two plane tickets to help pay for a week in Las Vegas for Marvin and Eddie, who'd drive up five days before Cheskis and Tommy. "We want to get him used to the climate," Eddie said. "There's less oxygen that high." Cheskis knew everything would be air conditioned anyway and learned later Las Vegas's altitude was only 2,000 feet. But it was important for everybody to have a positive attitude, and if Eddie thought things weren't right, Marvin would feel it.

Cheskis had offered the fight to Marvin without telling him he'd accepted it. "We can't find any tape of this guy," Cheskis said. "He's bigger than you, and he's been around the block."

"What's it pay?" Marvin said.

"Four thousand," Cheskis said. "Eddie and I take thirty percent of that."

"I want it."

"This is a gamble," Cheskis said. Eddie nodded.

"I fear no man," Marvin said.

The fight was on a Saturday and Cheskis and Tommy arrived Thursday. In the hotel room Eddie had covered an entire desktop with vials and bottles of vitamins and minerals. He must have been feeding forty pills a day into Marvin. "How you feeling?" Cheskis asked Marvin.

"Okay except for the wrist," he said.

"Wrist? Nobody told me anything about a wrist! Sonofabitch! How bad is it? Damn it, I knew it. I just knew it!"

Marvin and Eddie practically fell down laughing. "Man, you're so easy," Marvin finally told Cheskis.

"You bastard," Cheskis said. "You coulda given me a heart attack. If Garcia doesn't kill you, I'll do it myself."

Marvin went into a fighter's crouch and Cheskis came inside. They both threw fake shots at each other and laughed like little kids. *I feel good*, Cheskis realized. *I feel good.* They went down to the coffee shop for dinner, where Benny Diamond was waiting for them. Eddie had been working with Marvin in Benny's Vegas gym. It dated back twenty years. In the quick-to-rise-and-fall world of boxing, that made the gym an institution. Benny's nose was flat as a stop sign. He'd been wounded on Guadalcanal and fought as a sniper in Israel's War of Independence. Benny was one of those semi-famous people in boxing who'd found himself a gimmick to make TV viewers remember him. He always entered the ring with little action photos of boxing greats such as Sugar Ray Robinson and Benny Leonard pasted to his bald, white head.

It wasn't long before Benny and Eddie started swapping stories at the table. "Once I worked with this Panamanian lightweight? Navarro," Benny said. "His manager, Paulie Francini, he's from Baltimore, he hired me to work cuts. After this guy makes weight, me and Paulie, we go with him to get some spaghetti at this Italian joint I know. After they make the weight, pasta's a good thing to get into them. But this guy, he don't listen to nobody, he has to order a hamburger. Okay, Paulie says. We drove all the way there just to get the pasta, but what can you do? Finally the food comes, and Navarro, he starts eating this big hamburger, but pretty soon he gets up and goes to the head. I got a prostate like a grapefruit, so a minute later I go back there too, and the Panamanian guy, I don't see him, but there's this terrible stink in there, so I'm really trying to do my business fast. Sure enough, the guy comes out of the toilet stall and it's Navarro. He walks from wiping his ass straight past the sink to his hamburger. I get back to the table and there he is, eating. I couldn't watch. Later, I mention it to Paulie, and he says, 'Benny, welcome to the Third World.'"

Eddie had been waiting patiently to spring his Sonny Liston story. When he fought out of Sydney, he'd get occasional work hiring out as a sparring partner. "One day they bring Liston into the gym. He's in town for something and wants to work with someone fast, a tricky bloke, he says. Two hundred dollars a round and he promises to take it easy. Well, right away I found a way to hit Sonny. He was a clever bastard, but I was throwing this two-punch combination—straight right to the chest and a left uppercut to the body. That left kept landing and when he caught on, I started to fake the straight right, swivel over"—he rose from his chair to demonstrate—"hook him to the body two, three times and pivot out of there. It was driving him crazy, mate, and in the second round he countered with a body shot—it felt like getting whacked with an iron bar. I mean it was something. I knew I couldn't take any more of those, but I didn't want to quit." Eddie reseated himself.

"So when I take the shot I let out a scream like this. Eeeayowwww!!" Heads turned in the coffee shop. "Everyone's laughing.

Sonny, too. He was a good bloke, you know. We touched gloves, and after that, he behaved himself." Eddie started telling the one about the spear-carrying Indonesian witch doctor but stopped to stare at a huge scowling black man, obviously a fighter, with an aristocratic, petite young black woman, very dark, as he was. "That's Garcia," Eddie said as the hostess seated them.

"He always looks like that," Benny said. "Like he's ready to clock somebody." Garcia's head was shaved except for a lengthy thatch of wild hair at the front of his skull.

"Man needs a hairdresser," Tommy said.

"Why's he look so unhappy?" Eddie said. "Look at that Sheila of his."

"Take it easy," Tommy said.

"I just don't understand it," Eddie said.

"You know women can't resist sensitive guys," Tommy explained.

"But it's good, mate," Eddie said. "She's been with him all week, probably fucking his brains out. He'll be weak." Cheskis wasn't so sure. He'd read once that Joe Namath spent the night before his spectacular Super Bowl victory with a babe and a bottle. Marvin appraised Garcia with cold dispassion. After a while he went back to his menu, looking content. *I feel good*, Cheskis thought.

CHAPTER 13

THE CUBAN

Fight people scurried around the hotel like flight teams on a carrier—fighters in the eight scheduled bouts, plus all their support troops and media functionaries. Lucky fans caught occasional glimpses of the main-event fighters—tactile gods striding through the casino trailed by tough-guy entourages in matching, shiny athletic suits. Eddie was having a great time kibitzing. The fight world was a small one, and it seemed he knew half the people there. He'd taken Felix along because Felix had a title shot in two weeks, and leaving him unwatched for a week was out of the question. Felix had fought on TV many times and Eddie told Cheskis that wherever he appeared, squads of casino customers competed to buy him drinks. "He's not even sleeping in the room. He's got Sheilas all around. I can't do anything with him. Talk to him. Maybe he'll listen to you."

That night Cheskis found Felix smiling over a gift highball in one of the casino's bars. Cheskis had a hard time making himself heard over a crowd of disco droids delighting in the vapid din bursting from two speakers big as refrigerators. Cheskis wanted to speak tactfully, but a kind of madness was loose in the room, smothering good sense. "You're at a peak!" Cheskis shouted. "You don't want to lose it!" At first he wasn't sure Felix heard him. But then moving his lips close to Cheskis's ear, he replied, "I'm thirty-two years old, *jefe*. I'm not a kid. I been doing this a long time. I know what it's about." At least that's what Cheskis thought he said. Buried inside a trail of additional words, he heard the phrase "cut your throat" drift casually into his cranium. He tried to play it back in his mind as Felix continued talking. Cheskis couldn't be certain whether the "you" referred to a generic throat or Cheskis's. It may have been part of a story, a warning, a promise, or some mystifying combination. Cheskis chose not to respond or ask for clarification. Eventually Felix borrowed forty dollars and Cheskis excused himself. Felix had fought and won twice since getting out of jail, but he was always broke. Snaking his way through the Vegas bar bodies, Cheskis was unsure whether he'd just done a favor for a friend or been mugged.

"He may be doing something worse than booze," Cheskis told Eddie. "His eyes looked glassy." As for the throat reference, Eddie was neither surprised nor particularly curious.

"Yeah, he's promised to cut my throat," Eddie said. "Two or three times. I been sleeping with a gun. But I can't worry about it now. We got Marvin's fight and I'm thinking, we never saw tapes of this Cuban."

Most people would find it remarkable that Eddie passed matter-of-factly over the possibility that his fighter might try to murder him in his sleep. But Cheskis found himself dealing with the threat in the same casual manner. It was Felix's nature. A tiger eats.

Eddie, who swore that Benny's fingers were still nimble, hired him as cutman. "I can handle both jobs," Eddie said. "but it might help us with these Vegas judges to see Benny in the corner."

"That's smart, Eddie," Cheskis said. "I should have thought of that. You're doing my job too because I don't know how."

"You got us here, mate. You deal with all these sonsabitches better than me. They make me wonder about God sometimes. How could He make people like Borakovich and Powell? I don't understand it." Eddie, though brought up Catholic, regularly attended an African-American Pentecostal church. Cheskis suspected that originally he was motivated more by his passion for African-American church babes than religion. But the ploy, if that's what it was, had turned around and reeled Eddie in like a flounder.

The fighters weighed in Friday in a hotel ballroom where working fight-people mixed with ordinary fans, and waitresses took drink orders in a carnival atmosphere. Weigh-ins were a useless exercise for heavyweights. But they gave everyone a chance to see the fighters stripped down to their jockstraps.

121

This had to be a discouraging experience for your average Garcia opponent. Cheskis wasn't surprised by his tremendous shoulders and flat, muscled chest—evidence of a professional who'd taken no weight-training shortcuts. What startled him was the thickness of his thighs. Legs were the key ingredient in getting force behind a punch, and Garcia's legs looked like they could stomp hogs. As he raised his arms and flexed his biceps, a smirk flickered along the edges of his nonstop scowl. He came in at 241, Marvin at 216. "Those muscles won't do him any good," Eddie said yet again. "They'll get him tired." Cheskis wasn't sure these comments helped. They might magnify the danger in Marvin's mind. Cheskis thought abut all the small-time trainers who reached the edges of the big time and sank without a trace, like captivating actresses who made one or two memorable movies and slid back into toilet-paper commercials.

What Marvin thought about Eddie or Garcia or any of what lay ahead, was, as usual when it came to Marvin's thoughts, a mystery. From time to time he watched Garcia impassively, like a dog sniffing at a plate of food he would ultimately reject.

Next day, fight day, Cheskis spent an hour driving through foreign Las Vegas streets looking for a bucket to use in the corner. No one had thought to bring one from California. When he finally found something that would work he entered a checkout line that turned out to be cursed. A fat, frowning Russian who could barely speak English insisted on making a complicated exchange, and two consecutive women after him wrote checks. As he watched the other lines move lickety-split, Cheskis breathed deeply and tried to conjure up some tip from his anger management class. Instead he recalled too late what Stu once told him: "Always get behind the Mexicans. Mexicans are all cash."

"What the hell are these?" Eddie said when Cheskis pulled the buckets out of a plastic bag.

"I got them at Toys R Us," Cheskis admitted. "They're a little small, so I got two. You like the blue? They also had green or yellow." Eddie looked dubious. "What?" Cheskis said, "We're going to lose because our buckets are too cute?"

"It's not that," Marvin said. "It's just you shoulda got the green."

That evening Felix, acting as though everything was hunky dory, showed up in Marvin's dressing room while Eddie taped Marvin's fists in front of the inspector. Felix's eyes didn't seem glassy this time, but he had shadows beneath them and he didn't move with the panther steps of a tuned, world-class fighter two weeks before a big event.

Taping was a precisely ruled science—ten yards of gauze, two of surgical tape, no tape over the knuckles, the idea being to provide maximum protection for the fighter's hands while inflicting maximum damage on the opponent. Eddie's work looked beautiful, but his face showed he'd poured blood and soul into Marvin, and now he was sending him out to step in front of a truck.

The inspector signed the tape and left while Eddie pulled on gloves and warmed up Marvin. Marvin's punches were short and sharp, like daggers. "You look beautiful, man," Felix said.

The referee, a retired highway patrolman, made a perfunctory visit to assure everyone he would enforce all the rules.

"Watch how that Cuban uses his head," Eddie told him. "He's got a wire brush in front of it. I hear he likes to rub it in your eyes."

"I watch everything," the referee said, offended.

"Billy," Benny Diamond told the ref, "Eddie's just watching out for his fighter. We're not worried about you. You're the best referee in Nevada."

The ref flashed a microsecond smile which Cheskis figured was worth Benny's $300 share. "Benny, you gotta stop handing all of us the same line of shit. We talk to each other, you know."

Benny laughed and clapped the referee on the back. "Yeah, but with you I mean it," he said, giving everyone a wink.

As Marvin sat passively on a bench, Tommy kneeled down and started massaging his legs. "What the hell you doing?" Eddie said, rushing over.

Tommy stopped and looked up. "Giving his legs—"

"I see what you're doing," Eddie said.

"Then what'd you ask me for?"

"That's the worst damn thing you can do. It'll turn his legs to rubber. Can't turn my back for a minute around here." Things like that happened all the time. Fighters' jobs were so demanding and dangerous that everyone wanted to help them, but few helpers knew what they were doing.

The inspector returned to watch Eddie lace up Marvin's gloves and wind tape around the laces. A few minutes later another inspector opened the door and said, "Two minutes." Marvin glistened with sweat from his workout. Felix asked him, Eddie, Cheskis, Tommy, and Benny to form a circle with him and hold hands. "Lord," Felix said as everyone bowed their faces toward the concrete floor, "we pray no one gets seriously hurt in this fight. And we pray you grant Marvin this victory. He sure deserves it. We ask this in your name."

"Amen."

Cheskis might have been startled to see Felix pronounce such a prayer if chaplains hadn't blessed flight crews before they firebombed cities. And there was something else at work—the spirit of boxing brotherhood. It infused Felix with goodwill even as he hit on the break or threw an elbow. But each step he took away from the sport drained kindness, leaving only street venom in his veins.

Luck was with them. A knockout had been scored in the third round of the first TV fight, and Marvin's bout would be televised to fill the space before the main event. When they walked out into the casino auditorium, Cheskis estimated a crowd of 5,000 sprinkled around a venue that held 14,000. Vegas crowds always included high rollers and lesser gamblers who'd scored comped tickets from casinos. They were only taking a break from the tables and weren't serious fans. Strategy bored them. They demanded serious mayhem.

The announcer, decked out in a precisely-tailored, lint-free tuxedo, was a former used-car salesman who was always the handsomest person in the room and knew it. He was reputed to have bedded more beautiful women than the entire Rat Pack. Marvin had no robe. He wore a towel with a hole in it that served as a makeshift poncho. After Marvin and the team climbed into the ring, Garcia came out in his green satin robe with his name on the back in fancy script, his back looking big as a billboard. With the tuft of hair sticking forward, he looked like a creature from some other species. The same handler who'd accompanied him at the weigh-in sprang to the ropes first and held them open for his fighter, who climbed through without acknowledging him. Cheskis stared at another cornerman who followed Garcia into the ring. His hair was gray and thinning, and his face was broader than Cheskis remembered it, but he recognized him in an instant. Walking directly over to Cheskis, Staff Sergeant Valaitas smiled. From his attitude, you'd have thought they'd just talked yesterday. "How you doing, kid?"

I'll be doing way better than your fighter in a couple minutes. But by the time Cheskis thought to say this, Valaitas was already halfway back to his corner. Cheskis now recognized the third Garcia cornerman—team captain Caddington of Fort Ord, also heavier, but unmistakably Caddy. Cheskis tried to digest all this as he watched smiling promoter Ray Powell, a small black man with a beautiful silk suit, wearing his trademark lightly tinted glasses and goatee. Powell strutted over to Garcia, reached up, patted him on the shoulder, and told him something. If he really wanted Garcia to lose, Cheskis wondered, would he pose with him like this? But everyone knew Powell would cross a river of lava to get in front of a TV camera. "If you believe whatever Powell's telling you," Philyaw had said, "you must think cab drivers carry only five dollars in change. But meanwhile—his mind—it's working like a computer. The fucker's smart. But if you had something he wanted and it was behind your eyeballs? He'd rip out your eyeballs."

Years ago Powell had been one of the most successful bookies in New Jersey. But business suffered a setback when a dozen witnesses watched him kick and pistol-whip a customer to death over a $400 debt. Over the objections of the D.A.'s office, a mob-connected judge let Powell plead it down to manslaughter. He did less than four years and used the time to polish his boxing business plan. That was fifteen years ago. Now he was the

125

biggest, most powerful promoter in boxing. The homicide and subsequent soft sentence helped mold his reputation as a man who stopped at nothing and could fix anything.

The crowd had no favorite in this one. Cubans were no attraction in Vegas, and no one had heard of Marvin. But fans always got more excited over heavyweights, especially when both were carved like Greek statues. Obeying Cheskis's request, Marvin was introduced as "Quick O'Brien." Marvin was known around South Central L.A. as "Speed," his Crips street name, so they picked something close.

In the corner, Eddie told Marvin to punish Garcia's body. "Move around. Make him work. He'll be fast this first round, so when you throw those right hooks to the body, keep your left up. This fucker's ours, mate. But he doesn't have to know it yet. Take your time."

After they touched gloves and started circling, Marvin threw a jab, the safest punch, and Garcia countered with a lightning two-punch combination—a right-hand over the top followed by a left hook. As Marvin retreated, Garcia followed him to the ropes, throwing combinations, trying to end it fast. Marvin covered up peek-a-boo style, not throwing back. The referee shouted something that Cheskis couldn't hear over the fans' screaming and laughing about the prospect of a quick heavy-weight knockout. When big men went down, it could shake a building. The ref had probably warned Marvin to fight back or he'd end it.

Eddie yelled instructions, but Marvin couldn't possibly distinguish them from all the other excited voices. Finally he pivoted to his right and caught Garcia with a hard right. When Garcia turned into him, they traded a dozen blistering punches, but this time it was Garcia who moved out of there. Cheskis breathed again. It was turning into a terrific fight, but not for the fighters.

Marvin seemed okay back in the corner. "He likes that lead right," Eddie told him as Benny passed him a water bottle. Marvin swished the water around and spit it out.

"Take some more and swallow it," Benny told him.

"Swallow it?" Eddie said. "Nobody swallows it."

"Nobody's got any brains," Benny said. "Football, baseball, basketball players, all of 'em swallow water all the time."

"Cut the shit. Both of you," Cheskis said. "Eddie what do you want him to do?"

The warning buzzer went off. "Short punches," Eddie shouted. "Everything short. Just like we practiced."

At center ring the referee took one look at Marvin and called time, taking him back to the corner. "Where's his mouthpiece?"

"Crap!" Cheskis said. He frantically pounded his pockets, found it, and slipped it into Marvin's mouth.

"You guys get organized," the ref said. "Any more a this shit and I'll take a point, so help me."

"Ches's never been on TV before," Eddie explained to Benny. Out in the ring, Marvin and Garcia were already throwing thunder at close range. When Garcia tried to clinch, Marvin sidestepped him and kept punching. Garcia charged in with his head tipped, burrowing his wiry thatch of hair into Marvin's eyes. The referee stepped in and warned him, shaking his finger. He patted the top of his own head to make sure Spanish-speaking Garcia understood. But ten seconds later Garcia was trying to drill his hair into Marvin's eye socket again. Marvin thumped him behind the neck with illegal rabbit punches. When the ref moved in, Garcia wouldn't release Marvin's left glove. Marvin threw three right hands to the kidney. Finally the referee, sweating through his shirt, got them both under control. Cheskis spotted abrasions already forming on Marvin's cheek from Garcia's malevolent head. Marvin snapped off a combination and, when Garcia charged in with his head again, met him with a forearm to the nose. Garcia illegally beat Marvin's head with the side of his right fist as though hammering a nail. The bell sounded and Marvin returned to the corner leaking blood from somewhere around his left ear. The fans screamed and pounded each other in delight.

"Keep working the body," Eddie said.

"Swallow the water," Benny said as he examined Marvin's ear. The part that connected to the skull looked as though it had been sliced by a razor, and the whole ear was starting to swell. Marvin didn't ask about it. Benny bathed the cut in adrenaline, rubbed freezing metal over the area to fight the swelling, then applied Vaseline.

"He's tired already," Eddie said. "Make him work. He can't keep this up."

"You're doing fine, kid," Benny told him. "Just keep doing what you're doing."

Cheskis lost track of the rounds. Sometimes Garcia seemed to be tiring, but like a vampire gorged on fresh blood, he always revived. "When have you ever seen heavyweights throw so many punches?" one of the tuxedoed TV commentators kept asking his partner. The commentator was Ryan Upchurch, the network's lead fight analyst. Upchurch, whose real name was Giorgos Alogoskoutis, had a head of distinguished silver hair and one of those anchorman faces that TV audiences will put up with well past middle age, particularly when they're assisted by an occasional facelift. Upchurch had been a sportswriter at *The Times* while Cheskis was there. As far as he knew, they'd never met.

Every chance he got, Garcia worked on the ear. He punched it, elbowed it, butted it, rubbed the raw tape of his gloves across it, swiveled his wiry hair into it. Cheskis couldn't even imagine the pain. Bathed in blood, the ear stuck out like a megaphone and was gradually separating from the skull. The TV team increasingly focused on it. Twice the referee called time to summon the ring physician, who examined the bloated ear with a little flashlight and sent Marvin back out there. He looked at it between rounds, too. "Let me work on it," Eddie finally told Benny. Eddie went at it with astringent-soaked Q-tips and frozen metal just as Benny had done, but this time when he wiped it down with a towel there was no more fresh blood.

The two fighters touched gloves to signal the start of the eighth and final round. Both looked like they'd just gone thirty rounds with Bigfoot. Marvin's face didn't look like Marvin's face anymore, and his puffed-up ear was grotesquely askew. Garcia was cut above and below one eye, and the other was swollen. Blood leaked from a gash just above his forehead—the result of a clash of heads two or three rounds earlier. More blood seeped into his mouth from somewhere.

They immediately started banging each other at close range. Garcia came back again and again to the ear, trying to make the referee stop the contest and give him a technical knockout. Some of his punches were still quick, but then he threw a lazy right hand and didn't bring the glove back quickly. He'd done this several times earlier and escaped punishment, but this time Marvin slid underneath and ripped three left hooks to the liver. Garcia winced and reflexively raised his right leg off the canvas to help cover his right side. Marvin connected with a right hook to the body, but Garcia slammed him back with a right that missed and a left uppercut and shoulder to the chest that sent him flying off-balance. The ref called it a knockdown because only the ropes prevented him from hitting the canvas. After reaching the count of eight, the ref asked Marvin if he wanted to continue. He nodded yes but looked spent, lost.

As Garcia moved in for the kill, Marvin stunned him with a jab right down the pipe. Because Garcia was moving forward, the punch landed with extra force. Marvin slammed the liver again with two hooks. As Garcia lowered his elbows to protect his midsection he got caught by a big straight right to the head. Even with all the noise, Cheskis could hear the thump. Garcia pitched forward, hitting the canvas like a tree. The referee began a count, but after looking closely at Garcia, he raised his arms and signaled the fight over.

Cheskis and the other cornermen, all screaming, jumped inside the ropes and took turns hugging sweaty, bloody, barely-able-to-stand Marvin. One ring physician supervised as Garcia, now conscious, was helped onto a stool. The other doctor examined Marvin's ear. It was starting to look like a moose antler, but the bleeding remained stopped. A jumble of fight people filled the ring. Marvin worked his way through them and hugged Garcia, who hugged him back. They exchanged a few words across the language barrier. Upchurch, pink with TV makeup, worked his way in and placed one hand around Marvin's shoulders, pulling him to the camera. With his other hand, Upchurch held a microphone to Marvin's bruised lips. "Quick," he said, "how much were you paid to win the best fight we've seen this year?"

"I don't know, four or five thousand."

Upchurch chuckled. "You can bet it'll be more next time."

Eddie moved in on Marvin's other side and addressed Upchurch: "How much were you paid to ask the question?"

"I'll ask the questions," Upchurch said. "Who do you want next?" he said to Marvin. But before he could answer, Powell inserted himself into the shot. "How about this guy?" Powell told the camera.

"Who do you want him to fight next, Ray?" Upchurch said.

"When a fighter can put on a show like this—" Powell began.

Marvin turned to leave, but Upchurch shoved the microphone at him again. Marvin expressed his thanks to Garcia for taking the match. "He's a great fighter," Marvin said.

"Did he ever really hurt you?" Upchurch asked him.

"Sure, he hurt me just about every time he hit me. Punches hurt, same as head butts and everything else he did in there. But it's all part of the game. He's a great fighter. You want to know who's next, my manager's over there—Lee Cheskis. I'll fight whoever he puts in front of me."

"Do you feel ready for a title shot right now?" Upchurch asked him.

"I want to fight the best. I don't claim to be the best. I just want to fight them."

"Let's bring Lee over," Upchurch said. Powell, snubbed, kept smiling, but when he was left out of the shot he immediately breathed dark smoke. His face might change from rage to lunacy to good cheer at any moment. It was a source of his power.

"This was one hell of a fight for four or five thousand dollars," Upchurch told Cheskis. "And it was close. Any thoughts about a rematch?"

"We've got an ambulance waiting," Cheskis said, turning away.

Chapter 14

GOONS

Outside the emergency room, Cheskis asked Eddie how he'd managed to stop the bleeding. Eddie looked around. "Stu gave me the stuff," he said in a half-whisper. "It's what they use in operating rooms." Should anyone ask for a chemical analysis, Marvin would be disqualified and everyone in the corner screwed. But when you're up against a foul-master like Garcia, hitting him with a shovel wouldn't be out of line.

Cheskis asked Benny if he knew Valaitas. Excellent trainer, Benny said, who used to work out of Benny's gym. "I thought Garcia didn't have a trainer."

"He doesn't, the ignorant shit," Benny said. "Valaitas works for Powell on salary." Benny didn't know Caddington but had seen him around. "He's always with Valaitas. They work out of Powell's gym. He's punchy."

"Who?" Cheskis said.

"The guy, you know. The black guy. What's his name?"

"Caddington?"

"Yeah, Caddington."

This hospital had worked on more busted-up boxers than any medical facility in the world, and its doctors insisted on admitting both fighters. Before they were wheeled to their rooms, the two spent athletes lay side by side in the emergency room, fluids running into them. Like a soldier lying next to a P.O.W., mused Valaitas. Garcia's effort proved once again that courage doesn't always come in a nice wrapper. Valaitas had seen fighters in slugfests less savage who were never the same afterward. But you never knew. In their last bout, LaMotta survived one of the worst beatings in history from Sugar Ray Robinson, and decades later he still joked about it, all gears humming. You might not know the true toll of a fight like this one for twenty years.

Valaitas, knowing Powell's next move, managed to speak privately with Cheskis as the two teams drifted out of the emergency room toward their fighters' respective rooms. "Listen," he said, "I've only got a minute to explain."

Then he found Powell outside Garcia's room telling the others about a fight he'd once put together in Houston. Powell's fighter was knocked to the canvas in the first round with a hard right to the chest. The referee, hoping to earn Powell's gratitude, ruled it a low blow and deducted a point from the man standing. "The fans, they're throwing everything they can think of into the ring. If the ref hadn't been a cracker, they'd have lynched him. But they got rules about that in Texas. Finally, after the fight, I tell this ref—he's still got some of the beer, hotdog goo, you name it, on him—'Man, you got to learn finesse, understand?' He looks at me like I'm speaking Chinese or something, and that's when I realize 'finesse' is way beyond this man's vocabulary limit."

Everyone was still chuckling when one of Powell's goons showed up and told him, "Coast is clear, boss," meaning O'Brien's team had gone downstairs for coffee—or so the goon believed. Valaitas followed Powell, the two goons, and Powell Junior down the hall. Junior was carrying the briefcase his father called "the closer." When they reached O'Brien's room the goons waited outside as Powell entered with Paul Junior and Valaitas behind him.

"Here he is, man of the hour," Powell exclaimed with delight, closing the door behind them. Cheskis's kid looked even worse now, as Valaitas knew he would. Tomorrow he'd look worse still. He looked up from his bed, curious, as Powell, all smiles, gave him a Black Power salute. It wasn't returned.

"Young man, I came by specifically to tell you just how special you are," Powell said, and Valaitas tuned him out as he launched his spiel about destiny, Spartans, Kikuyu warriors, Buffalo soldiers, "Boxing Bonnie," a super-tough she-male who'd been in the joint with him, and all the rest of it. Had the kid been Latin, Aztec and Inca warriors would have been substituted for Kikuyu and cavalry.

Inside Powell's clown suit was a deadly serious businessman with the energy of ten. Taken from a more propitious womb, he might be running General Motors or the State Department. Powell kept all his files in his head, including a running count of favors owed and favors yet to be collected. He could pull people out of his pocket from Bangkok to Juarez. Corporate princes to the lowest stinkbugs. Whatever it took. Years ago, before he was a Colossus, he'd been cornered by two thugs sent by a competitor. Powell famously tipped them so they'd tone down the beating.

If they had to compete in his world, the pigmies who owned big-time, government-subsidized sports teams would be trampled. They commemorated paper warriors like them in statues all over Buenos Aires. Valaitas took a fighter there once and every time they turned a corner there was another statue of another pompous *commandante* who'd made his bones in a sandbox.

In the fight game, each event was a blank slate, with no date, location, TV network, or fighters. Promoters put it all together from scratch and negotiations never stopped. Powell was always trailed by a half-dozen or more lawsuits filed in various places around the world. On top of all this he had to spot all the finks and undercover agents dispatched by the feds. If they were doing the same kind of job against the Russians, the country was sunk. He'd already beaten two consecutive federal indictments. After the acquittals he flagrantly rewarded jurors with cruises, cash, trips to Bermuda. He made it all a joke, and it helped that he probably hated fighters. They said he had one fight in the amateurs and crawled out of the ring like a dog. Screwing fighters might be his way of getting even.

Powell was nearing the part where he opened the briefcase, and still no Cheskis. Maybe Caddy screwed it up somehow. "We have different roles—promoters and managers," Powell said. "See, I put it all together, kind of like Cecil B. DeMille. Managers, what they do is try to get a good promoter's attention. But your manager, he hasn't found you a promoter, has he? That's why you got what? Four thousand? If you had a manager like Ray Junior standing up for you—say hello to Ray Junior—it would have been twenty-five thou at least. Am I right, Junior?"

"More," Junior said. Junior didn't have much to do, but he could be relied on to do it before returning to his cocaine and broads. Most states wouldn't let a promoter double as manager, so whenever possible, Powell saddled fighters with Junior to cut himself a bigger slice.

"You want to keep your manager, go right ahead," Powell Senior said. "What I'm telling you is what I'd tell my own son. You need a promoter. So why not go with the best—if you can? And you can. You know how many heavyweight titles there are? That really count?"

"Four," Marvin said. He said it flat, betraying nothing, like an accomplished poker player. But the words came out just a little mumbled through his swollen lips.

"You know how many of those champions are my fighters?"

"I thought you can't own people anymore." Once again, the kid said it flat, no emotion.

"Listen, brother, see this skin? I know all about being owned, same as you." It was anybody's guess whether the brief flair of indignation was real or part of the act. The man was Shakespearian. "You think those white dudes are gonna look after you? Same way they looked after us when we came down the gangplank, brother, in chains. We didn't get hooked up with no promised land, did we? What we got was a cotton sack and a branding iron. We want to stop being field niggers, we got to work, like you did tonight. You're the real thing, my brother, and I don't deny it. I'm not driving a bargain. I'm yours already. Without me, you might get somewhere, sure. You're that good. But you can spend a long time scratching in a barnyard for bits of corn, understand? I'm the only man in the world can guarantee you a title shot. Right now, while you're in your prime. So you wondering—this man making lots of promises—can he deliver? I know. I come from the same ghetto. 'Cause it's all one ghetto, brother. Runs from Philly to Watts and every other nigger shithole along the way. Lookit here!"

134

The briefcase Junior had been holding suddenly appeared—a sleight of hand kind of thing. Powell Senior swung it on the bed with a flourish and clicked it open. He reached inside and tossed stacks of currency toward the kid. "This is yours. You don't got to share with anybody. It's the difference between what you made with them tonight and what you woulda made with me. Twenty-dollar bills. A thousand of them." Show a black man raw cash, Powell liked to say, and it does twice the work of a check.

The kid looked at the bills and smiled, but the smile wasn't readable. Could mean okay, fuck you, let's negotiate, anything. Which was when the door opened and Cheskis came in. He looked around pleasantly. "Say Marv, you holding a party?"

"In the morning maybe. Right now I wanna sleep," the kid said.

Caddy entered right behind Cheskis—not part of the plan. It made Valaitas slightly lightheaded because he knew that little slip-up would cost him his job. Powell showed no surprise. Nothing surprised Powell.

"Then let's all go," Cheskis said, presenting a problem for Powell, who'd received no signature and whose currency was spread out on the bed. He motioned to Junior to retrieve his goods. Junior had to rummage around to get it all. Embarrassing.

"We'll hold on to it for you," Powell said. But the kid ignored him. This had to be killing Powell. First Valaitas double-crosses him, next a lowly fighter treats him like a vagrant. When they filed into the hallway they ran into the kid's trainer—the Australian—and the two goons. When the goons saw Powell they tried to look fierce, not an easy thing to do sitting on a linoleum floor, back to the wall. The trainer had one hand inside his shiny jacket.

"You know," Cheskis told Powell, "you can talk to our guy. We don't object. But not tonight."

"Well *I* object," the trainer said to Powell. "I don't like the way you do business. Sneaking around like a spider. And don't give me that mad look, mate."

135

Ignoring him, Powell told Valaitas, "Catch you later, Benedict Arnold. You and your slave boy."

"Watch your mouth," Caddy said.

Yep, so much for that job.

"I found him after these gangsters in Milan had latched on to him," Valaitas explained to Cheskis at a small table in The Ship lounge at Caesars Palace. A crowd of standard Vegas Sinatra-imitators mingled with squads of hookers.

"They were shipping him around Europe under different names," Valaitas continued. "Wherever they needed an American to take a beating from a local hero. They kept his passport."

"You rescued him, then," Cheskis said.

"Caddy wasn't important to them. Just another piece of equipment."

Cheskis looked pretty good, Valaitas decided. No middle-aged paunch, fairly sure of himself, maybe less of a wiseass. Even had most of his hair. "What're you doing in this shitty business?" asked Valaitas.

"I could ask you the same thing," Cheskis said.

"Weren't you with *The New York Times* awhile?"

"How'd you know that?"

"I read it sometimes. I liked seeing your byline. I knew it had to be you."

"That was in another life. I don't even think about it." He didn't find it remarkable that an NCO read *The Times*. He'd come along nicely, Cheskis. But what had he been doing all these years? Managing small-time fighters? Probably, like the man said, living a life of quiet desperation.

"Powell's going to fire you, right?"

"Probably," Valaitas agreed.

"What about Caddy?"

"He works for me, not Ray. We'll be okay. I have my Army pension and my wife makes more than I do. I'll work for myself again. I was just about to leave Powell anyway," he lied.

"Your wife doesn't mind helping out Caddy?"

"If all we wanted was money, we'd have kept the gym. First we were in Oakland. I had plenty of kids coming in. But it was murder. Nobody paid their dues. So we moved it to San Francisco. Noe Valley. Brought in weight machines, kickboxing teachers, a juice bar. Natalie had the place looking like the Ritz Carlton. But I was always putting up with these spoiled yuppies and their spoiled dogs. They sleep with their dogs, half of 'em. Anyway, I sold it and came down here. What about you? Any kids?"

"No. You?"

"Girl and a boy." At Cheskis's urging, he dug out their photos, and Cheskis showed the proper enthusiasm.

"You know, Sarge, I'm—proud of you. The way you take care of Caddy and everything."

"Natalie says I'm doing penance."

"For what?"

"For being an asshole, she says. I'm nuts about her. What about you? Wives, girlfriends?"

"Girlfriend," he said.

Valaitas remembered seeing him once with an unforgettable girl, the kind of girl who honors you just by breaking your heart. He was careful not to mention Roybal. Because he sensed now what happened to Cheskis. Roybal. Cheskis blamed himself. Most people let life roll over them. Guys like Cheskis, they let it murder them.

"Let me tell you something, kid. You can't do everything right. I got my people killed in two wars. But carrying it around, it doesn't help."

Cheskis stared at him. That's all he said about Roybal. Nothing.

CHAPTER 15

OLD HICKORY

When Marvin left the hospital the next day his ear was so swaddled in bandages he looked like a barfly in *Star Wars*. The doctors had stitched up the skin where the ear met his skull and drained blood from the ear itself so it wouldn't turn cauliflower. He was banged up everywhere and moved like a man who'd fallen off a roof.

It was time for everyone to start back for L.A., but no one could find Felix, propelling Eddie into endless soliloquies about Felix's transgressions and his own sacrifices. He'd poured his life onto a canvas only to have a barbarian piss on it. Felix's wife hadn't heard from him but didn't seem alarmed. Living with him for years must have provided her with towering immunities.

Borakovich complained that Eddie should have watched his fighter. "Watch him yourself," Eddie spat back. "You got spare rooms at your place." Even if Felix turned up now, Eddie didn't see how he could get him down to the weight. He'd been three pounds above the 147-pound limit when they left for Vegas— just where Eddie wanted him. By now he might be ten pounds over. "They knew we had him sharp," Eddie said. "It's why they postponed it." Roundtree, the champion, had claimed a torn ligament a couple weeks before the first scheduled date. Postponement was a perfect ploy against a fighter like Felix, who, properly trained and conditioned, could box beautifully. But he lacked the discipline to stay beautiful.

Crossing the desert back to L.A., Cheskis was surprised by just how much he missed Lorraine. But it was a pleasant longing because it would soon end with fulfillment. Thoughts of Lorraine alleviated the highway tedium and transcended at least some of the morbid thoughts about all the other drivers zipping in and out of lanes who could kill him with one sneeze.

A weekend in Vegas seemed to vaporize drivers' fear of death. Sprinkled among them were who knew how many coked-up hysterics; sick, enraged losers; lunatics having various forms of sex with themselves and their passengers; feckless fools fiddling with radio dials, cigarettes, bra straps, beers, coffee, condoms, cosmetics, and ketchup containers. For much of the three-hundred-mile stretch across the sage the nearest hospital was more than an hour away. Traffic victims routinely bled to death or died of shock before they reached the emergency room.

Cheskis steered straight to his 2 P.M. class, where he turned back a set of papers he'd graded before leaving for Las Vegas. He used most of the class time—an hour and fifteen minutes— going over the results, measuring students' efforts against the who, what, where, when, and why building blocks of the sacred Tower of Journalistic Babel. "But the cop accidentally shot himself in the foot," Cheskis explained to the cross Adonia Fontaine. "You said he shot himself in the forehead. That's a big error, don't you think?"

"I just didn't hear you right," Ms. Fontaine said, staring him down like a bullfighter. "I know this is better than a C-plus paper." Ms. Fontaine wore $150 designer jeans, spent hours on her makeup and hair, took her day-to-day chances living in the Compton ghetto, and wasn't going to take any crap from Cheskis. Standing fast, he knew Ms. Fontaine would fix his wagon when she turned in her anonymous evaluation form at the end of the semester—rating him "poor" across the board, and ad libbing comments on his vile soul. McMasters would read it and smile. It was like getting paid to read other people's mail, and he was just the man to do it.

It was dusk as he drove up Lorraine's driveway in the virtually soundless cocoon of her neighborhood. No pots and pans, R&B, salsa, hollering, laughter. The affluent make very little noise.

She kissed him at the door with the intensity of someone validating a parking stub. The dog jumped around with dumb joy. At least someone was happy to see him. "Where's Marvin?" she said.

139

"His place. He'll take a few more days off work, but he's okay."

"Okay? I watched it. I watched it on TV. He's not okay." She looked uncharacteristically off-center, perhaps sleep-deprived.

"Can I come in?" he found himself saying as he felt a sink-hole form beneath his shoes.

She dropped to a sofa and nervously positioned her pert butt on its edge. They said nothing for awhile, listening to a Mozart piano concerto on the stereo. They had spoken on the edge of this issue more than once, but both of them had always pulled back. He'd forgotten the fight was televised, and now was foolishly unprepared. She got right up again and had him follow her out the white French doors to the old-fashioned porch swing hanging over the pool deck, the dog and cat trailing them. He caught a whiff of manure-based fertilizer from a potted plant somewhere, and perhaps the scent of sea air pushing up the canyon. They kept their hands in their laps as they finally got down to the discussion they'd been putting off so carefully.

"Look, I just don't see how you can profit from Marvin's suffering. It's impossible to ignore anymore." She must have practiced some of this.

"It may not seem like it, but I'm helping this kid, Lorraine. He never even worked a job until he became a fighter."

"It's not an either-or," she said. "The choice isn't between being a fighter or a criminal."

"To him that ring is a rose garden. Just one opponent, no guns, no knives. Besides, if I didn't manage him he'd still fight." But it was no good. She viewed Cheskis now as a functionary who packaged Christians for lions. "I can't just quit. It's wrong." Boxing, he wanted to explain, provided men like Marvin and Felix with a dignity they otherwise would never know—a dignity they could call on later and recall fondly, no matter how they ended up. But the more he told her, the worse it got.

Cheskis had made a point of reminding Marvin that down the line he could be paid off with pugilistic dementia, but the idea only amused him. Cheskis even took him to meet Paco Alganaraz in the shabby little harbor area gym where he'd just finished teaching a class to four neighborhood kids.

"You kids stay out of trouble, now," Paco told them twice. His words came out as though he had a mouthful of marbles. Cheskis introduced Marvin as a promising heavyweight.

"Paco was the flyweight champion of the world," Cheskis said, which impressed Marvin.

Flyweights compete at 112 pounds. Paco, who lost his title in Tokyo less than twenty years earlier, was pushing 200. "The thing about kids today," Paco said, "is they just run the streets and get in trouble. They got no program for them." The words were like the second act of a play. There was no opening scene. "Fighters, they got no one to look out for them." No one else was around now except for a middle-aged man with a teardrop tattoo beneath his eye who was tightening the ropes on the little ring that took up half the gym. "I never saved nothing. Nobody looked out for me."

"But you got a good job as a longshoreman, right?" Cheskis reminded Paco.

"Yeah, the union, they got me cleaned up. Weren't for them, I'd be dead from booze. But when I stopped fighting, nobody showed me nothing, you know? Just like today. The kids, they run in gangs, get in trouble, 'cause they got no place to go. Nobody does nothing about it."

Marvin tried to ask Paco about his boxing days, where he won his title, but Paco always drifted back to his mantra. After what Cheskis considered an appropriate time, he said it was time to go. Paco never asked them why they'd stopped by.

Cheskis and Marvin ordered fish tacos at a bustling seafood joint in San Pedro. "What was that?" Marvin asked him. "A field trip?" He didn't wait for an answer. "Everything happens for a reason. You believe that, Ches?"

"No, I think all kinds of things happen for no reason at all."

"Well, some things maybe."

"Everything that happens for no reason," Cheskis said, "that's what they call luck. And only some of it's good." Valaitas used to talk about luck—that it doesn't care about rabbits' feet or what sign you were born under. Luck is way beyond your powers. Which is why it's called luck. Or was it Kesey who said that?

"Us meeting up the way we did," Marvin said, "it happened for a reason."

"You'd have been a fighter without me," said Cheskis, flattered. "You were born for this."

"I wanted it too bad to actually do it. Understand what I'm saying? But then I said, 'You can trust this dude. There it is, right in front of you. What's your excuse now?' Well now I'm doing it, and nothing will make me stop. They'll have to kill me."

"You know you can't do it, kid," Philyaw said.

"Yeah," Cheskis agreed, taking a belt of scotch. "But I can't quit Lorraine, either."

"So you lose a dame," Philyaw said. "It's nothing a little bourbon and soda won't fix." Almost imperceptibly he briefly raised an index finger at the end of one trench-coat-sleeved arm, and as other customers clamored for attention, the lone bartender rushed over to present Philyaw and Cheskis with two more drinks.

"When's your guy fighting again?" the bartender asked Philyaw.

"I'll let you know," he said, brushing him off like a bug.

"Sometimes," he told Cheskis, "I think maybe I should do a special deal with Powell, the way Borakovich does. You know, he takes his cut on the side and he does okay. Guys like Eddie, they fight over crumbs, and they don't get to touch the cake. Felix, too. You know when he was a kid, nine, ten years old, they forced him into backyard gladiator contests over in Boyle Heights. Passed him around like a dog. Once after he lost they locked him in a closet for two days."

An ugly story in itself, but it also signified that Philyaw had given Cheskis's loss of Lorraine all the attention he felt it deserved. You didn't see Bogey crying when he passed Ingrid Bergman back to Claude Raines. Philyaw was a man of nice judgment and many resources, not one to spread false tales. His own origins were unclear, but he was hostile to anyone who'd grown up too comfy. "Whenever some rich bastard gives you a speech about how he worked for everything he's got, you know

142

you're talking to a putz who grew up with a pool, a pony, and a nanny." But he harbored no illusions about nobility among savages. He had it on good authority that Felix had been a trigger man on drive-bys, and at least once he'd forced his sister to take the wheel.

Tuesday Eddie got a call from Felix's wife. He'd been busted selling a pound of cocaine to undercover cops in North Hollywood. Eddie was calm. A crisis he could take. It was worrying about a possible crisis that defeated him. He made his call to Borakovich, who reported back that Powell advised patience. Powell's ever-ready legal team said the D.A. still hadn't filed charges. Maybe there was more to it. Wednesday they kicked Felix loose. He'd sold the cops a pile of laundry soap. But Eddie's elation was immediately deflated when Felix's wife dropped him off on Thursday. "He's soft," Eddie said. "He's ruined."

A couple nights later Eddie called Cheskis at home. "I need you to do me a favor, mate." Felix, he said, was at the Poop Deck, a bar in Hermosa Beach. Eddie wanted Cheskis to fetch him.

"He doesn't listen to me, Eddie," Cheskis said.

"If I go over there it'll get ugly, mate. I don't think he'll hit you." How comforting. Eddie didn't *think* he'd hit Cheskis. As it turned out, Felix watched passively, almost timorously, as Cheskis scattered the sycophants buying him tequilas. There was no talk of throat-cutting. On the drive over to Eddie's, Cheskis wanted to be encouraging. He found himself telling Felix about Andrew Jackson's duel against the best marksman in Tennessee, who'd insulted his wife's good name. Cheskis read the story when he was a boy and never forgot it. Old Hickory wore an oversized coat and positioned it so that when his opponent fired at what he thought was Jackson's heart, the bullet struck high. True to the code, the man stood his ground defenseless while the future president calmly took aim and killed him with one shot. "You can beat anybody," Cheskis told Felix. "All you need is the right strategy."

"You've come a long way, brother," replied Felix. "From when we were in County, remember?" Every day people asked Cheskis how he was doing. Yet how many of them cared as much as damaged, twisted, homicidal Felix?

"You can win this fight, Felix. Anything Roundtree's got, you've seen it before."

Eddie's apartment was at the top of an exterior staircase of fifteen or twenty steps. Cheskis considered accompanying Felix up there, just to be sure, but after all, he was a grown man. Later that night the phone woke Cheskis. "What happened to you?" Eddie asked him. Felix never made it inside.

Two days later, contrite, he limped into Eddie's. He'd been shooting dope in his ass, Eddie said. "You could see the marks." He'd also lost his shoes somewhere and the soles of his feet were torn and bleeding. His title bout was only a week off. The champion, Allen Roundtree, was a lanky kayo artist out of Atlanta who loved to train. He had 37 wins, 33 by knockout, no losses, and was being compared to Thomas "Hit Man" Hearns.

Felix weighed 161. He had to get down to 147. This late in the game, getting in shape for twelve rounds and making the weight were opposite, mutually exclusive goals. After Eddie and Felix got to Vegas, Cheskis and Marvin, at Eddie's request, flew across the desert to join them. Marvin and Felix played chess every day while Felix ingested only small amounts of water and no food. Various compounds brought along by Eddie helped him drain his bowels and bladder. The weigh-in was noon Friday, thirty-two hours before the fight. By Thursday Felix had stopped playing chess and lay face-up on his bed staring at the ceiling, licking his lips.

Eddie had what he considered an accurate bathroom scale. Two hours before the scheduled weigh-in, Felix was less than a pound over, and Eddie said they were home-free. Eddie, Cheskis, Tommy, and Marvin went downstairs for lunch. They avoided discussing a fight strategy or Felix's chances. When they got back to the room, Felix had perked up, which Cheskis saw as a good sign. But Eddie, looking worried, asked Felix to mount the scale again. It registered 150. "What'd you do?" Eddie screamed.

"Nothin'," Felix said. "It's the damn scale."

Eddie shook his head. "What'd you do?" he repeated, softer now. The weigh-in was in forty-five minutes.

144

"Gimme another pill," Felix said, but Eddie wouldn't even answer him. Felix tried to piss out any urine still hiding in his bladder. Then they went downstairs, where a lively, happy bunch of perhaps two hundred onlookers sat around the balance scale. Roundtree, looking sleek and taut in his jockstrap, registered at 147 exactly, drawing cheers. Stepping off, he flashed a beautiful set of teeth as he accepted an open bottle of Gatorade from one of his seconds and drained it. But he was in no terrible rush. As Eddie and Tommy held a towel in front of him, Felix stripped off everything, revealing jailhouse tattoos over his chest, back, and down his arms. "One forty nine and three-quarters!" the inspector announced. The Roundtree people and some of the fans slapped high fives and yelled like they'd won the Lotto. The chief trainer, a retired cop, applauded and hugged his fighter. News couldn't be more favorable if Felix had come down with stomach flu. Now they knew Felix wasn't in shape, and to make the weight, he'd have to get in even worse shape. The inspectors scheduled a last-chance weigh-in for Felix in four hours.

"If you'd held out, you'd be finished with it now," Eddie told him. "You'd be drinking Coke and eating pasta."

They all rode the elevator in silence. Inside the room Felix stripped off his T-shirt and plopped into bed again, face up. "I give him any more diuretics," Eddie said, "it could get dangerous." They could steam off the pounds or run them off. Steam was easier, but Eddie said it would leave him even more spent. Cheskis, watching Felix stare at the automatic sprinkler, spotted tiny tears in the corner of his eyes.

Eddie called Benny, who showed up a half-hour later. "Don't worry, kid," he told Felix. "We'll getcha there." Benny led them down to the basement, where they boarded an employees-only elevator and took it up to the gravel roof above the twenty-first floor. Stepping out, Cheskis felt the sun bake his eyeballs. Eddie and Tommy supported Felix, one on each side. "You gotta run now, kid," Benny said. "Run it off. The sun will help you. You can't feel yourself sweat in Vegas, but you're sweating already." Felix didn't move. "You can do it," Benny said. "You want that purse, right?" Felix closed his eyes almost a full minute, breathing heavily. Then he opened his mouth and eyes and let out a yell that didn't sound human. He began running in circles, stopping for jumping jacks, then running again. Occasionally he laughed like Richard Widmark in the film where he pushed an old lady in a wheelchair down the stairs. "He's Satan," Eddie said quietly.

Felix ran in circles for half an hour, grunting, laughing, sobbing. Then he sat down hard, gasping and crying more openly, but without tears. "Take this," Benny said, handing him a glass. He slammed down the mustard and warm water, gagged, and threw up a few particles of vomit still hiding in his digestive tract. Eddie handed him a towel, and he and Tommy helped him to his feet.

Felix approached the scale under his own power. There weren't nearly as many people around now. "One forty-six and three-quarters!" the inspector yelled.

"Your ass gonna be whipped," a member of Roundtree's entourage yelled. He was a black kid with a backwards baseball cap and an oversized sweatshirt. Felix declined the water bottle and stepped forward, looking right at the kid, smiling his psycho smile. The kid was perhaps twenty years old and clearly a fighter himself, used to stare-downs. He stared straight back, but had to look away. He tried to fake a little laugh, but it came out like a baby's cry. Felix sneered and grabbed the water bottle.

There's not much left to teach a fighter like Felix, who'd excelled in the ring more than twenty years as amateur and pro. It was too late to change his style even if you wanted to. Training was mostly a matter of getting him sharp, working on his timing, making sure he made the weight in top physical condition. A trainer between rounds might point out when Felix was forgetting something, perhaps lowering his right or crossing his feet, because everyone makes mistakes. A trainer might also spot an exploitable flaw in the opponent—or pretend he does, falsely claiming that he's a sucker for a right to the body or a left uppercut. Even the most polished fighters have to be open somewhere for the split second they're throwing a punch. Trouble is, opponents trying to capitalize on it can present an even bigger hole. That's why commentators liken boxing to a chess match. But in chess, players take turns. In boxing, when a fighter lands a punch, he's entitled to land another and another.

Early that morning one of Felix's former trainers, Bud Fallows, came in on a flight from Memphis, where he was training someone for a fight the following weekend. "I wanted to be here when Felix gets his title shot," Bud said. Well-known around L.A. gyms, he was an almost white-looking black man, a stuttering ex-fighter who always wore a postman's cap.

When Eddie warmed him up in the dressing room, Felix's punches had no snap. He failed to turn his feet into his shots or bob his head. He looked like a gob of shit, and it created a shocked, funereal silence. There was a communal understanding that he was going out to be sacrificed. Before leaving the hotel room, Cheskis had watched Eddie slip Felix some kind of hormonal boost that he dissolved under his tongue. Cheskis didn't want to know what it was. Felix wasn't his fighter. Whatever the stuff was, Eddie said one pop cost him forty dollars. It didn't seem to be helping. Bud, seeing Felix's awful warm-up, looked even sadder than everyone else, like an old-time bluesman who projected centuries of gloom in his song.

After getting everyone to hold hands, Felix prayed for himself and his opponent. For the ceremonial walk to the ring he pulled up the hood on his robe and put on a pair of dark glasses he always wore into the ring. L.A. was a lot closer to Vegas than Atlanta, and the crowd let Felix know they were on his side. By the time he climbed through the ropes he'd perked up considerably, almost enough to make his team forget all the wrong cards he was playing. Felix was home again. A boxing ring made him more comfortable than family, friends, booze, drugs, crime, jail, sex, or God. Meanwhile Bud complained to Cheskis that Felix was flat because of Eddie, that when he'd trained him, Felix always turned his elbow when he threw hooks. Cheskis, trying not to be overheard by the others, explained how grievously Felix had broken training. But Bud was sure his superior regimen would have worked its magic.

"He's never had a champion," was the way Eddie described Bud. But in truth, neither had Eddie, except for a few diminutive or debatable titles—champion of Queensland or some "world" sanctioning body no one ever heard of. But this title was the real thing, and every day Felix spent on the lam from training, every drink, every shot of crystal meth, had been a sword thrust to Eddie's heart. With a title, Felix's next purse would break into six figures. As for Bud, it was difficult to tell whether he preferred to see Felix win a title or fail under another trainer. Probably Bud didn't know himself.

Borakovich, who hadn't bothered to stop by Felix's dressing room, sat with his ex-soap queen two rows in front of Cheskis, Marvin, and Bud. Nobody said hello. Sprinkled among the crowd were easily two hundred Latino L.A. gang members. Even blood enemies coalesced on select issues, and this was one of them—a homey fighting for a world championship.

When Felix removed his dark glasses and robe, he revealed muscles that weren't as precisely defined as Roundtree's, but his shoulders were broader, and under his tattoos he was all bone and muscle. Roundtree glistened like a snake.

The first round was a shocker. Felix was a different fighter than the zombie in the dressing room. Moving side to side in a fluid ballet, he slipped punches and gave more than he got. Somehow he'd erased the effects of all his self-destruction over the last few weeks. Within his classy routine he paradoxically integrated virtuoso elbows, head butts, forearms, and low blows. Despite his natural skill, he always took that dirty edge, delighting in the delinquency of it. Felix seemed to have eyes all over him like a fly, allowing him to insert most of the illegal repertoire when the referee was at the wrong angle to see it. But there was more to it than that. His speed and finesse played tricks on the mind. It's difficult to spot an elbow when it's sandwiched within split-second, legal mayhem. A right, two lefts, a head butt, an uppercut, an elbow. The ref cautioned Felix twice in that first round, but referees generally hate to deduct points in world title fights. Roundtree's ex-cop trainer shook his fist and screamed.

Rage would cloud his thinking—another reward for Felix's extraordinary skills.

Because Roundtree was the taller man, it was easier for Felix to move in and inflict damage with the top of his head. Also, Roundtree's longer trunk gave Felix a bigger target for his body shots. The best course for Roundtree was to get some distance for his devastating right hand. But challenged to a duel inside, the beast in him refused to back off.

A moment after the bell ended the second round, the ref turned to speak to an inspector at ringside and Felix reached behind his head to whack Roundtree in the face with the palm of his glove. The blow couldn't possibly inflict serious harm. It was more like a prank. Roundtree lunged at Felix, which the referee did see. Both Roundtree and his cop had to be restrained while Felix laughed.

In round three Roundtree caught Felix with a solid hook to the jaw, momentarily buckling his knees. Felix moved inside, slamming Roundtree in the kidney as he tried to clear his head. Roundtree caught him with a right uppercut, but even as their heads collided, Felix threw a three-punch combination to the head, nuts, and head again. As Roundtree complained to the referee, Felix blasted him with an overhand right that put him on the canvas, sending the crowd to its feet. That included Cheskis, Marvin, and ex-Felix-trainer Bud, who'd already yelled himself hoarse. Cheskis wasn't sure whether the referee would call the low blow, the knockdown, or both. What he did was start a count, signaling an official knockdown. At this point Cheskis spotted Powell and his son sitting across the ring. Powell was enjoying himself. Why not? He had contracts with both fighters.

Roundtree, who rose immediately, shook his head and quarreled with the ref. He pounded his own head in fury as blood flowed from a fresh slash above his right eye. It was impossible to hear anything above the crowd noise. The ref called time and brought up the ring physician, who examined Roundtree's cut, careful not to treat it. The fighters spent the last twenty seconds of the round trading angry shots to the head. That round was the apex of Felix's good fortune. Thereafter, Roundtree, sobered by his own blood, kept Felix at a distance with his jackhammer jab and took over. Yet even as Felix's supernatural energy source gave out and his sustained beating accelerated, he showed no marks. No perforated eardrums, slit eyelids, hematological growths that jut out like alien spores. Benny had little to do in the corner. Felix's clean canvas of a face defied science. He's Satan, Eddie repeated.

Felix went down in the fifth and eighth rounds. After the second knockdown the ref looked into his eyes and signaled the contest over. There was the usual exuberance in the other corner and the fighters hugged, all transgressions forgiven. Back in Eddie's hotel room some equipment was missing. Where's Felix? Everyone asked. "I got screwed again," Eddie said. "Just watch. And I already paid Benny out of my own pocket." Sure enough, Borakovich and Felix quarreled over training expenses and other costs. Eddie, caught in the middle, got screwed by both.

AUGUST 1985

Chapter 16

ROAD TO PARIS

"How many?" asked Cheskis, coming through the door. He saw Lucretia's lips move but couldn't make out her reply over the noise from the Gulliver-sized TV next to the storefront window. She tossed her dough with magical precision, showing equal doses of contentment and pride. Cheskis stepped closer, placing his hands on the shoulder-high counter. "Sweetheart, what're you doing? Running a business or watching TV?"

"What?" she shouted.

"Jesus, I said what—"

"I heard ya," she said, tossing up the dough again as a smile broke across her broad, brown face.

"You're such a nasty little person," he said. "How come you smell so nice? Doesn't seem right."

"You don't smell nothing, liar."

"I could smell you in a blizzard."

"We got three deliveries stacked up," she said, deftly throwing onion bits on a raw pie. The TV screen showed a brunette knock-out reading a statement. The camera swept down the faces of a mostly attentive panel of immaculate men with styled hair and handkerchiefs in their lapels, then returned to the brunette. It was a Senate committee hearing, and the witness was clearly an entertainer of some kind. Ordinary women didn't look like that. She filled the screen with the glow of rehearsed passion, sometimes bringing her voice down to a whisper to dramatize a point.

Cheskis stepped behind the counter. "Don't go looking for my remote," Lucretia said.

"You have a suspicious mind," he replied, fumbling for it. "How you going to find true love if you don't open up your heart? Ahh, there." She slapped his hand, but he held on and punched down the volume.

"I found more true love than's good for me," she said.

"Who's she?" he asked, pointing to the TV brunette.

"You'll just make fun."

"Come on, I'm interested."

Lucretia said a name that meant nothing to him. "From *Green Corridors*," she added. "Don't you know nothing?" She slung two pies into the big metal oven with a shovel and slammed the door as the brunette recited mental health statistics.

"Let me guess," Cheskis said. "She plays a psychiatrist?"

"How'd you know?" Lucretia asked him, tilting her head ever so slightly, like a puzzled terrier.

"She plays a psychiatrist on TV and she's explaining mental illness to a Senate committee. That's it, isn't it?"

"Quiet," she said. "I can't hear."

"These people are making me crazy, Lucretia."

A thirty-second commercial ended happily when the dim-witted everyman took laxative advice from his smarter, loving wife. Cheskis looked through the short stack of pizza cartons, noting dollar amounts and addresses as David entered from out back. "Somebody called," he told Cheskis, shoving a piece of paper toward him. A practiced pizza guy, David took perfect notes: Valaitas, his number, ten minutes ago. Cheskis stepped into the tiny office and closed the door.

"You want a fight in Paris?" asked Valaitas.

"It's in three weeks," Cheskis explained to Eddie and Stu an hour later in the gym. Once again, he conversed against a tide of electronic amplification, this time some kind of demon-clanging rock 'n' roll from speakers placed around the room.

"I don't know. That's not much time," Eddie shouted back. But he knew better than anyone that Marvin was in shape. And restless. He hadn't fought in thirteen weeks. Managers looking to build up their fighters wouldn't get near him, so it was hard to move beyond palooka contests. With a record of 12-0-1, he'd reached the point where he could knock off one of the minor titles if he could get a shot, but they were all controlled by Powell.

"What about that fight Reynolds told you about?" inquired Eddie.

"You want to pay that burglar? This purse is twelve thousand," Cheskis said.

"You can get a bad screwing going for the quick money, mate. I've seen it many times. . . . Wait a minute." He turned toward his stereo receiver. "What the hell's playing on this thing?" The lead singer of a heavy metal band sounded like he was gargling and hollering at the same time.

"Picciolo, he did it," Stu informed him.

"Picciolo! Picciolo!" Eddie yelled as he searched through stations. Picciolo, a tallish MBA, was practicing his defense, bobbing and weaving beneath a sandbag swinging from a rope. When he turned toward Eddie, the bag knocked him on the noggin. Rubbing his skull, he approached Eddie without enthusiasm.

"Didn't I tell you never to touch that dial? What was that shit?"

"Iron Maiden," Picciolo said.

"Well keep them out of my gym, understand?"

"I'm the one who ratted on you," Stu informed Picciolo.

Eddie found Marvin Gaye on his rhythm and blues station. "Where were we?"

"You know he's moving to Indianapolis?" Cheskis said as Picciolo returned to his sandbag.

"Who?" asked Eddie.

"Picciolo. He told me last week."

"What's he doing that for?"

"His company's moving him," Cheskis explained.

Stu said: "You know, people fought a revolution so nobody could send people to Indianapolis. Men froze their nuts at Valley Forge. Now these assholes get herded around like sheep. Baaa!" he yelled toward Picciolo, who doubtless failed to grasp the reference.

"You're the weirdest fucking doctor I ever saw," Eddie said.

"He's no crazier than you are," Cheskis said.

"What're you talking about, mate?"

"How many two-hundred-year-old men tell heavyweights to throw punches at them?"

"It's what I do, mate. The good Lord lets me." He was pleased to be called crazy in the context of crazy courage. "Now where the hell were we?"

"You were saying how we're gonna get screwed in Paris," Cheskis said. "But you can get screwed waiting, too. Valaitas says this French guy's got a good record, but he's a typical European. Stands right in front of you. Not much pop, either. And the promoter doesn't care who wins. He just wants a guy who comes to fight."

"If he can't move and he can't punch, how come this bloke is seventeen and one? Sounds like bullshit, mate."

"Quick hands. But Marvin will handle him."

"Is it for TV?"

"European TV."

"So what, mate?"

"Somebody will see it. When we're at the La Brea, it's a tree falling in the forest."

"What the fuck you talking about, mate? Trees? That Sheila's made you cuckoo. Forget her. She'll be back anyway. You watch." Eddie always had advice. If two scientists were inventing a formula, he'd tell them they were using the wrong beakers.

"We'll get some attention over there," Cheskis said. "It'll get covered in the papers." Cheskis had learned that fighting in L.A. was next to useless in terms of getting anyone to notice. *The L.A. Times* considered boxing no more important than college volleyball. Because the Associated Press relied on *The Times* to supply it with local sports, Marvin's L.A. fights went unreported. Cheskis had tried complaining to the sports editor but couldn't get past the punk-ass clerks who answered phones.

"Funny things happen in Europe, mate. Besides, I don't trust your mate."

"Valaitas? He lost his job helping us. Remember?"

"Maybe he wants it back. Maybe he never lost it. What if it's all a trick, mate?"

"You watch too much *Perry Mason*, Eddie."

"You blame everything on TV," Stu told Cheskis. "So who's the real paranoid?"

"I don't blame TV for everything. Sometimes I blame doctors."

Eddie told Cheskis, "A trip would do you good, mate. You meet some nice French Sheilas, you'll forget all about Lorraine."

"So you'll do it?"

"Sure, mate. I was just fucking with you. But it's going to cost more than you think. It always does."

Marvin was hitting the speed bag when Cheskis told him. He raced around the gym, hugged people, yelled, laughed. Over the course of the last year his wall had been coming down two or three bricks at a time. Now it was barely knee-high. The metamorphosis amazed Cheskis, but not Eddie, who saw boxing as a higher power. He figured you could clear up cancer if you just trained properly and found the right vitamin store.

Of course Lorraine refused to go to Paris. She still took his phone calls, but that didn't mean much. She didn't hang up on telemarketers either. "You're the only woman I've cared about in I don't know how long," Cheskis told her.

"You're a tough guy. You can handle it."

"I'm weak and helpless. You're the tough one. Too tough."

Eddie was right. It cost them more than Cheskis figured. For starters, Eddie insisted they arrive ten days before the fight to shake off the jet lag. The promoter would pay only three days' expenses. Cheskis, playing with the numbers on a pad, decided it was time to take Eddie's advice and pull in some investors. "We're cutting too many corners because we're so broke all the time," he told Marvin. "Let me see if I can work out a syndicate deal, and I'll bring it back to you, okay?"

"We're still going to Paris, right?"

"Absolutely."

Tommy and Stu required about thirty seconds of convincing. Philyaw and Valaitas not much more. Everybody knew there was no quicker route to serious boxing success than latching on to a talented heavyweight. The four new investors would each kick six thousand into the kitty in exchange for each of them reaping five percent of all future purses. Cheskis and Eddie reduced their cuts to ten percent, which left Marvin sixty percent. From now on he'd draw a salary for days he had to miss work at the warehouse. If the kitty needed a boost, Stu, Tommy, Valaitas, and Philyaw would each put up seventeen and a half percent, Cheskis and Eddie fifteen percent each. Were Quick to reach world-class territory, a million-dollar purse wasn't out of the question, paying each five-percent shareholder $50,000. A lawyer who trained with Eddie put it all in writing just before Marvin, Eddie, Tommy, and Cheskis left for Paris.

"I'm gonna work extra hard now," Marvin said.

Cheskis told him, "Don't even think about it. For you, nothing's really changed."

"No, it's all different now. Getting damn serious, you know? Shit! I don't like everybody depending on me like this."

"Marvin, nothing's—"

"I need to sit down, man. I'm wobbly. Oh Lawdy."

"Goddammit, don't fuck with me like that! My whole life just passed in front of me."

"Any juicy parts?"

"Not nearly enough."

"Don't be silly, man. Just stick 'em in front of me."

Everybody was a little uncomfortable putting Marvin in with a fighter no one had ever seen, so, bolstered by the new funding, Cheskis called Batman Berkowitz. Philyaw gave Cheskis the directions but refused to accompany him. "Last time I went over there I had an asthma attack," he said. "My first asthma attack in thirty years. The whole place is an environmental hazard."

Cheskis found Batman east of Venice in a dark, low-rent, New Yorky apartment with walls of grayish purple. The rooms were filled with metal shelves, even the kitchen. The shelves, which also covered the windows, were jammed with videotapes and reels of film, top to bottom, every space filled with something, including old pizza cartons and newspapers. "Yeah, I got your guy," Berkowitz said. "Batman's got it all—tapes, fight records, films. I got everything. From all over the world. Got Mabous against Pierre LeMieu, some Englishman too. What's his name? What's his name?" Batman kneeled down at a card table in what once was a living room and searched through index cards with thick, strangler's fingers. An impossibly long ash dangled from the cigarette in his mouth, making Cheskis nervous until at last it fell to the floor. Cheskis paid ninety dollars for two tapes of Frenchman Mabous.

Mabous was almost completely bald, which made him look older than he was. But he looked like a real fighter, very light on his feet for a big man, whose style was exactly as Valaitas described it. In both tapes he wore down his opponents and knocked them out in the later rounds.

Next Cheskis tracked down sports writer Carol Grantz in the La Brea bar. Grantz, who looked like a burned-out social worker, was a defrocked Navy pilot who wore floppy Hawaiian shirts, carried a tire around his waist, and shook hands with a sweaty palm. Cheskis would later discover he perspired under all circumstances. He wrote for the *Herald-Examiner*, L.A.'s last remaining afternoon daily. It had been dying for twenty years and paid reporters like fruit pickers.

Following Philyaw's instructions, Cheskis bought Grantz a drink and slipped him two twenties to mention Marvin's upcoming Paris fight in his Saturday column.

"No problemo," he said.

Valaitas had told them about a little kickboxing gym in Paris where they could fly under the radar. The proprietor, a former South Vietnam major named Huc, was built like a broom handle and could kick holes in masonry. He was expecting them. "When Sergeant Valaitas asks a favor," he said, English rolling easily off his tongue, "it's done." Valaitas had told them very little about Huc, who didn't give the impression he welcomed personal questions. Whatever he did in the war, it wasn't taught in finishing school. Huc steered them to a cheap but tidy hotel only two blocks from the gym, on Place Clichy, Henry Miller's old turf. Everything seemed perfect until one afternoon when Huc, watching Eddie put Marvin through the paces, tried to give

Marvin a tip on how to counter a straight right. "I'm the one training him," Eddie shouted down from the ring. "I been doing this a long time, mate." Huc nodded, showing no emotion.

"He was just trying to help," said Marvin.

"Happy now, mate?" Eddie said to Huc, who wordlessly walked off. "There's rules," Eddie said. "You don't talk to another trainer's fighter."

Eddie didn't like Marvin running on hard surfaces, which he said punished joints, particularly knees. So every morning at 6 A.M. Marvin took the Métro to the Tuileries Gardens for five miles of roadwork past statues and flowers, within sight of the Louvre, Musee d'Orsay, and other landmarks. Marvin bought guidebooks so he could identify each structure. He'd fallen for Paris as only a young man could. He was desolated to learn they'd just missed Bastille Day but bounced back when he discovered admission to the Louvre was free the first Sunday of every month. "We're just in time, man, and look at this—Marie Antoinette's jail cell is only a few blocks away."

"But she's dead, mate," Eddie said. "After you take care of this Frenchman, we'll find you a nice live Sheila instead. You want chocolate or vanilla?" Eddie could sniff out romance anywhere in the world. He had the gift. But it was one talent he never bragged about.

Tommy and Stu showed up four days before fight night, and after an early workout that evening Stu took everybody to the Café de la Paix across from the Opéra. It drizzled off and on, but not enough to bother Right Bank pedestrians. From their outdoor table under a canopy the O'Brien team watched the sidewalk parade of faces and fashions. At tables all around them self-assured customers were served by quick, inscrutable waiters. Everything down to the slightest detail seemed geared toward creating an array of casual yet precise pleasures—the silverware, the faces, the wafers that came with the coffee.

Cheskis told Stu, "This is nice, but maybe later you can show us where you really rich bastards go, you know, the joints you don't tell us about."

"No fucken way," Stu said. "I took an oath."

"Man, this is the coolest place I've ever been," Marvin said. "Let's come here every day."

"I used to come here every day," Cheskis said. He never spoke of his past, and now as they looked at him too intently he realized it was something they discussed.

"When was that?" Eddie said.

"In another life. A long time ago. They say if you sit at one of these tables long enough, you'll meet everyone you know. Or maybe it's someone you know. Actually, I'm not sure what they say. What do they say, Stu?"

"Another life? What's with all the secrets? Jesus, I tell everybody how my partner stole my wife, how my pecker's only moderately huge. All we know about you is your middle initial."

"You have trouble with your sausage, try a chocolate Sheila," Eddie said. "Right, Marvin?"

"Call me Quick," Marvin said. "Quick. That's me. Quick O'Brien."

Tommy raised his glass, and everyone followed. "Okay, mates, from now on it's Quick." Tommy had been pulled so deeply into Eddie's *Weltanschauung* that from time to time he called people "mate." It was a useful word.

"So what about it?" Stu asked Cheskis. "When were you here?"

"I was here with my ex-wife," Cheskis said. "Eight, maybe nine years ago. I was crazy about this town, too, just like Marvin—Quick, I mean. After I got here, I never wanted to sleep. We just walked and walked. We lived in New York."

"What'd you do for a living?" asked Tommy. Cheskis asked the waiter for another coffee, but the man moved past without acknowledging him.

"Hey waiter!" Stu yelled out. Heads turned. The waiter disappeared inside. He was back in two or three minutes with a tray of drinks for three Germans at the next table. He looked a bit old to be charging around restaurants. He was bald and somewhat overweight, but also broad-shouldered, with a neck that was red and rough as a carrot. A farmer's neck. "Monsieur?" he said to Cheskis.

160

"What's your name, dude?" Stu asked him.

"Charles," the waiter said.

Cheskis decided to forget the coffee and ordered a serious drink instead. They all switched to alcoholic beverages except Marvin, who had another coffee *au lait*, this time with chocolate ice cream.

"So what'd you do in New York?" Stu asked Cheskis.

"I was a reporter for *The New York Times*."

"Why'd you leave?"

"I had an opportunity to get into the pizza business."

"You should do that again," Eddie said. "Reporting. You'd be the only boxing writer who knows what it's like to take a punch. You could write my life story. Put it in a book." When he'd been a reporter, Cheskis ran into half a dozen people a month who said he should write their life story. In this case it was true, but publishers preferred memoirs of movie stars and political hacks whose ghost writers spun out the same forgettable bullshit as forgettable Renaissance princes.

"You guys'd make a fortune," Tommy said.

"I don't know if the world's ready for Eddie's story," said Quick.

"You're right, mate. Nobody'd believe it. I ever tell you about Wandurra fucking a horse?" He'd told everyone about Wandurra fucking a horse, but no one stopped him from telling it again. They were like kids who like to hear bedtime stories repeated, Cheskis decided. He wished he'd heard bedtime stories when he was a kid.

"We were in the outback training for this Korean," Eddie said. "A bloke who owned this big Italian restaurant—it was a famous restaurant in Sydney—he used to let me use his place up there. There's nothing around, no town, nothing. He had this aborigine who looked after the place—Arthur. Arthur told me one day, 'Look,' he said, 'don't tell Wandurra, but I saw him fucking one of the mares.' He'd been suspicious because somebody kept moving the stool. He couldn't figure it out. And then one morning he spots Wandurra up on the stool banging the horse. 'Be sure you don't tell him I said anything,' he said. He was scared."

"That would make a great chapter right there," Tommy said.

"Was the horse cute?" Stu asked.

"The bitch was probably asking for it," Cheskis said.

"Some a these damn horses, they'll break your heart," Quick said.

"That's why I never wanted to get involved with one," Stu said.

"Wandurra was the craziest fighter I ever had. There's nothing he wouldn't stick his sausage into. I'd go to wake him up in the morning, I never knew what I'd find. Old ladies, other blokes, farm animals, you never knew."

"Those must be some hotels you've got in Australia," Stu said.

"You fuckers're all crazy, you know that?" Eddie said.

"This is a good place for it though," Quick said. "I'd rather be crazy here than crazy in L.A."

Cheskis, relieved the question period was over, was so used to revealing little about himself that he didn't always remember why he did it. It had long since become a reflex. The longer he held on to his regrets, the deeper they burrowed into him, so far down inside they were almost a secret to him, too. But sometimes they tumbled through his mind, a hailstorm of self-rebuke. What he'd done to Roybal was worse than anything ever done to him by his father or anyone else. "Your father's a good man," Cheskis's mom would say, which was as much complaint as she'd offer about her sour, inflammable husband.

Charles served their drinks, leaned close to Quick, and said, sotto voice, "Monsieur, I am not, what do you say? A pimp."

"Never said you were, Charles."

"But the young lady over there, in the flower dress, she . . . glances at you. Have you noticed?"

"Yes." She was less than ten yards away and had the genetic perfection of a top-end fashion model except for a minor bump in her nose and a smile that might be crooked. She sat with a woman perhaps ten years older, also beautiful.

"She's not a pro, is she Charles?" Cheskis asked him.

"Excuse me?"

"A professional. A prostitute," Stu explained.

"I don't think so, but she is very interested in—"

"Quick. Quick O'Brien," Quick said. "She speak English, you think?"

"She is Swiss. She probably speaks everything."

"Marvin—" Eddie said.

"Quick," Quick corrected him.

"You fight in less than a week," Eddie said. His no-Sheilas-before-a-fight rule was no joke to Eddie. Most trainers would agree sex drained fighters. Others reasoned that at the very least, pre-fight abstinence made them meaner. It had been part of the training regimen as long as anyone could remember. Boxing didn't change much over time. You could watch a fifty-year-old film and see fighters throwing exactly the same hooks and uppercuts, skipping ropes, hitting the bags, doing the roadwork. Team athletes and their coaches were always finding new training gimmicks to give them an edge. But fighters from decades ago could walk into a gym and find everything pretty much the same.

Quick glanced at the young woman, who smiled boldly in return. He turned away. "This fight business ain't easy, is it?" he said.

"Eddie, what if he just gets her number?" Cheskis said. "That's okay, isn't it?"

"See her after the fight," Eddie said.

"What about I invite her to the fight?" Moments later Quick was at her table, crouched down, talking to her and her companion at face level. They were all grinning. Cheskis was glad to see the kid get his day in the sun. But watching the courtship dance made him ache all the more for Lorraine.

When Quick returned, he said, "They invited me to lunch tomorrow. They're coming to the fight."

"You're not going," Eddie said.

"It's just lunch, Eddie."

"You'll have time for Sheilas after you're champion."

Quick didn't have it out with Eddie in front of everyone. That wasn't his way. But he kept his lunch date. Later Eddie confronted him in the gym. "This fight can be easy, or it can be hard. It was up to you," he told him, according to Tommy. "Now it's gonna be hard."

Tommy related the story to Cheskis and Stu in a little brasserie near their hotel.

"I don't like the sound of this," Stu said.

"He's planting doubt in Quick's mind," Cheskis agreed.

"In the industry," Tommy said, which back in L.A. meant the TV-film industry, "people hammer on the door so long sometimes, by the time they get inside they're nuts."

"He's already got us spending all this extra cash for food," Stu said. Eddie insisted they eat no meals in the promoter's hotel so no one could contaminate Quick's food. "I'm telling you," Eddie had said, "funny things happen over here." Lots of fight people believed Europeans spiked opponents' food. It was one of those rumors that never get chased to the source.

"You have to talk to Eddie," Stu told Cheskis.

"Why me?"

"It's gotta be only one of us or he'll think we're ganging up on him."

"We are."

Tommy wouldn't do it either. So Cheskis spoke with Quick about it. "I don't worry when he talks like that," Quick said. "It's just Eddie." On this day his sinewy aura was augmented by crisp, ironed jeans and a black T-shirt just tight enough. He wore white athletic shoes that were tied and even scuffed a little, which he'd have considered unacceptable a year ago. You had to strain your eyes to see the scar on his ear, as invisible now as those years he'd spent on the street. Cheskis knew the guys probably discussed Cheskis's missing years more frequently than Quick's. Even in the boxing world, possibly the least racist segment of society, it was assumed that black men all had the same stories to tell.

According to rumor, the promoter was backed by gangsters from Cherbourg, and Eddie had predicted trouble prying the purse out of him. But he was handed 120 crisp hundred-dollar bills right after the weigh-in, as agreed. Returning to their hotel rooms from dinner they saw someone had gone through the closets, bathrooms, everything. The culprits didn't make a mess, but they didn't bother to disguise their search, either. "Still think I'm batty?" Eddie said.

"You're a goddamn genius, Eddie," Stu said, kissing the top of his head. Eddie had demanded they shun the hotel safe and carry the cash with them to the restaurant. He also made them divide the stash among them to insure against one lucky grab. They kept the group together after that, and Eddie's perfect call cemented everyone together again.

The crowd was 4,000 at most, sprinkled around an arena built for at least three times that. There was so much tobacco smoke, it seemed like the place was on fire. The crowd cheered Quick almost as much as the French fighter, which didn't amount to much cheering. Previous bouts had been stinkers. Mabous, who'd weighed in three or four pounds heavier than Quick, was calm as a cumulous cloud. At the bell he came out churning big punches like a madman, looking nothing like the tapes. Cheskis read the shock on Quick's face. No feeling-out stage. Mabous was out to kill or be killed, and he drove confused Quick into the ropes several times before the bell ended the round—a big one for the Frenchman. His cornermen were delighted in two languages—French and Arabic. But in round two the Frenchman ran into a couple of right hands that made him less sure of himself. Halfway through the round Quick stepped in with a left uppercut and hook to the liver that made Mabous wince. He fought back. There was no quit in this guy. At least that's what Cheskis thought, but after the bell Mabous shook his head, giving up on his stool. In Europe, when things don't go a fighter's way, the fans will let him surrender, unlike America and Latin America, where they expect him to keep battling if his eyeballs are hanging from strings.

"The bloke didn't train. You could see it," Eddie said in the restaurant later. At last they could eat in the hotel. "He figured he'd knock us out right away or else." Eddie announced he was going to see his wife across the Channel.

"Wife? What wife?" Tommy said. So it turned out Eddie had his secrets too.

165

CHAPTER 17

POWELL

Cheskis, foggy from jet lag, searched ten minutes to find a parking space. Each summer Inlanders from as far as Riverside and San Bernardino swept over the beach like locusts to compete with locals for restaurant booths, sexual partners, and the biggest prize of all—choice waves. As Cheskis coaxed clumps of mostly junk mail from his mailbox, the phone rang. Fumbling with his keys, he lost hold of a package no bigger than a card deck. It bounced inside the door and Cheskis heard glass break. As he grabbed the phone, a blast of cheap perfume instantly made his little place smell like the ghost of Liberace. The package must have contained some kind of free cologne sample. His caller, obviously reading from a prepared text, invited him a hundred miles across the desert to inspect a time-share condo in Palm Springs next to a world-class golf course teeming with sports and entertainment celebrities. "Aaargghhh!"

Slamming the receiver, he retrieved the wet, ruptured box and walked it out to the dumpster like the corpse of a skunk. Groggy but unable to sleep, he popped a Valium. When he woke four hours later he wasn't sure where he was—a jail cell? No. He played a message from Lorraine:

"Lee, I thought I should let you know I'm going to England, probably for awhile. I leave Sunday. If I'm already gone when you get this, I'll be in touch later. Be well." A message that sounded more suitable for a co-worker in the next cubicle. What day was this? Sunday. She didn't pick up at home. Maybe he could catch her at the airport. How many airlines could be flying to London today? Too many. Popped another Valium. Woke up believing he was in Samantha's bed in Santa Cruz, only Bedford Falls had become Pottersville and the angel Clarence was giving him the old George Bailey treatment from *It's a Wonderful Life*.

166

But something wasn't right—Samantha's place wasn't this orderly. Realized it was a familiar dream, something he'd dreamed many times and only remembered this one time. Unless of course he was dreaming about all the previous dreams.

Still in gamey airliner clothes, he found shoes and stumbled over to the Dead Mackerel. Looked inside to see a crowd of regulars sprinkled with seasonal Inlanders talking loud, drinking beer, watching ballgames. Backed out, drove twenty miles down the freeway to Barney's Beanery in West Hollywood, where Janis Joplin was last seen alive. Entered to find a crowd almost identical to the one he'd left at the Mackerel. Tried for five minutes to get a bartender's attention, never got it, turned around, drove home and changed into gym clothes. Eddie's gym was closed. Using his key, he let himself in, stretched, turned on the bell-timer, did four-and-a-half rounds shadow boxing and moving from bag to bag when Tommy wandered in. "You hear about Felix?" he asked.

"What?" When Felix was concerned, such questions never had a jolly answer. In this case he'd beaten up his wife in a bowling alley.

"They're holding him without bond," Tommy said. "He's in deep shit. This is a very bad time to be beating up your wife."

"When's a good time?"

Apparently the beating wasn't life threatening. "He was a real psycho, you know?" Tommy declared. They were already talking about him in the past tense. "Wanna do a little work?" asked Tommy.

Sparring with Tommy helped him, at least for awhile, shove Lorraine into a rear corner of his mind. Finally they got so tired and sloppy they had to stop. Cheskis showered at home, went down to the pizzeria. David and Lucretia asked about Paris. "Great," he told them. And how was he doing? "Fine," Cheskis replied, his mind on London again.

A man Cheskis didn't recognize—probably another fight manager—had just concluded his business with matchmaker Art Reynolds as

Cheskis and Tommy arrived at his Hollywood Park box. Walking past them, the man shook his head in a signal of disgust, distress, failure, anger. Now it was Cheskis's turn. Reynolds, his gaze fixed on an overhead TV screen, had the look of a gambler on tilt, as though the very next bad turn might blow his ears off. His companion this day was a slim-muscled black woman with a shining, precise Afro, low-cut blouse, and dynamite green eyes. Another lovely woman for another degenerate creep. Ah, sweet mystery of life.

"God damn fucking shit!" Reynolds yelled out. "I knew I should a boxed this race. I knew it, I knew it. Look what it would a paid!" There were no horses at Hollywood Park today because they were running at Santa Anita. California's screwy laws allowed off-track betting accompanied by closed-circuit TV screens at the other tracks on the circuit, creating a kind of phone sex for horseplayers.

"Awright, awright, goddamnit. What ya want, mon?" Reynolds barked.

"It's not our fault your horse ran slow," Cheskis said.

"Slow? You dumb cracker piece of shit. He won." It was one of those remarks that could be taken in jest or seriousness and the speaker was unconcerned with your choice. Like sick gamblers everywhere, Reynolds had reached a point where he was angry when he lost and angry when he won because he hadn't bet more.

"There aren't any crackers named Cheskis. Not one. So what have you got for me?"

Reynolds looked at Cheskis the same way Drill Sergeant Fuslinger looked at him the day he slammed a slim metal rod across Cheskis's thumb because it failed to lightly touch his index finger as he cradled his M-14 at right shoulder arms. Within moments the thumb began swelling into what would soon look like a mutant turnip. The rangy Fuslinger, straight back from Nam, had served as an advisor to the good gooks and apparently was driven stark raving mad by the bad ones. No one wanted to be the sad sack within reach when he finally bit off a recruit's nose or scooped out an eyeball.

As his thumb turned black, Cheskis, still at attention, stared at Fuslinger's purple-fury features and recognized that the spring was sprung, this was the moment, and he was that sad sack. Instead of satiating Fuslinger, banging Cheskis's thumb had only raised the level of his fury. Cheskis could wait for this over-the-top fiend to tear him to pieces or he could save himself and smash the stock of his rifle across the side of Fuslinger's homicidal head, earning a trip to Leavenworth. He had only milliseconds to decide, and no decision was a decision. That's when Cheskis lost it, bursting into mad giggles of surrender and hopelessness. A glob of his spittle flew onto Fuslinger's cheek.

But as the sergeant absorbed this indignity and beheld the crazy man in front of him, his maniacal rage instantly transmuted to wide-eyed, weak-kneed panic. He must have been back in the bush beneath a mortar barrage, or perhaps picking his way through a minefield.

Laughing hysterically because he was in fact hysterical, Cheskis watched, astonished, as a gasping Fuslinger clutched fearfully at his own throat and slunk away in terror, leaving his platoon at attention. At that moment Cheskis became a legend in his basic training company. He'd never have a better day.

"Four thousand to fight Alex Cordoba," Reynolds said in a tone one might use with a child molester. He named a date four weeks off.

"Cordoba is a good fight," Cheskis said, "but four's ridiculous. "What're you paying Cordoba?"

"That don't matter to you."

"I can find out from the commission," Cheskis said. "It's public record, you know." But they both knew whatever he paid Cordoba on the record was of little importance. All the untaxed, unaudited, secret dollars flying around would tell the true shape of the deal, and they were invisible.

"Look anywhere you like. Crawl under the commissioners' asses like a cucaracha. See if I care. Thing you still don't understand is your fighter is a big nigger. Our fans, they're not interested in big niggers. They're little Mexicans, see? So they like little Mexican fighters. You want more money? Find yourself a Mexican. That nigger a yours, he such a big attraction, take him down the street. See what you get."

Cheskis, his smile intact, answered almost dreamily. "Know something? You remind me of a guy I used to know. He was kind of a hero, actually. Guy by the name of Fuslinger."

In Nicaragua Reynolds had competed as a heavyweight, and since turning matchmaker he had on at least a couple occasions thrown down on managers. But now he was confused, unable to determine whether Cheskis was praising or insulting him. Tommy seized the opportunity to steer back to business. The purse ended up at $4,500, with ten percent going to Reynolds. Plus the team would receive $800 in training expenses, half of that kicking back to Reynolds. Quick's bout would be the main event, and Philyaw's Boris would be in the co-feature with a heavyweight yet to be named.

"What do we do with that four hundred for training expenses?" Tommy asked Cheskis in the car.

"We just throw it in with the purse money and split things legit," Cheskis explained. "Reynolds isn't comfortable with a clean deal. You have to make him think it's at least a little dirty."

"You know, Eddie gave that fucker a car once," Tommy said.

"I know."

It was an old, neglected Mercedes convertible Eddie had restored with his own sweat, finding parts, sanding out the rust, and ultimately handing it over to Reynolds to get a welterweight he used to manage into a tournament at La Brea. Reynolds gave the car to a girlfriend. Eddie's welterweight won the tournament but returned to Puerto Rico to work in his father-in-law's carpet business. Later, when the transmission started to slip, Reynolds brought the car back to Eddie to get it repaired.

"We just have to be patient," Tommy said.

"You know how much Evolo Scanlon is making to fight Castle? Five hundred thousand," Cheskis told him.

"Quick would murder Scanlon," Tommy said.

170

"Garcia was tougher than either of them, and Quick knocked him out."

"All we have to do is keep winning," Tommy said.

That's what Cheskis wanted to think. But it was as though Quick fought his bouts down in a basement. He could be right around the corner from Madison Square Garden, but no one would venture down the sidewalk to see him.

Alex Cordoba was a rarity—a tawny Mexican big enough to compete as a heavyweight. He'd gutted through some tough contests, and local fans adored him. His manager had achieved his own kind of fame in the fight business only a few months earlier when he turned down $300,000 for a fight in Atlantic City against a flawed contender. Not enough preparation time for a big fight and not enough purse for his star, the manager complained. The promoter agreed to find the contender another opponent and let Cordoba take the winner thirteen weeks later for $400,000. Okay. The date was set. Handshakes all around. The networks were happy, the Atlantic City casino was happy, everybody was happy. Meanwhile Cordoba took a little tune-up in Fresno with a smallish white guy from Idaho with a joke record accumulated in tank towns around the Pacific Northwest. He caught Cordoba with a double hook in the first round and knocked him to the canvas. Cordoba struggled to his feet, listed to portside, and fell again. The referee had no choice but to stop the contest. Now the white guy from Idaho was getting the equivalent of the title shot in a ballpark and Cordoba was back in Palooka-ville, taking on Quick for maybe $6,000 in a non-televised event. And Quick would probably knock him out.

Training Quick for Cordoba, one day Eddie lost focus or perhaps grew a millisecond too old. He told Quick to throw a right but left his left out of position, and Quick's shot went right through his gloves to the target, sprinkling teeth and blood around the canvas like spilled soup. "What're you looking at?" said Eddie,

171

his face a red, gory mask. "Keep going! We got five minutes left." At least that was the story that went around the gym. Cheskis wasn't there to see it. It was Eddie's way to mine additional melodrama out of such a scene. But the fact remained: he was one tough sonofabitch. Quick, conditioned to obey his trainer, pushed on, which was, said eyewitnesses, the scariest part, watching them continue. Over the next few days Tommy took over Quick's training while a dentist from the gym crew repaired Eddie's mouth and fitted him with dentures.

A week before Quick's bout with Cordoba, Reynolds asked to meet Cheskis. "Sure," Cheskis said. "But not at Hollywood Park."

"Okay; where, then?"

"Eddie's gym in Redondo," Cheskis answered.

"Okay. Two o'clock?"

Cheskis immediately called Eddie, who said, "Maybe we're finally getting respect, mate. It happens. But watch out."

"For what?"

"I wish I knew, mate. Just watch out."

Reynolds extended his hand. Cheskis shook it and led him out back to the folding chairs next to the ring. "I gotta tell you," Reynolds said, "I respect the way you bringing your kid along. I know how hard it is. I wanna do more business with you, not like we been doing." Cheskis, totally in the dark, figured the best thing to say was nothing. "Buddy Lancaster, he's coming to our show Friday. You know who he is, right?"

"Gary Goldberg's matchmaker."

"He's looking for somebody to fight Jake Trinidad for a big card he's setting up for December third. They gonna advertise on TV, announcers in tuxedos, all of it. And listen to this, he been looking at tapes of your boy."

"How do you know?"

"He got the tapes from me. If everything works out Friday, you get the fight."

Goldberg, perennial Number Two in the promoter sweepstakes, had pretty much ceded the heavyweight division to Powell. But recently he'd signed Trinidad, a tough, heavyweight Puerto Rican out of Philadelphia. "Goldberg and Lancaster, they looking for a good opponent. But not *too* good, understand? Your boy blows out Cordoba, they'll get scared, see?"

"You really think I'm going to ask Quick to throw a fight just 'cause you say it's a good idea?"

"You got me all wrong, Cheskis. You can let your guy win, don't worry. Just don't blow Cordoba outta there, understand. Let him look good, but like I said, not too good. Then, you get the December fight with Trinidad, you give me three thousand. And from now on you get special treatment at La Brea. You bringing a kid up, he goes to the head of the line. I take a straight ten percent without no more bullshit, no more bargaining. Just a straight partnership. I like the way you work. Eddie too. Most guys out there, I can't trust, can't do serious work with them. I'll give you my home phone, man. Anytime you want something, you don't have to come down. Just call."

"I don't have any other fighters."

"Don't worry, I gonna bring them to you. I'm hooked into every gym from Tijuana to Buenos Aires. But when I bring them over here I need somebody I can trust what he's doing."

"I'm not paying you any three thousand. Forget that."

"What?" Anger, like a touch of lightning, crossed Reynolds's face and disappeared so fast Cheskis was unsure he saw it.

"All you're telling me is an eclipse is coming. But you don't make eclipses. You're just a guy who reads the almanac."

"But I got Lancaster ready for you."

"This kind of deal you make ahead of time. You know that."

"Two thousand."

Cheskis shook his head slowly.

"A day will come—soon—when you pay it out of gratitude. Just make sure your kid's good Friday night, but, you know—not too good."

"I think he's telling the truth," Philyaw said. "He does that once in a while just to throw you off. Everybody I checked with, it came out the same. You like, you could talk to Lancaster, but what's the use? He won't spell out what he wants. We know

173

they've got a lot invested in Trinidad. They need credible opponents, but they don't want to really gamble till there are millions on the table."

"So what do we do in the Cordoba fight?"

"Pretty much the way Reynolds described it. Beat him, but don't let Quick go right through the guy and scare Lancaster off. Settle for a decision."

Cheskis looked down and without even thinking about it, grabbed the back of his own head, as though it didn't deserve to be there, alive on his neck.

"What's the risk?" Philyaw said. "We still get a good win. He doesn't have to knock every ball outta the park. That's the way styles match up sometimes. Everybody understands that. Ali won some squeakers on his way up. Joe Louis, even Marciano. Quick can afford a few close ones. Not like Boris. He's got so much scar tissue around his eyes he starts bleeding when they touch gloves. He's got nothing after four, five rounds anyway."

Philyaw had been talking more and more about pulling the plug on his big Bohemian. "Wait'll you face that," he told Cheskis. "It's like telling somebody he's got cancer." Discarded fighters usually tried to move on to another manager who'd find them a few more fights. But Philyaw was that manager—the last house at the end of the dead-end street. With his wrinkled trench coat, pulled-down, forties hat, and dour, knowing, Bogey face, he was perfect for the part.

Sure enough, matchmaker Lancaster—a young man with even features and large, sparkling teeth—was ringside, where he acknowledged a steady stream of fighters, managers, hangers-on and their girlfriends, all coming by to schmooze him because he put big cards together for Goldberg. Fighters may bleed and break to scramble out of the pit, but Lancaster would always have a gold Rolex and a pleasant home in Scarsdale. Seated not far away was a surprise attendee—Powell, who, an hour before the opening bout, had found Cheskis and invited him into his limo. There they sat in the parking lot, just the two of them.

Cheskis sipped eighteen-year-old scotch. Powell had a Perrier he never touched.

"One hundred thousand dollars," Powell said, enunciating each syllable with slow precision. Cheskis, doing pirouettes in his head, just nodded his head slightly. It was difficult to discern Powell's facial expressions in the dimness of the limo. "What I want for that is controlling interest in your fighter. My son becomes lead manager. You get twenty percent of whatever he gets."

That meant Powell would take the standard one-third of all purse money for his son, snip off an extra ten percent for the trainers who would kick back a chunk of it to him, plus Powell would take twenty percent for promoting, plus who knows how much he'd divert for training expenses, fees, licenses, payments to the barnacle people who sold rankings, and other obligations real and imagined. A lawyer who'd seen some of Powell's contracts had told Cheskis that his fighters ended up with eighteen to twenty percent of a purse before taxes.

"For starters," Cheskis said, "I have a handshake deal with Quick. I can't sign over a contract that doesn't exist."

"Not a problem. You just write up a contract, get your boy to sign it, and sell it to us. Now look, you're a bright fellow. You understand that in this business the difference between making hundreds or making millions is a thumbs-up or thumbs-down. And this is the thumb," he said, holding his right thumb next to his ear. "To start I'll guarantee three fights a year, purses at a hundred fifty thousand, minimum. But it'll be more—way more—when we get him into a big casino on national TV, plus foreign rights. All that will be spelled out in the contract, and it's in my interest to make it happen."

"A hundred fifty thousand for each fight?"

"It's an aggregate figure for the three fights. But that's a worst-case scenario anyway. There'll be money from TV, money from casinos. We're gonna build your kid, make people notice. The total for all three fights will probably be ten times that. And that hundred K signing bonus? It doesn't go on paper. How you split it is up to you and your conscience. I'll make Quick O'Brien's next fight against Leopold Qawi December third. The winner challenges Elmo Cunningham for the title."

"Isn't Goldberg's putting together a card for December third?"

"He'll have Trinidad against some walking corpse. If I've got a title elimination between two legitimate contenders, Trinidad's own mama won't watch him."

Making a deal with Powell was like joining the Teamsters. He'd take a big slice of the pie, but he'd likely serve a bigger pie. Cheskis knew he could make a deal without giving Junior controlling interest, which had to be just one of Powell's bargaining tactics. The real problem was pitting Quick against Leonard Qawi. Big even by heavyweight standards, Qawi had a flashing right hand that was likened to Joe Louis's. He needed only about seven inches of space to knock his opponents senseless and was widely expected to win the title from Cunningham, whom he'd already knocked out in the amateurs. Powell controlled both fighters.

Goldberg's heavyweight, Trinidad, was no walk in the park either. A left-hander, he threw one or two punches, then clinched before opponents could fire back. As he wore them down he hypnotized them with his rhythm—one or two punches, clinch, repeat. Eventually, when they stopped looking for it, he'd pounce with his lethal left. Eddie had already sized him up as an easy fight for Quick. Cheskis told Powell he'd have to discuss the offer with his partners.

Powell waved an index finger to signify no. "Somebody said he who hesitates is not only lost, but several miles from the next freeway exit."

"Shakespeare?"

"He's overrated," Powell said. "I'm a Chaucer man myself. Milton, too. They dealt with the whole range of human experience and emotions, and they did it more poetically than Shakespeare. You'd be surprised how many scholars are on my side. '*When I consider how my light is spent, E're half my days in this dark world and wide*—' There he is, man, contemplating his blindness, asking the question. Why me? Sooner or later, everybody asks. Milton, he decides '*God doth not need either man's work or his own gifts.*' See that? We take ourselves too seriously, Ches. We borrow a tiny speck of space for a moment so brief and even those of us who truly understand it—we understand it only in quick flashes. But we're also, some of us, blessed with some understanding of the Lord. Like Milton says. There's the answer. Leave it to Him. You do believe that, don't you?"

"No."

"Me neither. We have to have dinner, you and me. All the people I got working for me, not one of 'em would know what the hell we're talking about. You're not surprised to see a nigger quote Milton, are you? But I guess you heard about that prison library. It's the only story they tell about me that's got any truth in it. I ordered books by mail, too, working four cents an hour to get the money. The Man dealt me lemons, so I made lemonade."

"You're a charming man, Mr. Powell. But I guess you know that."

"I *know* what you're thinking. 'Don't listen to this man. He ain't no good. He tried to steal my fighter.' Am I right?" More precisely, Cheskis was wondering how the charming Mr. Powell could order someone's arms or legs broken as easily as ordinary mortals ordered extra mayo on a ham and cheese sandwich. Something was amiss in the species.

"So what you want? Revenge? 'Cause I tried to sign your fighter? We know each other better now. We both learned. Don't give in to revenge. It's the ghetto talking to you, tempting you. 'Cause I'll be damned if you ain't got ghetto in you, Ches. I can tell. Tells us we're nothin', that only those whiteys off the May-flower are worth a damn. Fuck that. It's bullshit. But you already got that part figured, don't you. Listen here, we got a deal?" Powell stuck out a beefy hand.

Cheskis waited until after the inspector had signed the tape over Quick's laces and the referee finished making his complimentary visit to the dressing room. "When you win tonight," Cheskis told Quick, "it's okay if you don't knock the guy out, at least not right away." His voice sounded funny, he thought, warped or something, too high-pitched.

"What're you talking about?" asked Tommy. But Quick and Eddie understood right away.

"What'd you hear?" asked Eddie, no anger in his voice, just curiosity and a touch of anxiety.

Cheskis quickly explained the possibilities—a deal with Goldberg and Lancaster to get at Trinidad, or a deal with Powell and a fight with Qawi.

"What do you think?" asked Eddie.

"Powell's a snake," Cheskis said. "If we can get that Trinidad fight instead, sign with Goldberg, we won't be looking over our shoulders every five minutes, and we get an easier fight."

"What about Qawi?" asked Quick. "I want that guy."

"He'll keep." *And after you get more experience, maybe you'll have a chance against him.*

"No matter which way you turn," Eddie said, "it's still a dirty business."

"Well, let's see what this guy's got tonight," Quick said, neither agreeing nor disagreeing to carry Cordoba for awhile.

Out in the arena the crowd was expectant, noisy, big. Cheskis cursed himself for not getting a bigger purse out of Reynolds. Both fighters had local fans, but Cordoba's were clearly more numerous. He entered the ring, as always, looking trim. Gang tattoos were etched across a flat belly. They fought ten action-packed rounds. Both men had their moments, but at no time did either look to be in serious trouble. Cordoba drew on what seemed like an infinite reservoir of energy, but he was mostly outhustled by Quick, who, artist that he was, got a little more done. At the closing bell the two fighters were toe to toe in the corner, oblivious to the world around them. The referee bravely jumped between them. Realizing now that it was over, the fighters embraced, then walked around the ring with arms around each other's shoulders as the crowd cheered.

The announcer proclaimed the decision was unanimous and, according to custom, read the scores without attaching the fighters' names to them. Cheskis had given Quick at least eight of the ten rounds.

The announcer named Cordoba the winner, throwing out the name like a grenade. There must be some mistake! But no, the announcer didn't correct himself.

A barrage of paper cups, beer, peanuts, and other debris flew into the ring from all directions as the crowd hollered in amazed rage. Everyone in the ring covered up, as though ducking helicopter blades. They double-timed toward the safety of the dressing rooms as the crowd found its voice together—"Bullshit! Bullshit! Bullshit!"

In the dressing room Eddie said, "To beat a Mexican in this town, you have to knock him out, mate. And we made it close enough to steal." As he spoke, he picked bits of peanut shells and other debris off his shirt.

Cheskis knew all the grievous tip-offs he'd ignored were racing through every mind on Team O'Brien. Two of the judges were barely known in L.A., smuggled in from lettuce country as though on a mission. The third was a retired sheriff's deputy, from Orange County who, Eddie had heard, could be bought with the right hooker. "I should have smelled the rat," Eddie said. "It was my fault."

If Quick had knocked out his opponent, crooked judges wouldn't have mattered. But no one rebuked Cheskis. It was as though he were a Down syndrome child who'd accidentally burned their house down. Meanwhile, they digested the meaning of the previous bout, in which Philyaw's Boris the Bohemian, though shaky at first, had eventually taken over and scored a knockout in the fifth round. His opponent was a trim college kid from the San Fernando Valley with nine wins and no losses and cornermen with monogrammed satin jackets. But the kid's manager was just another dreamer who didn't know the score, moving his powder-puff cruiserweight up in search of heavyweight money when he couldn't punch his way out of a *piñata*. The perfect opponent for a crude slugger like Boris, who was the star on the night boxing's two promoter lions scouted heavyweights. Cheskis, blind-sided by Reynolds and Philyaw, had failed to heed the Number One fight rule: protect yourself at all times.

An inspector came in looking for Quick to monitor his urine test. He found him crumpled in the corner, face to the wall, sobbing quietly.

NOVEMBER 1965

Chapter 18

NAKED PRESIDENTS

After their baptismal breakfast with Kesey, most weekends Cheskis and Roybal drove Cheskis's junker—a Buick with no reverse—to Kesey's salon in La Honda, where odd varieties of people drifted on and off the grounds just as soldiers drifted in and out of Headquarters Company. Kesey and his wife Faye were delighted to share the bounty from his two books with their makeshift tribe. "It beats buying Polaroid," Kesey said. Though his success in the wider world paid the bills, it was the force of his personality, not the power of his literary reputation, that made even Hells Angels deferential. Along with everyone else, they debated the meaning of his pronouncements as though studying Jesus's parables.

Meanwhile iconic Neal Cassady strode out of *On the Road* and among the mortals at Kesey's like Aeneas, the half-god son of Aphrodite. Neal, who could get himself laid under the most adverse circumstances, found no adverse circumstances at Kesey's. When Cheskis pointed out to Samantha that he was a bit nuts, she answered testily, "He did two years in San Quentin for one joint."

"That gives him the right to put acid in the food?"

"Only once, I think. But he's such a beautiful man. And stop with the pouting. You're not so bad yourself." She gave him a little smirk that told him she knew plenty more than she was saying, including whatever he was thinking.

As far as he knew, Cheskis had never been around when Cassady chemically doctored the food, but everyone believed it happened, just as everyone believed he'd done serious time—one, two, or three years—for possession of one joint, two joints, or in one version, a single seed. Even the women who slept with him were reluctant to bother this mythological creature with trivia, making facts hard to come by.

"You think Cassady's crazy enough to spike what little kids might eat?" Roybal asked Cheskis. So they quietly decided they'd eat the food but drink only straight from bottles, cans, or the faucet. Making too great an issue of the spiking question would be unwise. In the paranoid fog that swirled around La Honda, government soldiers could easily be mistaken for government agents. The cops had raided the place at least once, and Kesey had a marijuana bust working its way through the courts. Meanwhile, the glacial California law was too sluggish as yet to outlaw LSD, which was used as a perfectly legal condiment by the Kesey crowd. Hot dogs with acid, Coke with acid, sex with acid.

Although Kesey was, as far as Cheskis could determine, apolitical, he found it unsettling that Cheskis and Roybal could be whisked away to another foolish war cooked up by crazed Homo sapiens and their defective hunter-killer genes—no sense looking into it more deeply than that. War was another sorry symptom of the square world's persistent inability to grasp the obvious. "Presidents," he said, "always have pimples on their ass. We should get to see them naked before election day."

On a moonlit evening in Kesey's hot tub, Cheskis massaged his elbow, injured somehow in a bout with a scared, skinny kid in San Jose. The strong smell of raw cedar overpowered the chlorine. They'd smoked all the joints and were down to the last of the beer—a handful of naked souls. On this trip he and Roybal had brought Talagos, a freckled, red-haired reservist. In civilian life Talagos guided city folks on bear hunts in the Upper Peninsula of Michigan. He'd been dumped into the post's Headquarters Company with all the other soldiers whose orders were screwy in some way or other. "I'm sorry," he kept telling Cheskis and Roybal. Talagos was sorry because the angel of death had miraculously passed over reservists and national guardsmen. Because he was high on grass and beer, he was sorry over and over.

"Forget it, man," Roybal said. "It ain't your fault LBJ's got it in for Mexicans and Jews. We don't mind taking a bullet for you, do we Ches?"

"I wouldn't take a bullet for the fucking queen of England," Cheskis said, "and I'm one of her biggest supporters."

"Monarchy is sexy," somebody said.

"Absolute monarchy is even sexier," Samantha said. "Whippings, lust, decadence, obedience, more lust."

It had taken a while for Cheskis to be unbothered that everyone could see her naked and he still wasn't always comfortable with it. "Look," he told Talagos, "Roybal and I, we aren't taking bullets for anybody. We're gonna travel the world with the Army boxing team while some bear is chewing your ass in the woods. But even if we don't, even if we end up in the shit, it's not your fault, Talagos. You think we wouldn't trade with you if we could?"

"Ches has a point," Roybal said. "Maybe it's better if you dodge bullets in the jungle and I own the WASP bank."

"I'm Greek," Talagos said. "I don't own any fucking bank."

"A gringo's a gringo," Cheskis said.

"See? Ches knows," Roybal said. "Whatsa difference?"

"Not a dime's worth of difference," Samantha said. "They're all evil white bastards."

"Anyway, I'm not picking lettuce and I'm outta the wooden barracks," Roybal said. "I'm in a squad room in a nice brick building that won't burn down in forty seconds." Fort Ord, like so many other military installations, still used wooden buildings that had been thrown together during World War II and were intended as only temporary. The Army claimed that any fire in these old structures would engulf the entire building in forty seconds. Sergeants repeated this as though it were a statistic that came straight out of M.I.T. Forty seconds. No variables. Those poor souls quartered in a death barracks took one-hour turns on fire watch throughout the night, one on each of the two stories. This regularly robbed them of sleep that was in short supply anyway. It was all part of a life that made the redwood tub in La Honda seem as though it were on another planet. Sometimes Cheskis felt he commuted between two selves, like Superman and Clark Kent.

"No, I'm not one a the gringos," Roybal said. "You're one a the Mexicans. I'm making you an honorary Mexican. Right now." They clinked Coors bottles.

"Companeros," Cheskis said.

"Why don't you two just fuck each other already?" said a voice. It came from a tall, thin brunette with a problem complexion who was some kind of insurance factotum in San Jose. Cheskis didn't know her name. But she'd tried to tell everyone's fortune earlier. He noticed that women who told fortunes tended to be unattractive.

"I know you didn't mean that," Kesey said to her in his relaxed Oregon drawl. Kesey had been unusually quiet and contemplative this evening, but clearly not inattentive.

"I was kidding," she said. She looked around from face to face like some trapped creature.

"I know that, dear," Kesey said. "Because if you said that in the malicious sense I'm certain you didn't intend, you'd have been shitting out a big, gratuitous turd in here, a dark, secret turd, and I know that's not what happened."

"Men bring that out in us sometimes," Samantha said. "You won't let us into your little men things." Cheskis knew this was a heroic attempt to provide some kind of relief to the tall brunette who had just, it appeared, been barred from return visits. Kesey did this occasionally. The rules were not as loose as they might seem. It was a lovely thing Samantha was trying to do. She was a lovely person. Why didn't Cheskis love her? She went up on her toes and hugged Cheskis and Roybal simultaneously, then kissed them. "Be well," she said. "You're my noble ones. I love you both."

At 4 A.M. Cheskis, Roybal, and Talagos pushed the Buick with no reverse into position so they could get back in time for physical training and the three-mile run. That was as far ahead as Cheskis wanted to think. Samantha and her girls would catch a ride later.

As Cheskis fought to stay awake at the wheel, Roybal, next to him, settled on a radio station out of Seattle playing Sonny and Cher's "I've Got You, Babe." "Ches, let me ask you something," said Talagos, sprawled across the back seat.

"Sure."

"If you don't mind my asking," he said.

"His sister's all mine," Roybal said. "Forget it."

"Keep your gentile ass away from her," Cheskis said.

"Maybe I'll convert."

"Get yourself circumcised."

"I am circumcised. You know I'm circumcised."

"Yeah, but where was the rabbi?"

"Maybe there was a rabbi. You don't know."

"I was standing right there in the lettuce patch. I remember."

"Fuck you were. You were never in a lettuce patch in your life."

"Makes no difference," he said. "I don't have a sister anyway."

"The hell you don't."

"Far as you're concerned I don't," Cheskis said. "When can I meet your mom?"

"What I was gonna ask," Talagos said, "was how'd you get into boxing? You don't seem like a boxer. I mean—you really know how to beat guys up? Expert-like?"

Watching the road, Cheskis told him, "It's a skill like any other. You just learn it."

"You make 'em miss, make 'em pay," Roybal said.

"Funny thing is," Cheskis said, "it doesn't even require that much courage."

"Really?"

"At first, maybe, but after a while you get comfortable with it. Jumping out of a plane, now that's got to be scary. Heights."

"I don't like 'em either," Roybal said.

"How would you know?" Cheskis said. "You're from Fresno. Everything's short in Fresno. Short little buildings, short little Mexicans."

"You never got near Fresno."

"I smelled it once from the freeway."

"Smells like lilacs, is how it smells," Roybal said.

"How the hell does a dumb Mexican know about lilacs?" Cheskis said. "And Kesey, you knew who he was. I'm the one who went to college, but you're the one who knew. Remember?"

"Do you get scared in fights?" Talagos asked Roybal.

"Sometimes," he said. "All the time, at first."

"Me too," Cheskis said. When he started out he would bounce around nervously, wasting energy, thinking he was mimicking a real boxer. But gradually he learned to remain calm, to move around his opponent and throw combinations, to startle him with quick jabs, summon the Hun inside himself.

"What about a street fight?" Talagos asked. "Is that scary?"

"I don't know," Cheskis said. "I'm too much of a coward to find out."

"No he's not," Roybal injected. "He just lets guys off. Anyway, street fights, most of 'em last a few seconds. A few punches and it's over. Inside that ring, that's a whole other step."

Hearing Roybal stick up for him, even brag about him, provided Cheskis a rush of pleasure. He'd thought Roybal was like a kid brother. But maybe he was also a kind of father, a nonresentful father. That was a sweet gift he'd observed but never tasted.

"How'd you get into it?" Talagos asked Cheskis. "Into boxing?" Talagos clearly assumed there was no reason to even wonder why Roybal, a Mexican, would be a fighter.

"Ches got into fighting 'cause he's angry," Roybal said. "All fighters are angry."

"Is that right?" Talagos said.

"Yeah," Cheskis said. "It's right."

"But you two don't seem angry. You're mellow, both of you."

"Yeah, that's right, too," Cheskis said. Although he'd never reveal the answer to Talagos, he knew precisely what got him into boxing. Someday when the question came up again, he might tell Roybal, though, even if it was a little embarrassing, maybe *because* it was embarrassing. *The Sun Also Rises*. That sparked it. Hemingway clearly disliked Jews, but he had a grudging respect for his character Jake because Jake was a tough Jew, a boxing Jew. Hemingway must have known tough Jews. Cheskis knew there were lots of them before Jews flocked to dentistry and accounting. He also knew that amateur fighter Hemingway was a bully, though most fighters channel their rage inside the ring. Cheskis was proud he hadn't returned fire against the brunette

187

in the hot tub. When he was an angry kid, before he learned to box, he'd clash—sometimes violently—with other angry people. He thought he'd learned his lesson when his first high school expelled him and his family had to pay to fix some jerk's broken teeth, but rage could be a patient beast, always ready to take over. Willing himself into a tough Jew was only half an answer.

Talked out, beat, and still a little drunk and stoned, all three of them stayed awake in the pre-dawn light, listening to the unisex radio voices of Sonny and Cher.

I got you to talk to me
I got you to kiss goodnight
I got you to hold me tight
I got you, I won't let go
I got you to love me so
I got you babe

Chapter 19

VALAITAS

Cheskis faked a jab, crouched, hooked a right to the gut, then swiveled to safety. "Pathetic," he said. "Like drowning kittens."

"Wha'd you do, man?" Roybal said.

"Made myself small, moved my feet, got your number."

Roybal charged in, exploding with a triple jab, scoring on all three.

"Eat shit and die," said Cheskis, who stepped in and clinched. Talking through their mouthpieces put the words through a kind of blender. They'd agreed to put more zip in their punches but had a hard time with it, which wasn't unusual among fighters who worked together regularly. Sometimes Valaitas arranged sessions with boxers from other gyms, but that didn't always work, either. Against a stranger, somebody would put some thunder in a shot, his opponent would react, and next thing you knew they were throwing murder bombs. Afterward they'd be dealing with inflamed ears, busted noses, jammed thumbs—souvenirs they'd carry into an upcoming tournament. Only occasionally did Valaitas's fighters fall into cock fights with each other, although it's what many of them were used to in the rough gyms back home, where kids from enemy gyms looked them up and ringside kibitzers wagered on the outcome.

Once a session turned sloppy, it was practically impossible to ratchet it back to respectability. Finally Valaitas, holding pads for the team's only officer, a middleweight lieutenant, stormed over disgusted. "Doing nothing is better than that shit. Just hit the showers." He seemed more sorrowful than angry, which brought more shame on them.

Sitting with his spit-shined boots in his little office, Valaitas prepared yet again to chew out Cheskis. A chore in the same category as playing an Army tuba, walking the general's schnauzer, or polishing all the handles on the HMS *Pinafore*. Teaching the guys was good. All the military crap surrounding it was just that—crap. But there had been chicken shit in the copper mine, too. Chicken shit was everywhere, even when something very real resulted. He knew the mine couldn't possibly have been as pleasant as his memories of it, but it was a cloister that gave him time to think, to imagine alternate universes. What if he'd zigged instead of zagged? Had never met Toni on that bus in Seattle? Two minutes later and he'd have missed it. She sat there stunning and smart and knowing it. "I have to ask," he'd blurted out finally. "Could I buy you a cup of coffee?" Not much of a line, but the sight of her had knocked out his brain engines.

She looked him up and down, appraising him and his uniform like he was marked-down pottery. "Don't make me laugh," she said.

"Well, let's try. A priest, a rabbi, and a midget walk into a bar—"

"It's my stop," she said, getting up.

Several passengers watched them like they were a hot TV show. "It's not easy for a guy to do this in front of everybody," he forced himself to say. Suddenly she offered her hand, then hung on to his, smiling so prettily. They stepped off to laughter and applause. He knew this must be the best day of his life.

Next night she dragged him to see *La Dolce Vita*. He splurged on a taxi back to her place. The movie, he discovered, was an aphrodisiac for both of them. She'd already seen it three times. So many people in the film, she said, understood the value of dignity, but they just couldn't hang on to it because of their lust, their thirst for pleasure. "It stole their souls," she said. "They were helpless. Marcello, everybody in the film, almost."

"Anita Ekberg's not my type," he said, massaging her belly under the blanket.

"And I suppose you prefer small breasts," she said.

"If they're yours," he said.

"Come off it," she said.

"You don't want the truth?"

190

"Always tell the truth, buster. That's why I keep you around."

"I'm already nuts about you," he said.

She threw the blanket around her shoulders and went straight to her bookshelf. "Here it is," returning with *The Brothers Karamazov.* "Have you read this?"

"I'm an infantryman, for Christ's sake."

"It'll take you a while. That's okay. But I'll be quizzing you. You want to get lucky, you better pass."

"Know something? You're going too far," he said.

"Anybody can see that. I don't have any clothes on."

Marriage. Talk about dumb ideas. *Poof*, he went from being someone exotic in her life to just another inadequate provider. Next step was obvious: Dump soldier boy and get yourself a jerk like the one she had now. If the IRS ever caught on that half the time the loudmouthed silly bastard had no tape in his cash register, he wouldn't own all those New England shoe stores and the heart-stopping wife who went with them.

But Valaitas was the true fool, expecting her to live the life of a noncom's wife at Fort Benning in one of those crappy little look-alike houses with tin tricycles and government shrubbery all around. Wasn't any *Dolce Vita* around Columbus, Georgia, that's for sure. All the time he was playing infantry he knew she was sitting around on the Kmart furniture listening to one of Ingmar Bergman's ticking clocks.

It was afterward, down in the mine, when he learned he wasn't finished with the Army after all. He *was* the Army, which the Army understood all along and explained why after two years on the lam there was no jolt in Leavenworth. Relax, they said, coach boxers awhile, then engage the latest enemy. If you're alive afterward, you get your pension. Fight for capitalism, retire in a socialist bubble.

With everybody moving around all the time, a soldier's deepest connection could be the Army itself. No good keeping in touch with Army buddies. Cheskis probably never even understood they'd *been* buddies. Along came Roybal, and that was the end of Stanley and Livingston. It was almost time to roll out the Valaitas farewell system anyway: On the last day, tell everyone you have one more day tomorrow. So much smoother. No hand-shakes, awkwardness, jokey gifts. As far as he could tell, none of the guys knew about his Vietnam orders. But eventually some clerk would spread the word.

Now to deal with the showered, summoned Cheskis who stood blank-faced before him. "You know how you looked out there today?" Valaitas paused, giving him time to provide an answer that would not come. That was Cheskis's way. He knew it was time to eat dirt. But he'd eat as little as he could get away with, even though there was no one to see him do it. Once again, the kid reminded Valaitas of himself. Why, he couldn't say. When Valaitas was Cheskis's age he'd already fought his way back from the Chosin Reservoir. Been frozen and starved and bayoneted by a Chinese major. "You looked like shit. You know that, don't you?"

"I know," Cheskis said.

"You think that takes care of it? All you gotta do is agree and life's a bowl of cherries?"

"Sarge, what do you want me to say?"

"It's what you *do* that counts. No more dragging in here Mondays like you just crawled out of a train wreck. I won't send you to Carson out of shape, stepping all over your own feet. Even if you make the team, you'll end up losing to those fucking swabbies and jarheads, and I won't stand for it. You'll make a jerk out of me."

Truly, just the thought of one of his fighters losing to a Marine was revolting. The jarheads had hauled all their wounded and most of their dead out of Chosin. But his chicken shit 7th Division abandoned their dead. Some of the wounded, too, to freeze or be murdered. Valaitas killed four of their pursuers up close, slicing, shooting, and strangling them as they watched, eyes wide with terror and understanding, including the major who'd managed to get a bayonet in him first. Valaitas making squad leader three weeks off the boat, one of the last decisions Captain Coe made before getting chewed up by a grenade. He was a good kid, Coe, tried to look out for his men, who kept dying on him anyway. And that's all he was—a kid. Leaning against that ridge, legs crossed like a swami, trying to smile as the outfit trudged off through the snow, everybody hoping without much hope to get south. Valaitas never forgot watching Coe's breath in the frozen air that smelled like nothing, like clear poison. Coe, an only child. When his parents died, if they weren't dead already, no one would know he'd ever lived except for guys like Valaitas. No one would visit his grave even if he'd had one. Valaitas should get another chance, to not let his buddy die because of orders from a panicked commander somewhere up the line. That's how it always went for him. He figured out the answers after he flunked the test. Somebody said you should get another life after you wasted one figuring out how to live.

"I'm winning my fights, Sarge. I'm winning all my fights."

"Winning!" Valaitas spat out the word like it was a bug. "You shoulda knocked that kid out in San Jose. He was nothin'. Nothin'!"

"I won every round."

"You leave it to those judges, half of 'em couldn't find their ass with both hands. The rest are crooks. We've been lucky so far, but if you don't start finishing these guys off, it'll—Ah, crap, you can do it. Twist your legs into your punches. Knock 'em out, make 'em quit. I keep showing you." But Cheskis would never have a big punch. It was like red hair. You had to be born with it.

"Changing my style, I could get caught."

"So you eat a punch once in a while. You want the Army team, you gotta walk right through these guys. Understand? You're a soldier." With no preliminaries, Valaitas sprang out of his seat, tore open a locker, fumbled around, and found what he was looking for. Two pairs of beat-up training gloves, laces gone. Black gloves with the impact areas worn almost white. Wordlessly, Cheskis followed him out to the gym floor. No one left out there but the lieutenant, still working on the up-and-down bag, bobbing, weaving, punching, covered in sweat. A light-skinned young heartthrob from the ROTC program of a black college in Louisiana. Stopped what he was doing and tried to figure it out.

Two guys in their fatigues, boots and everything, with gloves at the end of their sleeves. "What's up, coach?" he said.

Valaitas gave him the best answer he could think of, which was not to answer. Cheskis caught Valaitas with a jab to the forehead just about the time Valaitas finished saying "Jab me."

"Now one-two," Valaitas said. Cheskis let loose a jab followed by a right hand. Very quick, both blocked by Valaitas's gloves. "All of a sudden your jab turned to shit. You're thinking too hard about the right. Throw 'em both like you mean it, understand? Whenever."

They circled, looking for position. Cheskis threw the one-two again. Valaitas slipped underneath and hooked to the liver. A stamping machine hook, a giant spring of a hook, all business. Cheskis blocked part of it with his elbow and came right back with another one-two, turning into the right and thumping Valaitas in the cheek. Bam, Valaitas hooked him to the ear, hard but not deadly. A souvenir. Cheskis kept his envelope, stepped left. Valaitas, coming out of his crouch, smiled. "That's the way, kid." He dropped his gloves.

"Lieutenant?" Valaitas said, "How about some ice."

"Right, coach."

Later, Valaitas asked them both over to the NCO club. And Cheskis said okay for a change. "Sorry," the lieutenant said. "Got a date."

"Use two rubbers," Valaitas said. "It's a nasty world."

The lieutenant smiled. "You got a dirty mind, coach." He wouldn't have come anyway. He knew officers in the NCO club made the sergeants uncomfortable.

At the bar, Valaitas ordered them each a shot of twelve-year-old scotch. "It's only ninety calories," he told Cheskis. "Sip it, like a gentleman."

Cheskis said he was sorry about the welt on Valaitas's cheek.

"No you're not," Valaitas grinned, then huddled closer, talked softly, as though they were fishing a lake at dawn. "Listen kid, you're tougher than you think. But you have to work. You can't come in beat to shit every Monday, skipping rope with your tongue hanging outta your mouth. Your buddy Roybal, he's shaping up better 'n you, you know that? When you two aren't waltzing, I mean."

"I caught you, though."

Valaitas had to smile. "Yeah, that was a good right hand. Would have put some guys out of there."

"Not you."

"When you're fighting just three rounds, you gotta be all business in there all the time. No matter who's in there with you. You can't afford to start bad habits."

"Okay, coach."

"Listen, I'm thinking of sending Roybal up to Carson."

"Honest?" You could see Cheskis was really pleased for his buddy. Didn't even ask about his own situation. A good kid, Cheskis.

"Yeah, but don't tell 'em yet, understand?"

"Sure."

The lying bastard. He'd tell him first chance he got.

"How many are going?"

"You have to know everything?"

"Just asking, Sarge."

"Probably four guys," Valaitas said, not naming names. Four guys getting a pass from fire and fear, from the kind of regret that's just too much for a man. Didn't somebody smart say you should never get in a land war in Asia? LBJ was smart, but it wasn't doing him any good. He might see things differently if he'd had to pull that gunner out of the Huey. It was actually only two-thirds of the gunner. The rest of him got left in the Huey. Funny part came later, when they wouldn't even give Valaitas a star for his Combat Infantry Badge. Worried some Communist spy working in a post laundry or something would spot it on his uniform and put two and two together. The whole world knew we were in Laos, but some fools in the Pentagon thought it was a secret. The same fools telling LBJ how to win the war. LBJ should spend a few minutes with the half-crazy master sergeant who greeted Valaitas's group when they filed off the plane into the Laotian furnace. These little fuckers weigh maybe ninety-five pounds, he said, but they'll jump up and kick you in the teeth, no preliminaries.

Wednesday night, sitting alone in a typically Carmel joint. Tropical décor, plants, brightly-colored fish in clear, well-tended tanks, bartender probably sitting on a master's degree, everything spotless. Not a place you'd expect to find other enlisted men. But Cheskis found it anyway. Wandered in with Roybal and a couple of babes. That's when Valaitas read it in their eyes. They knew. Not just them. Everyone. Knew he'd been a master sergeant who took a mind spill, went over the hill, finally returned with his tail wagging. If everyone knew, then everyone must be secretly pleased, which was only human, after all—acting like hyenas. Pleased to find him on his fifth drink, pleased his wife ran off with a golf-playing creep who wore a hairpiece. People had that in them, that streak of ugly. It's why they laughed at clowns getting hit with big fluffy hammers.

Valaitas caught himself looking at their girls probably too carefully. Cheskis's, with those perky little breasts, was a real babe. Didn't chew gum, talk TV, toe the line. She looked older than Cheskis. She didn't care, either. Valaitas tried not to think carnal thoughts about her. But for a while now he'd run into walls trying for the high-caliber waitresses, precision instruments that picked up on the tiniest hint of desperation or middle age. Soon he'd have to settle for the ones with resentment and crow's feet. Set 'em all up, he told the bartender, plotting yet another escape.

196

CHAPTER 20

THE HUN

"You look like a couple a queers in there," said Kenny. "Stop talking, damnit."

Without consciously trying to, they'd sunk again to a forbidden level of insufficient violence.

"We're not really sparring," Roybal said.

"We're making love," Cheskis said. "Join us." But he knew they better step it up.

Kenny would be an awful poker player. His face folded into his latest emotion at the speed of light, and now he was nervous about the Fort Carson trip, just two days away. But no one was more aware of it than Cheskis, whose breakfast was a thin slice of wheat toast dipped in a soft-boiled egg. Still, he hung around the mess hall long enough to hear the one topic on everyone's lips—the Air Cav. Fighting for its life in a place called Ia Drang, where there were human-wave attacks and hand-to-hand combat. The casualty toll was whatever rumor you heard last. Discussions were more excited than somber, like descriptions of a back-and-forth ball game, not spilled guts and burnt limbs. None of the talk managed to get Cheskis's mind off his hunger. One advantage of gym work—even sloppy gym work—was that it took his mind off food.

Bam! Bam! Suddenly Roybal changed gears, catching Cheskis with a nice right hand, left-uppercut to the body combination. Okay, give Kenny something to ease his mind. Cheskis answered with a sharp double-jab. "You think that makes up for it?" shouted Valaitas from down below. Where the hell did he come from? Hadn't seen him all day. "You just got hit by a big right hand. A piddly fucking jab won't impress the judges. You lost this round, period. I warned you about this, Cheskis. I told you.

197

This isn't patty cake. Show me something or stay behind. Either you want this or you don't."

The bell ended the three-minute round. Cheskis and Roybal touched gloves and retreated. "Yeah, sure, touch gloves, you fucking pussy sonsabitches!" Valaitas's words bounced off the walls in the hollowness of the gym. "You don't need a rest. You haven't been fighting! Keep working, goddamnit! Show me some *work.*" Other guys who'd been punching bags or shadow boxing made a point of not looking toward the ring as Cheskis and Roybal went back at it. Cheskis feinted and landed a stiff jab right behind it, a real jab, to the brown, unprotected nose.

"Don't jab just to land a jab!" Valaitas yelled. "Use it to set something up. All by itself one little jab is shit, understand? Shit! How long I been trying to teach you? Combinations!"

Roybal, nose bleeding, stepped in and threw the right hand, left-uppercut combination again. The right missed, but the uppercut, landing just below Cheskis's chest, felt like a hammer. If he weren't working his midsection every day he'd be unable to breathe. Roybal would do as he was told, and sure enough he bobbed underneath and came up with a one-two. Not a huge right, but no friendly slap, either. Cheskis instinctively threw two left hooks, one low, one high. The second one landed clean, staggering Roybal, who countered immediately with a hook of his own. Cheskis stepped right, feinted a right hook to the body, and switched his weight, coming in with a left uppercut that caught Roybal in the jaw, knocking him back as he winced in pain. His headgear had no padding under the chin. Who designed this crap? Roybal crouched lower, finding the ropes at his back. Cheskis followed, pushed his right glove out a little, holding Roybal's head in place—an illegal move—and hooked him to the head. Roybal threw one back and they traded simultaneously, looking for defensive holes. The bell sounded to begin a new round. They'd fought through the rest period, so they weren't sure what to do. They were breathing hard. Cheskis wiped sweat out of his eyes with his arm.

"Time!" Kenny called. He jumped up to the ring apron and squirted water into their mouths, one at a time.

Valaitas yelled "What the fuck you doing? Let 'em work."

It occurred to Cheskis that Valaitas had been drinking. Middle of the day. Kenny stepped down from the apron and said something to Valaitas that Cheskis couldn't hear.

The two fighters stepped inside and clinched. Valaitas started yelling specific instructions at Cheskis, acting as though Roybal were a stranger from another gym. "Plant your lead foot between his feet. That's it. Now throw up and down. It's legal. Don't let 'em live! Stay on 'em!" Cheskis couldn't see Roybal's face now. Each rested his head on the shoulder of the other as they struggled for advantage. Roybal took a quick step back and rocked Cheskis with an uppercut to his naked chin. Cheskis, clearing his head, dived back in, trying to hold Roybal's arms. Roybal pushed him away, looking for punching room. Cheskis skipped left, putting himself out of reach. He wasn't thinking about making the Army team. He thought only about winning. He worried about his stamina now, knowing Roybal's was better. Neither of them knew how many rounds lay ahead, or whether there'd be a rest period.

"Don't forget the body!" Valaitas yelled. When a trainer shouts instructions at his fighter, you'd think opponents would take advantage of the information. But they don't. Concentrating on what's going on and what they're going to do is all that computes. Cheskis jabbed, not thinking about whether it landed. He thought about speed. Speed is power. Huns move, don't hesitate. Simultaneously he stepped left and swung a half-hook, half uppercut to the body while he covered his right ear with the other glove and swiveled on the ball of his foot, leveraging his weight behind the punch. He'd made this same move many times against Roybal, who'd learned to watch for it. This time he must have been thinking ahead to his own next move because the door to his ribcage was open. Cheskis tightened his fist at the last possible moment, maximizing force, and felt the glove sink deep. Roybal exhaled, sounding like a dissonant harmonica. Anyone but a fighter or a psychopath would have cried out. He sank to his knees. "That's the way!" Valaitas shouted. As Kenny bounded into the ring, Roybal looked up, spotted

Cheskis and transformed a mask of agony into a smile, which, in the loony logic of gym war, was even more evidence of damage.

Their chests heaved as they sucked in air with a terrible desperation mixed with relief because they were done. Cheskis, knowing each breath stabbed Roybal like a spear, may have smiled back before looking away. In the locker room, no one looked at Cheskis as he worked hard to disguise his need to get away.

OCTOBER 1985

CHAPTER 21

TRANSFORMING THE MIND

After the loss to Cordoba, Cheskis sneaked out as Quick took his urine test. Minutes later he exited the parking lot. Instead of taking the freeway, he soon found himself driving south along Crenshaw Boulevard through the heart of historically black L.A., where these days an occasional *carcineria* or *panateria* marked a slow but steady influx of Mexicans and Central Americans. If Cheskis were to turn onto a side street he'd cruise past stucco bungalows with bargain window shades and bars on the windows, but also flowers out front and mostly well-kept lawns. When out-of-towners stumbled across L.A.'s slums they were puzzled by the neatness.

Cheskis barely noticed where he was and drove without purpose. His mind, as it had done so many times before, played back the split second it took to break Roybal's ribs. What had Cheskis been thinking? Time gave him no perspective. It was a fog that obscured motive. Maybe he hadn't been thinking at all, just surviving, like one of those men on the *Titanic* who put on a dress. Like his father, he had someone to watch out for, but he watched out for himself instead. Roybal wasn't expecting the Hun, who would make the team at Fort Carson and spend the next year traveling to competitions, living like a bird colonel until another lightweight who'd eventually become a pro contender bumped him off the team.

Cheskis served out his hitch, found a job on a Bay area weekly, and milked his friendship with Kesey to write a series of articles about the counterculture. He made a name for himself, earning a spot on The *New York Times*. Next thing he knew he was married to an anesthesiologist and vacationing in Paris and Venice, which was where, in 1976, he ran into a heavier Monk, his lieutenant at Fort Ord. As their wives shopped, Cheskis and

Monk drank hard liquor at an outdoor table in the sticky heat of St. Mark's Square.

Monk had made a Herculean, possibly compulsive effort to stay in touch with men he'd served with, including Cheskis, who never wrote or called back. Cheskis, waylaid by chance, now had to hear the rest.

Roybal had volunteered for jump school after his ribs healed and fought in Nam with the 101st Airborne. Near the end of his tour a new guy tripped a mine that killed the new guy and maimed Roybal, blowing off a leg, a thumb, and making a mess of his face and intestines.

"Which thumb?" Cheskis asked numbly.

"Can you believe it?" Monk said. "The one on his *other* fucking hand—the one with five fingers." Six months after getting home, Roybal slammed his car into an abutment on the Interstate. Whether it was intentional no one knew.

"Just driving down the freeway full of booze, maybe that's suicide right there," Monk speculated. What are the intentions of a drunk? And if he has any, do they count for anything? "I wish I'd been there to talk to him," Monk said. Monk had that kind of attitude. He thought you could fix anything.

Cheskis wasn't up to pretending that it was Monk whose actions or lack of them were in question. You can't babysit everyone you ever knew. But you're supposed to at least try to help your closest friends, especially after you slice them, dice them, and leave them for the buzzards. If Roybal had never met Cheskis he'd probably be living a sweet life. He had an aptitude for it. He'd have gone to Nam right out of infantry training with the rest of his unit, upsetting the whole chain of events.

"He didn't even get his name on the wall," Monk pointed out. "It wasn't a war death." That's what started Cheskis sobbing, but he was able to stop in just a little while.

It had taken not much time at all for no one to care who did or didn't go to Vietnam or why. No one cared about savvy insiders whose shrinks wrote them the right letters for the right price or about the politician Cheskis knew who'd hidden out in Divinity School. No one cared about the high school friend who spent the eve of his physical chain-smoking bare-chested in the cold to trigger an asthma attack. No one was aware of schemers who joined the Air Force in exchange for training so technical they were guaranteed to get nowhere near a battle zone, or that six out of seven Vietnam vets were actually rear-echelon motherfuckers as safely removed from Viet Cong violence as McGeorge Bundy or Jane Fonda.

Grunts with mud in their teeth were tortured by moments of cowardice, shame, or guilt while their contemporaries—perhaps vaguely disquieted, perhaps not—lined up for Stones tickets. Cheskis had written many thousands of words about protestors, breathed the same teargas and marijuana smoke, drank their wine and slept with their women. He'd watched them ditch the movement when the draft ended in '72, though the Vietnamese they cared about so passionately kept dying another three years.

Cheskis and Maggie left Venice the next day for Lake Como. Along the way, Cheskis got into a fistfight with another driver. A year later Cheskis had no wife, no *Times* job. He felt sometimes that his decisions back then were performed by a previous occupant of his being. But it was he who had to live with their consequences.

Cheskis stopped when he saw a green neon sign on a store window: "Cozy Crenshaw Lounge," with three of the letters burned out. Inside was a dark, dark joint. Just a trace of light behind the bar and a bit more from the inside of a jukebox that played Stevie Wonder on low volume. Cheskis had to stand in the door awhile to see anything at all. When he finally seated himself at the bar he could barely make out customers in the shadows. The bartender wore a gray mustache, a gray, nondescript shirt, and no expression, not even a weary one. Hints of ghostly conversations drifted across the darkness like fluttering cobwebs. Cheskis drank a quick drink and left what he hoped was a dollar tip on the bar.

Still heading south, he found a "Nude Girls" joint with no name stuck on the far side of a gravel parking lot as big as an infield. Total nudity was legal in California only if no alcohol was served. Near the airport, the joint was presumably positioned to catch widget salesmen between planes or conferencing in nearby hotels. But the clientele looked primarily local. Men, mostly young ones in small groups, drifted in and out past two security men built like buffalos. Another buffalo inside collected a ten-dollar fee from Cheskis, then tried to stamp his hand with an ultra-violet gizmo that Cheskis declined.

Inside he found a fair-sized crowd, loads of gaiety underscored with sexual tension, people trying to shout over the disco dreck spun by a wise-ass disk jockey on a raised platform. Young and sometimes not so young women, no clothes, all races and colors, cruised in heels among the tables toting colorful, little-girls' tips purses. They were alternatives to the risk of disease in an age of sexual panic. Some were startlingly pretty and possibly spent their daylight hours trying to crack studio gates. But beauty requirements here weren't absolutely rigid, judging by the occasional sagging butts and mottled complexions. The hostesses sometimes gave the impression they enjoyed the social interaction, but their mission was to get hired and tipped for a quick lap dance, to writhe above and around a male and tease him while he sat foolish, helpless, and entertained. Most of the hostesses probably had boyfriends. By what happenstance did men fall on the free side of the line while others were designated schlubs who had to lay out cash, keep their pants zipped and their hands at their sides? This was an easy place for a man to feel sorry for himself.

The events of the last few days replayed in Cheskis's mind. He even had occasional moments when he half-believed he could step back in time and play his hand differently. Each time the inevitable weight of reality had him disdaining himself all over again. It felt much too familiar.

Cheskis didn't really want one of the faux cocktails or eleven-dollar Cokes. But after awhile he was annoyed that no one tried to sell him one. Finally he noticed a short, redheaded waitress on her way over, but she was stopped by a young man at the next table. Probably Iranian, he had the kind of dark, delicate looks that made life easy, with long lashes over big, black eyes. The skimpily-clad waitress listened attentively as his drink order segued into an amusing story about the California driving test. She was skinny, with drugged eyes, bad teeth, and freckles everywhere. Cheskis shouted a Coke order. The young man looked straight at him and said something Cheskis couldn't hear above the disco. His four friends all laughed. The waitress continued to ignore Cheskis, who shouted at her again. The handsome kid pointed an angry finger as, showing off, he half-rose out of his chair. But before he could get to his feet, Cheskis got there first and hit him with two jabs to the face, then thumped him with vicious speed and precision as the companions, yelling what may or may not have been Farsi, came to life, grabbing him from all sides.

The kid crouched and tried to cover up as Cheskis slammed repeated uppercuts into his solar plexus. When he dropped his arms to protect his middle, Cheskis went back to work on the face. Bouncers with bad intentions swooped in and something knocked the wind out of Cheskis. They had all his limbs restrained now, and as they dragged him toward the door he felt someone bending back fingers on one hand. He tucked his chin as a fist with a sharp ring on it periodically slammed him in the head. With an explosive burst he wriggled an arm free and managed to grab someone's ear, twisting until he retrieved his bent fingers on the other hand. Now they were out in the parking lot. Tasting his own blood, he sat in gravel with his arms at his sides, trying to focus on his surroundings. Resisting the urge to assume the fetal position, he was paid with a couple swift kicks to the back. "Let's do this again," he pronounced with surprising clarity. This was answered with a kick to a bicep. Hurt like hell. "Forget him. He's an asshole," someone said, and suddenly he was alone.

Early next morning Cheskis threw some belongings in his back seat and drove up to Lorraine's house. The key was still under the same rock. Providing no excuse, he called the pizzeria and left a message that he'd be unable to come in and didn't know when he would. Lorraine had left some of the windows locked in a partly open position so the house didn't have that closed-in smell. The cat and dog were probably with a friend in Ventura. Someone had been watering the plants. He resisted peering into cabinets and drawers. After moving his belongings into a spare bedroom, he took another look at his face. One eye was almost completely shut and his nose was swollen and probably broken. Lots of scrapes and aches, including painful rips in his skull. His mouth and tongue were puffed and throbbing. He could barely move two swollen fingers, and much of an arm was discolored. Could be worse. And the Iranian kid would be all right. At least that's what he tried to believe.

Cheskis found the classical music station, which seemed to suit his circumstances, and played it on low volume when he wasn't watching TV, his primary occupation the first couple days. He ignored a phone message from a plant sitter asking why the key wasn't under the rock. He pulled some Buddhist books off the shelves but made little headway.

When someone whom I have helped,
Or in whom I have placed great hopes,
Mistreats me in extremely hurtful ways,
May I regard him still as my precious teacher.

One of Geshe Langri Thangpa's eight verses on transforming the mind. He found few instructions on dealing with the tides of remorse that could punish a guilty soul like the vultures eating Prometheus's innards. The credo was to behave decently from here on out and everything would take care of itself.

Each day Cheskis briefly considered putting in an appearance at the gym and each day he put it off. Mornings he drove ten miles to a newsstand in downtown Long Beach where he picked up a *New York Daily News* and looked through the sports section. Eventually he found the story he hoped not to find. Boris the Bohemian had signed a contract to fight Trinidad in Atlantic City. Cheskis knew he had to get in touch with Quick and the others, but he spent the rest of that day and the next stretched out on the sofa, trying to lose himself in the nothingness of the vaulted ceiling.

Lorraine's home would have been a perfect escape had it not reminded him she was no longer his. It became increasingly difficult to dismiss visions of her in a king-sized bed with some slick British rake. Michael Caine, Sean Connery, Cary Grant. There was no end to them. She had plenty of time on her hands and was probably hanging around some Buddhist temple full of cunning, Anglo-Saxon Casanovas with irresistible accents. People didn't end a romance and go into isolation. They went out and proved they were still attractive, even if they weren't. And Lorraine was. Damn fucking hell.

On the third day he called her office, claimed to be her sister's husband, and said his wife was in a coma. Because he knew Lorraine was in London, he sounded fairly legitimate and finally found a concerned, gay-sounding young man who took the time to find him a London lead. Moments later Cheskis was talking to Lorraine. "I've been trying to reach you," she said, sounding half relieved, half angry. "Your message machine is full. What's going on?" He told her his location but gave no reason for being there. "Why were you calling?" asked Cheskis, preferring the role of questioner to questionee.

"Because I'm weak."

Why London?

"Something back there has gone wrong," she said. "Just the feel of it, the strip malls, the ugliness. Something's twisted. They elected a bad actor president."

"Okay, so the architecture and the politics stink," Cheskis replied. "But people don't leave people they care about over that kind of crap."

"I'm in Bayswater next to the park. It's raining. Again. Maybe you could visit."

"Listen, kid, I want to see you too, but I've got serious problems here."

"What kind?"

"I turned out to be a lousy fight manager. I probably ruined Quick's career."

"You mean Marvin? What happened?"

"I got double-crossed by Philyaw because I'm stupid, and we lost a fight. It's complicated, but I screwed everything up. Now we have to start all over again."

"I don't believe it."

"What do you mean?"

"The part about Philyaw. Bogey would never double-cross anybody. He's the hero."

"It's not funny."

"Then how come you're laughing?"

"You picked a funny time to disappear," Eddie said. "If I didn't know you better, I'd think you were in on it with Philyaw and Reynolds."

"That's not what it is, Eddie."

"The other thing is, you've got our money. What were we supposed to think?"

"You hold the money if you want. I fucked up, but I didn't steal, Eddie. It's all there."

"I know mate. I'm just fucking with you."

"What about Quick? How's he taking all this?"

"You don't know? Play your messages! Quick's in jail, mate."

Details were incomplete, whatever Eddie could get from Quick, who'd gotten through to him with a couple collect calls. The jail was still processing him in, so he was denied visitors. It was a federal rap. Possession of crack with intention to sell and firearms possession—all found two years ago in a Portland apartment shared by two men—one of whom, according to the charges, was Marvin O'Brien. Evidently no one was home when the cops burst in and no one showed up to claim the booty, which left the cops feeling only half-smart and plenty angry. "He says he doesn't know what they're talking about," Eddie said.

"What do you think?"

"I don't know," Eddie said.

"But why arrest him now after two years?" asked Cheskis.

"I don't know," replied Marco Antonio Zaragoza, Quick's court-appointed attorney, who didn't seem to know much about

209

anything. He had a brown suit that smelled like petroleum residue and a toupee that looked like the corpse of a possum. After three minutes in his shabby ashtray of an office above a beauty salon in Whittier, Cheskis decided Zaragoza couldn't free a cocker spaniel from a cardboard box. His files were scraps of paper and napkins scattered around the office. Cheskis had to remove a pile of them to seat himself. Zaragoza didn't know the precise nature of the charges or the name and whereabouts of the accomplice. He didn't know whether bail could be arranged. He probably wouldn't know a Magna Carta from a Margarita. Leaving the case with him would be like sentencing Quick to the Gulag.

"From what I'm hearing, it looks like twenty thousand," said Paul Castro. His Santa Monica office was not quite as neat as he was, but it was clean and comfortable, all black and white. A few tasteful plants. He'd probably hired a decorator.

"Christ, can't I get some kind of discount?" Cheskis pleaded. "I'm a return customer."

"I'm already giving you a discount. I borrowed a mint so I could go to that fucking *conquistadora* law school they got over at UCLA. Besides which, I don't have time for this case, which means if I take it I'll see my wife and kids even less than I do now. You know the last time I got laid? Ah, forget it. What do you care?"

"Not true," Cheskis said. "Night and day I worry about your sex life."

Castro put his two hands together to form a tent, stared over it awhile, and said, "All right, I'll take off three thousand. I want two thousand by tomorrow, the rest by next week. Okay? If the case is less complicated than it sounds, it'll be less. But don't count on it."

Cheskis, relieved, knew he could pull that much out of the management kitty.

"Incidentally, where'd you get all those bruises? You still talking shit about Roberto Duran? No, forget it. I don't even

210

want to know. But grow up, for Chrissakes. This town's full of maniacs. I heard a case the other day, somebody got stabbed for sitting on a toilet too long. Not ten blocks from here. Now if you don't mind, I'd like to get to work on Marvin O'Brien."

"What are you going to do?"

"Check with the U.S. Attorney's Office. See what they got and who's got the case. Then I go over to the County Jail and see my client. Call me in the morning. No, don't call. Get over here with my two thousand at 8, no, 7:30, before I go to court."

By this time Cheskis had moved home and checked his old messages—mostly repeated entreaties from Eddie, Tommy, Valaitas, and Stu, some spare, some detailed, all growing more desperate with time. Three times Cheskis played back a brief, tantalizing recitation from a woman in Powell's office. Call him, she said. Maybe Cheskis could still make some kind of deal if only he could present Powell with an unjailed Quick. The most telling message was the one that didn't exist—from Philyaw.

"You think you're the first fella got took?" Valaitas told Cheskis. Calling his partners one by one, Cheskis realized Quick's arrest had an unintended consequence he tried not to enjoy. No one cared anymore about his disastrous role in the Cordoba fight. Had Quick kayoed his guy in round one he'd be in jail anyway.

"One thing," Valaitas said. "Don't tell anyone—I mean anyone—about the arrest."

"What's the difference?"

"Let's find out what we're dealing with, okay? Letting the world know can't possibly help us. I told everyone else the same thing—except that fucker Philyaw. He's hunkered down somewhere."

"Sorry about all this, Sarge. I thought I was letting you in on a good thing."

"It's not important."

"You think Philyaw and Reynolds were planning this all the time?"

"Maybe," Valaitas said. "All I know is they're getting a $60,000 purse for the Trinidad fight, and they got it cheap. The six thousand Philyaw put in the kitty, plus whatever he paid the judges and the split with Reynolds. Not much, considering."

Next morning Cheskis fought his way up the San Diego Freeway in rush hour to Castro's office. "This case has ugly written all over it," Castro said. "For starters the prosecutor is a little Ivy League prick who's looking to be chief justice or something. I can handle that, but this case—" According to the charges, Quick and an accomplice—both using fake identities— were selling crack all over Portland, drawing on what appeared to be an inexhaustible supply back in L.A.

"This was what? Two years ago? How can they get you for possession from two years ago?"

"It happens all the time," Castro said. "Somebody gets busted on another rap and he tosses some pals on the fire. Quick's not active in the gang anymore, so that makes it safer to rat him out."

"Eddie thinks they found Quick because of the Cordoba fight," Cheskis said.

"When was it?"

"A week ago in the La Brea."

"On local TV?"

"Yeah."

"It's not hard to imagine some FBI guy seeing Marvin O'Brien, he knows the name, goes down to the boxing commission, and bam, he's got everything." All this time it appeared boxing saved Quick. But in the end it may have destroyed him.

"What about bail?"

"I got him a bail hearing tomorrow morning," Castro said. "They're going to ask for the moon. This prosecutor acts like he brought in Al Capone."

"Is he guilty?"

"Will they convict him? That's the point," Castro said.

"Will they?"

"Probably."

"So what do we do?"

"The courthouse is a big bazaar. You make deals. You don't, they'll ship him up to Portland for trial. I'll refund most of your money and you'll have to find another lawyer up there. I can help you with that. But as they get closer to trial they have to nail down their case, take depositions, analyze physical evidence, file subpoenas. The more time and effort they put in, the worse the deal gets. Make them go to trial, they'll be looking for thirty-three years."

"Are you kidding?"

"And if they prove their case, they'll get close to that because of mandatory sentencing. Even if you draw a bleeding heart judge, you're still screwed. Also, Mr. O'Brien has a prior for possession."

"What if he makes a deal right away?"

"I can get him five years, maybe even three."

"How long would he serve? Two years?"

"There's no parole in the federal system. If they give you three years, you do three years minus maybe a few months."

"What's Quick say?"

"Won't cop to anything. He's a bright kid, but he doesn't seem to get it. Talk to him. I already set it up."

Cheskis and Eddie spent nearly two hours on folding chairs in a crowded, lime green waiting room that hadn't been swept since the hula hoop. Eddie fell in love with two or three women. "I shoulda got some phone numbers," he'd complain later. "It's perfect. Their boyfriends are all in the clink."

Eventually Quick in an orange jumpsuit was smiling at them through dirty glass and holding a phone to his ear. Cheskis had almost forgotten what a formidable-looking man he was. It wasn't natural for a tall man with those shoulders to move with such cat-like grace. Cheskis couldn't believe he'd ever been stupid enough to spar with him. Quick thanked them for hiring Castro, but showed little interest in his case. "I just want to get out and get another fight," he said. "That's all I care about."

CHAPTER 22

PHILYAW

Castro pulled out a formidable weapon at the bail hearing—Dr. Stu, who cancelled all his morning appointments and showed up in a seriously expensive suit. He was completely convincing playing the part of a community luminary and gave the impression he could get a freeway rerouted by calling a couple numbers on his Rolodex. The two prosecutors, not used to establishment figures testifying in behalf of crack dealers, were thrown off their game. But after a quick huddle, they regrouped, insisting that the judge hold Quick without bail. Failing that, they wanted it set at a cool million, implying that any lesser figure would be like handing Charles Manson a ticket to Peru.

But no matter what the prosecutors asked him, Stu found a way to portray Quick as a spiritual heir to Gandhi. Sitting at the defense table with Castro, Quick tried to look beatific in the jail's orange pajamas. Trouble was, after more than a year of hitting bags, skipping rope, running, tearing up sparring partners, hardening his washboard torso, and eliminating the last elusive fat cell, he looked like a killing machine. If the judge let his imagination run free, he might envisage Quick ripping the table in half and throwing it at the judge's exposed, balding head. Still, the judge, without comment, set bail at $50,000. Cheskis and Eddie rushed across the street to pay a bondsman ten percent and spring Quick. But after he filled out the papers and got home, Cheskis received a call from the bondsman. "They took it to another judge," he said. "Bail's an even million."

"They can do that?" Cheskis asked Castro, whom he called seconds later.

"Yeah, but they almost never do. I told you. This prosecutor's a total asshole. How'd you make out with your kid? Will he make a deal?"

214

"He's not going for it," Cheskis said.

Quick got a collect call through to Cheskis that night. He still wanted a trial. It would most likely be in Portland, Cheskis reminded him.

"That's okay, man. I'll take my chances with a public defender up there. But I'm not agreeing to no five years. I'd never get another fight."

"Sure you will."

"No, I'll be some middle-aged fucker. I'm at my peak. I feel it. I can't do time, Ches. Five years, thirty, it doesn't matter. For me, it's all a death sentence."

Philyaw, who rarely drank at home, was on his third bourbon when the cat popped in from somewhere and rubbed against his leg. He picked her up and held her close, then slowly twisted back and forth at the waist, as though trying to calm her, even though she was calm already. He felt his eyes begin to tear. "What the fuck is wrong with me?" he yelled out. His voice sounded crazy, echoing around his three-bedroom house with no one to hear it but him and the cat. He gently placed her back on the floor. Screw this, he was going out.

Moving at a determined pace, Philyaw shaved, showered, and put on the usual get-up. He slowed down to appraise himself in the full-length mirror in a bedroom that could pass for a room in a Motel 6. Un-fucking-believable. He looked more like Bogart than Bogart. Even when he was a kid the resemblance was unmistakable, and it got more so every year. He'd try new haircuts, practice alien expressions in the mirror. But the inescapable image mocked his efforts. And there was no hiding such stuff at Hollywood High, where the other kids knew all about his mom and Bogey. Even the teachers whispered about him, laughed about him. He was sure of it. No one said the name directly to his face, but it floated all around him, teasing him like flicks of a lash. He heard it everywhere but the tiny apartment he shared with his mom.

He'd beg her to move, without spelling out why, to Idaho, China, anywhere. He'd bring home library books and read her flattering passages about Tahiti, Acapulco, Mauritius. He knew she was partial to the tropics. Good jobs hang like ripe fruit in Australia, he'd exclaim. But producers, she'd reply, don't hang around Mauritius or Sydney. They dined at the Brown Derby, grabbed quick cocktails at the Polo Lounge. When they ducked into Schwab's for a milk shake she wanted them to find her this time instead of Lana Turner. She and Philyaw ate fried bologna so she could get the right cosmetics and clothes. "They're investments," she explained, "like stocks or bonds." She spent hours preparing herself, and then, while he waited up nights, she circulated, sometimes until morning.

She papered the town with her studio portraits. "Everybody says I look like Marilyn Monroe," she'd remind him, plead with him, eventually in one of her food-stained waitress outfits, when she was putting on pounds. The touched-up portraits did make her almost a dead ringer for Marilyn. Along the way he came to realize that moving to the sticks wouldn't help anyway. Things might be even worse because what else would they have to talk about out in Fuckville if they had a face like his in town? At least in Hollywood, periodic scandals took the heat off. Somebody's dad arrested for marijuana, an older sister getting kicked off a soap. Why didn't he ever invite friends over? she used to ask him. So she could bring out cookies with her boobs hanging out. Measured against what he'd been through, the problems of Quick, Cheskis, and all the rest of them didn't amount to a hill of beans in this crazy world.

Philyaw tried out different expressions for the mirror. Might have to get the trench coat cleaned one of these days. But not pressed. He opened the door to the garage and flipped the switch, but the light didn't turn on. Crap. Moving toward the car, he sensed something in the darkness. "Oh Jesus! No! Oh God, please, give me a chance. No no no no." No sound from the waiting figure in black raising the pistol, pointing it at Philyaw's chest. Blam! Philyaw sank to his knees. "I'm sorry, I'm sorry, I'm sorry." Curled up in a fetal position. Blam! This time in the temple. He felt his tears, was conscious of the odor, knew he'd moved his bowls. Noticed after some interval that he was still alive. The shooter might be standing over him. Tried to remain still, but his breath came fast, and finally he started to sob, howling a little as he waited for the third bullet. He strained to hear something, maybe a long time, maybe not. Finally reached down to feel his chest, felt the stickiness. Oh Jesus. No pain there, but he must have bitten through his lower lip. Felt his temple. Sticky. Barely moving his head, looked around. Finally sat up. No sign of anybody. Forced himself to look down. He saw better now—a yellow splotch on his chest. What the hell? "Stop whimpering!" he yelled into the darkness in a voice not his own.

Powell's receptionist put Cheskis right through. "I'd tell you how it all happened, but you wouldn't believe me," Cheskis told him.

"I got eyes. You guys were shaving points. But see, those judges in California, they're not all straight. There's bears in the woods and you're fresh meat." No mention of the arrest. He didn't know.

"I own the management contract now," Cheskis said. "There are no partners, no syndicate. For a hundred thousand he's yours. I'll give up my percentage. That's a discount for the loss on his record. You know it's a bargain. He can beat Qawi right now. Let him have that date on December third."

"What you got? Alimony? A gambling jones?"

"I'm doing what I need to do. Look, you don't want to risk Qawi against Cunningham right now? Let Quick at him. He doesn't need any tune-up, either. Quick's a dangerous weapon. If you don't sign him, he'll end up with someone else."

"When I made that offer I was bidding for an undefeated guy, not somebody with a loss against a used-up Mexican."

"Then why'd your office call me?"

"So I could say I told you so. Ain't it fun to hear?"

"I'm giving you a discount. After he beats Qawi and Cunningham no one will remember the Cordoba fight. One thing, though. Quick has the right to hire me, Eddie, anyone he wants to train him. None of that will come off your end. And Quick has to get Qawi or Cunningham December third. In writing."

"I'll let you know."

"No time for bullshit. I need the cash now. It's a fire sale."

"I might—*might* put up eighty."

"Check with me later then. He might still be available. But the numbers won't change."

Next morning Cheskis flew out to New York with a phony, post-dated contract between him and Quick to sign over to Powell's son. He waited in the lobby only a few minutes before Powell's secretary sent him into a conference room where Powell, Powell Junior, and a lawyer sat at the table. Powell was all business. No mention of Milton or Chaucer. Junior neither nodded nor spoke to him. The lawyer was a skinny, clerical-looking man with a pot belly who held the contract at arm's length as he pored over it. Cheskis read the agreement Powell put in front of him but only enough to avoid suspicion. He didn't care what it said. He'd sign anything as long as he got a cashier's check for $100,000 and Quick got on the December third card for Qawi or Cunningham. As it turned out, the contract specified his opponent as Qawi.

Cheskis barely made it back for his flight out of JFK, wondering the whole time what Powell would do when he learned he just bought a fighter looking at thirty-three years in stir. Cheskis imagined an enraged Powell lunging at him from various places inside the airport, teeth bared, goons in tow.

Back in L.A., Cheskis met the bondsman in his little dump of an office near the jail and signed the check over. The bondsman resembled an inscrutable great-uncle of Cheskis's who, it was whispered, used to hijack bootleggers along the Canadian border. Tiny black eyes, raw cheeks, Dumbo ears. He was risking nine hundred thousand to make a quick hundred thousand and he barely blinked.

Next day Cheskis, Eddie, Tommy, and Quick met at the gym before it opened. Quick, in sweat pants and T-shirt, passed around grateful hugs. He'd been rescued from a cave-in, but for how long?

Why, Eddie wondered aloud, didn't Powell know about Quick's bust by now?

"Maybe because there's no one to report it," Cheskis surmised. To a court reporter, the name Marvin O'Brien was just another on a long list of accused felons.

"Powell's going to find out, mate," Eddie said.

Cheskis knew it was preferable to inform him himself. But picking up the phone to do it would be like putting a scorpion to his ear.

Quick said, "I can't be worrying about Powell. Next six weeks I think about Qawi. Only Qawi. I'm gonna put his picture next to my bed so he's the first thing I see every morning and last thing at night."

"You do your roadwork this morning?" Eddie asked him.

"I'll suit up," Quick said, heading for his locker. This broke up the meeting, if it was in fact a meeting. They'd launched their syndicate with exactitude, but the status of everyone's obligations was no longer clear. No one, including Cheskis, even knew the size of the purse. Powell would screw them out of it anyway when he learned of Quick's legal troubles.

Cheskis considered calling Lorraine that night but found himself dialing Valaitas instead. He wasn't around, said his wife. "May I ask who's calling?" She had a lilting voice with precise, pleasing diction. Cheskis identified himself and asked when she expected him.

"Ches, I'm so glad you called. This is Natalie. I've heard so much about you. From Sam and Caddy both. You're a big deal in this household, you know. Come out and see us. Please."

"I will."

"This isn't idle chatter. Please come out and see us. But I warn you, Sam will bore the hell out of you with all his photographs. You look awfully cute in that uniform." Valaitas never snapped photos. He must have chased them down from everyone else. A sentimental sleuth. Cheskis wondered whether Natalie knew Valaitas had sacrificed his job to help him.

Valaitas, she said, had just boarded a plane for New York. "I'll have him call you when he gets back." New York? What was he doing there? She didn't know.

CHAPTER 23

THE TONIGHT SHOW

Powell took the news better than Valaitas expected. There's probably no kind of double-cross he hadn't seen—or done. "What's a Turkish honorific?"

"What?" asked a puzzled Valaitas.

"It's on the tip of my tongue."

"What is?"

"Three letters."

Oh. Powell's religion—*The New York Times* crossword puzzle. "I don't know, Ray. Listen—"

"This always happens to me. I get all the hard ones and get stumped on the gimmes." He grabbed some newspaper pages off his desk and shook them in frustration. "What kind a fiends write these things?"

"The way to get your hundred thousand back is to go ahead with the fight. The money all went to the bondsman. Let them pick up their purse so they can pay you back."

"Oh, they'll pay me, all right. But they better not count on any purse. That contract had fraud written all over it. Fraud. Talk to a lawyer."

Powell's office was warm, and Powell was in shirtsleeves. Immaculate shirtsleeves. He always looked like he was stepping out of a catalog. Valaitas took off his herringbone, thrift-shop jacket and set it on the arm of his chair. Natalie constantly combed thrift shops—grubby, dirgeful places that smelled like landfills. She brought home lamps with switches that fell off, electric fans that rattled, ready-to-rip cashmere sweaters, vacuum cleaners that worked a month or two, always expecting a pearl in the next oyster. She dressed the whole family in second-hand clothing. But he drew the line at wearing second-hand trousers, which he considered only a short step from second-hand jockey shorts.

"These pals a yours," Powell said, "they went way beyond the edge of my tolerance. Besides which, I'd have to be crazy to let O'Brien in the ring with Qawi. He can't beat him, but what if he did? He still goes in the joint, so he can't fight Cunningham. Meanwhile it puts a big turd on Qawi's record. That's the business end of it. On the personal side? This Cheskis motherfucker conned me. Now you say if I don't let him con me some more I'll get screwed worse."

"Ray, he always planned to pay you back after the fight. He was trying to help a friend, that's all. Ches can be a little stupid sometimes. But I flew all the way out here to let you know. He's an old Army buddy. He's like family."

"I don't care if he shot Ho Chi Minh in the ass. Means nothing to me." Powell addressed this to the goon as much as Valaitas. It was the first time Powell paid any attention to the goon who stood across the office between his goon chair and the American flag on a pole. The goon was a white man stuffed into his suit like a muscled potato. Probably a cop, maybe retired, definitely carrying a pistol under his jacket.

"I'm just trying to straighten this out," Valaitas said.

"And what if you can't? Straighten it out." Powell looked into Valaitas's eyes and all the way down to his liver. "Hell, I'm just blowing off steam," he added, changing direction and smiling for the first time. "I'm not even mad at the cat. It was a storm. It passed." Which was exactly what he'd say if he had retribution in mind. For the life of him, Valaitas couldn't think of one good reason Powell should put Quick in the ring with Qawi. After six hours on the plane he still came up short.

"What if I guarantee you the hundred thousand, Ray?"

Powell squinted a little and looked up at the ceiling as though it held answers. "I hear you got hold of a couple good prospects."

"They're people, Ray. I don't trade 'em around like cantaloupes."

"Ever hear a baseball? Football? What you think goes on there? Niggers on the auction block showing their teeth. You know if I want to go to a Super Bowl I gotta line up for tickets with everybody else? 'Cause those team owners, see, they're what

221

you call *sportsmen*. They look out for each other. But Ray Powell? That nigger's poison." Powell didn't use the supposedly friendly niggah appellation of rappers. He was old-fashioned. "Now listen, you said what you got to say. I need to get some work done. Someone just shot a hole in my heavyweight schedule."

Valaitas picked up his jacket. "You know, Ray, if you'd take my calls, I wouldn't have to fly all this way to talk to you."

"Had to register my displeasure. For that night in the hospital room. You remember."

"Like I said. He's an old Army buddy."

"Don't start that again."

"You do what you have to, and I'll do what I have to."

"Agreed," Powell said.

"Ray, you don't mind my asking, how'd you find out about O'Brien's legal problems?"

"I ain't sworn to secrecy. We got a call from some prosecutor in L.A. They sure hate crack-dealing niggers out there, don't they? Hate 'em worse than me. I hear the man's calling boxing writers, too."

"You got a name? The guy who called?"

"I didn't even talk to 'em. What's the difference? One cop's same as the next." The goon squinted, just for an instant. Definitely a cop.

Looking for a cab back to JFK, the only thing Valaitas knew for sure was that nothing was settled, not even whether Powell would proceed with any kind of fight card December third. If you believed him, Powell now considered the hundred thousand a trivial matter.

Just when Cheskis thought he had Grantz persuaded, he realized the putz still didn't get it. "This is a big feature story, human interest," he explained again.

"I can't write any pretty stories about a drug dealer," Grantz said. "They'd fire me."

"You just have to show them what's underneath it all. Quick threw away everything just to get his shot, and now they're taking it away from him. That's a good story. He's reformed. Works, goes to church. And they're setting him up for the penitentiary so they can give a pass to a real drug dealer somewhere."

"Who?"

"I don't know who. Who do you think gave them Quick's name? A Red Cross volunteer? Some sleazeball who got caught."

"So you're saying he's innocent."

"Grantz, I swear to God. I don't even know. I never asked him. That's not the point. The person he is now, what he's achieved, what he's willing to give up just for a shot at the title— that's your story."

"But he's not getting a title shot. Hey, I never asked you. How was Paris?"

"Paris? Fine, it was fine."

"I've never been to Paris. Can't afford it."

Cheskis had no experience with journalists like Grantz. He'd seen publicists buy reporters with flattery, introductions to celebrities, party invitations, that sort of thing. Never cold cash. But he'd never covered the boxing business, where no one seemed to pass up any opportunity to swipe a few bills off the table. And Grantz could see his urgency, which loused up Cheskis's bargaining position. So much of the boxing world crackled with urgency. By the time a fighter fought his way up to some meaningful level he was already slipping.

The nearly empty La Brea bar was cool, but looking across the booth, Cheskis saw sweat on Grantz's upper lip. His hair, skin, and the frames of his glasses were all slight variations of the same dishwater hue. Only his Hawaiian shirt had any color to it. Plus the red rubber band that held the ponytail identifying him as an adventurer.

"Let's say Quick keeps his date with Qawi because of your piece. They'll have to mention you, right? On TV? That makes you a hero."

"Not necessarily. Those TV bastards steal what they please."

"So what are you supposed to do? Stop looking for good stories?"

Grantz yelled over to the bartender for two more. Cheskis wasn't even halfway through his. That's the way it was with drunks. They wanted everyone to stay with them so they wouldn't be peculiar.

Cheskis said, "If Quick does what he says he's going to do—and I think he will—he'll stay out as long as he can just so he can fight while he can."

"But what's the point? You said yourself he'll never get two fights in before the trial. So he'll never get a shot at Cunningham anyway."

"That," Cheskis explained, "is what makes the story beautiful."

Cheskis wanted to infuse Grantz with curiosity, shoot him with a talent dart, shake him like a rat. Briefly he considered trying to chase down some reporters he used to know in New York. But he was just about out of time and they'd end up screwing him anyway. A public relations pro once told him the hardest stories to plant were the interesting ones. Appealing to *The L.A. Times* was another road to nowhere.

Eventually Grantz accepted $300 upfront to interview Quick and Eddie in the gym next day, and if his editors wouldn't use the feature, he'd get something into his Saturday column. If the fight went off, Cheskis would set him up with a room and reasonable expenses in Las Vegas for the weekend. Cheskis went to bed thinking maybe he could handle this job after all. What seemed like only moments later, the phone rang.

"Look, you're not queer, I'm not queer, see?"

"Thank you, Sarge. That's something I really needed to know. What time is it?"

"I don't know. Late," Valaitas said.

"Sarge, you're not one of those people who get drunk and call everybody at three in the morning, are you?"

"Shut up a minute. Yeah, I'm kinda drunk, but here's the thing, see, I'm older and smarter now."

"Okay," Cheskis said, followed by silence.

"We're not queer."

"You said that."

"But see, I think I resented Roybal 'cause you were closer to him, understand? 'Cause you were both young and I was—I wasn't. Maybe, I don't know, maybe that's why I wanted you to beat the hell out of each other. Can't say for sure. Half the shit we do, who knows why? But listen, Roybal? You didn't kill him, understand? I'm the—I was supposed to be a coach, to look out for my people. But you make choices sometimes. You can't look out for everybody. That's how it was in Korea, The Nam—you make choices."

Finally, "I gotta go now, okay? But thanks for calling, Sarge. Thanks."

"Okay, kid. We'll talk again."

"Carol? What kind of people name a boy Carol? They must be idiots, mate."

"Just be nice to him, Eddie. Please. It wasn't easy setting this up." Powell had told the press he was still hoping to put together a fight card for December third, so Carol Grantz's story had to land before he signed another opponent. Meanwhile, Castro called every couple of days begging Quick to change his mind and make a deal with the maniacal prosecutor. Quick and Eddie trained each day, looking for a miracle.

As it turned out, Cheskis didn't have to worry about Eddie. He charmed Grantz down to his toenails and the very next day had him training alongside all his other stray fuck-ups. Eddie, though contemptuous of humanity, loved people. To him Grantz was a fertile field that only needed the right farmer. Quick revealed just enough of himself to help Grantz's story sing, and Grantz even brought a photographer.

The story ran two days later buried in the sports section under the headline **Defendant, Focused on Title Bid, Shuns Sentencing Deal**. It wasn't as badly written as Cheskis had feared. Eddie and Quick both spoke respectfully of Powell, as Cheskis had begged them to do, and the article was accompanied by a big, compelling photo of an intense Eddie wrapping one of Quick's huge hands in gauze. Quick stared off into space as though watching a ship on the horizon.

It was no easy matter getting a copy of the article to TV wise-man Ryan Upchurch, whose network was supposed to carry the fight. Finally convincing someone at the network that he wasn't an assassin, Cheskis reached Upchurch's personal assistant and arranged to overnight the article to him. He also sent copies to every name he found listed as a sports programming executive at the network and another one to Powell. The next day Cheskis, practically broke, pleaded his way back into the pizza delivery line-up. But as soon as he walked in the door, Lucretia told him, "You gotta go see Eddie. He sounded double crazy."

Cheskis had to park two blocks from the gym because of all the TV trucks. Inside, the place swarmed with rival cameras and crews. There were beautiful TV reporters of both genders. Crews included beefy bodyguards whose principal responsibility was to protect their jumble of cables and gadgets. Holding her own next to a bewildered Quick was a former Miss America, stunning in a lime-green, silk sheath with a flirty neckline. She clung to the sleeve of Quick's sweaty T-shirt with one hand, and in the other wielded a microphone as though it was a gendarme's baton. Trying to get past her was an ex-Miss Delaware from a rival station. Miss Delaware, in her alluringly simple little black dress and pearls, was arguably even more gorgeous than the ex-Miss America, but reportedly had hit a wrong note on her saxophone in the talent competition.

Strutting unscathed through the mayhem with an unlit cigar in his teeth was Junior Powell, dressed impeccably, just like his dad. But his fly was open. Gym members tried to find space to work out, but they were inevitably defeated by all the cables snaking across the floor like tripwires. Someone tugged at Cheskis's shirt. He turned to see potbellied Grantz decked out in gym attire. "I told you the TV guys would steal the story," he yelled above the din. A bodyguard beefcake shoved past Grantz with a sneer. Grantz, willing but raw, shoved him in return, and the bodyguard twirled 360 degrees, aiming an elbow at Grantz's exposed Adam's apple. Before it arrived, little Eddie snapped a clean left hook to his jaw, and the bodyguard collapsed in a heap.

"Mate, I have to throw them out," Eddie told Cheskis. "Is that okay?" He conversed over the comatose body as though it wasn't there.

"It's your gym," Cheskis answered. "But—"

"Everybody! If you're not training, get the hell out!" Eddie yelled. He turned to Grantz. "We got to get your feet right. But you got balls, mate. You'll be there in no time."

TV people looked over at Eddie like he was one of those odd sea creatures stuck in the tank of a Chinese restaurant. Few of them had seen him deck the bodyguard, which happened in an instant. But they couldn't help noticing the body at his feet. Junior Powell reacted like someone had poured ink on his three-hundred-dollar hat. As he bounded over, Cheskis threw himself between him and Eddie.

"Junior, here's what you do," Cheskis said. "Hire a hotel ballroom. The Portofino's just a few blocks away. Get all these people to meet you there in half an hour. Tell the hotel to set up a dais. You're moderator, understand? You speak, then Eddie, then Quick. Take their questions. Then we'll make everybody available for one-on-one interviews. I'll put together a list of who's here." The idea of taking turns in front of TV cameras soothed both Junior and Eddie. The bodyguard at their feet moaned, then stirred a bit.

"How do you know all this shit?" asked Junior, impressed.

"He used to work for *The New York Times*," Eddie said.

"No shit. Can you get my dad the answers to the crossword puzzles? Before they're published, I mean."

"I'll work on it," Cheskis said.

The crews were annoyed that they had to set up all over again, but Cheskis promised them everything would be organized at the Portofino and they'd end up finishing sooner.

Tommy showed up for a workout just as everyone was leaving, so he bummed a ride to the hotel, where he pleaded with Quick, "Mention my name to Miss Delaware, will you?"

"Mention you how? Like we were together in County?"

"Come on, Quick."

"Okay, buddy. Far as she's concerned, you're the man."

"Beautiful."

Junior told the reassembled multitude what a fantastic fight everyone would see December third. The crews taped the spiel without enthusiasm. Eddie, who'd changed into a crisp blue and white athletic suit, gained their attention with just a few words. "Quick is the finest fighter I ever trained, and I've trained some great ones. If anyone can beat Qawi, it's him."

Cheskis, responding to a hotel message, picked up a house phone. "Don't let him say anything!" the voice said.

"Who's this? I can hardly hear."

"Castro. Don't let him say anything about the case."

"Have you ever sold crack cocaine?" was the first question from reporters.

"I've done a lot of things I'm not proud of," Quick replied into a bank of microphones. He was remarkably cool. "But if I talk about things I did or the things I didn't do, my lawyer's gonna kick my butt."

"Would you plead guilty and make a deal if you didn't have a fight scheduled?"

"Same answer. Sorry. Want to talk about the fight?"

"What got you into boxing?"

Quick scanned the audience, and as he paused, the murmur out there gradually subsided. "Good question," he replied. "What happened is, there was this nasty kid in the hood, I mean one big, tough-talking dude. Scary. One day he like, well, he beat me up, I admit it. And worse than that, he walked off with my sister's Barbie dolls. My sister and me, we went home crying. Next thing, my mama took me to a gym to learn how to defend myself. Time went by and finally I called out the dude. We got into it out on the playground. But eventually, him and me, we became friends. But you know to this day Leopold Qawi, he won't part with those Barbies."

Dead silence. A couple snickers, followed by giggles and finally laughter, which tipped off the TV reporters that Quick was joking, so they laughed too. After that, the room belonged to Quick. News people adore a kidder. If Hitler could deliver one-liners he'd have gotten better press.

Cheskis had planned to call Lorraine, but by the time they wrapped up the news conference, it was already past midnight in London. Instead he took a call from big daddy Powell, who was

228

on New York time. Cheskis still didn't realize what kind of legs this story had. Powell, spiritual heir to P. T. Barnum, did. "All is forgiven," he told Cheskis.

"What's the purse?"

"What the hell you care? You sold your fighter, remember?"

"Where's Quick's copy of the contract?"

"He's got one."

"His contract for the fight? No he doesn't. You have to give him a copy. Those are commission rules."

"You look up those commission rules, my friend. See if they say *when* he has to get his copy."

All his life Cheskis cited rules he'd never read. This was the first time it didn't work. Powell *had* read them. He wrote them. In this business, the negotiations never ceased, and Powell was always prepared.

"I understand somebody raised the question of your getting that hundred thousand back."

"What else did Valaitas tell you?" asked Powell.

"I'm telling you, not Valaitas; *I'm* telling you. If Junior manages, we don't owe you any hundred thousand. If he wants to tear up the contract, fine. You get the hundred thousand after the fight. But however you slice it, Quick gets $300,000 to fight Qawi. And you don't deduct any bullshit expenses."

"The deal was $150,000 to cover three fights."

"Those were minimums pending the specific contracts. So where's the first contract?"

"The single-minded pursuit of a trivial object can destroy a man," Powell said. "That's Chaucer."

"If it's so trivial, stop trying to screw us out of it," Cheskis said.

"Just 'cause you fried some Viet Cong babies don't give you no special privileges," Powell said.

"What gives you that idea?"

"Valaitas says you were war buddies."

"No, you got that wrong," Cheskis said. "I never got near Vietnam. I ran away. But the running's over. We've been getting screwed from the beginning, and it ends right here."

Next day Eddie was fielding calls from all over the world, not always patiently. In his frustration he nearly hung up on a Johnny Carson assistant who wanted Quick and Qawi to tape a *Tonight Show* tomorrow.

"Mate, it's nice to get attention, but we have to train," Eddie told Cheskis. "Qawi's in camp in North Carolina. While he's training we're fucking around with Miss Delaware."

"How'd Tommy do with Miss Delaware?"

"I don't know. He hasn't been in," Eddie said.

"Well, Qawi's got to fly in from all the way down there to go on Carson. That'll set him back. But after the show we have to get Quick out of town. Trouble is, the syndicate money's just about gone."

"And nobody's made a dime," Eddie said.

"I don't get it, Eddie. No matter how much we win, we never seem to make a profit." From time to time he recalled that he and Maggie used to have a Picasso print and a doorman.

"Don't get discouraged, mate. We'll just have to beat Qawi, and then we'll go as far as we can."

"Why don't we put Castro on Powell's ass?" Cheskis said.

"We still owe him six thousand. He can deduct it from anything he collects."

"Might work. We'll train in Vegas. I know where we can live cheap. Benny's got good security in that gym. He'll keep everybody away."

A *Tonight Show* limo picked up Quick and Eddie, and they glided off to Burbank like tycoons. Cheskis didn't go along because he was determined to get in touch with Lorraine, but all he got was her machine. Minutes before the show aired he got a call from Eddie. The show had just been taped. "Just watch it, mate. I don't want to spoil any of it for you."

Everything stayed friendly, even after Qawi made a show of presenting Quick with a skirted Barbie. Quick, nodding in appreciation, announced he'd also bought a gift, something he knew Qawi was dying to have. "Eddie," he called out. Eddie in suit

230

and tie walked out from stage left and handed Quick Barbie's boyfriend doll—blond, pretty Ken, which Quick offered to Qawi. In comedy, they say timing is everything. Thunderous laughter erupted in the audience. Hysterical Johnny pounded his desk and gasped for air. Ed leaned back and bellowed as though giving birth.

Qawi refused the doll, so Quick placed it on Johnny's desk. The cameras alternated from shots of Johnny, Ed, and their guests and close-ups of the doll. Gradually everyone became aware of the silent interaction between the two fighters. Qawi, watching Quick, was wide-eyed, as though fighting an internal eruption. Quick, meeting his gaze, showed a touch of amusement. Neither seemed aware of the cameras anymore. Johnny tried to get the mirth back on track, but he might as well have been speaking Albanian. Cheskis watched with anticipation, excitement, and dread. Johnny stopped talking. No one cut to a commercial. Someone in charge decided that whatever transpired should go out on the air.

Finally Qawi addressed Quick: "Fight time I'm going to take you down into hell. And when the flames are licking your ass, Mr. Drug Dealer, see if you feel like joking then." It wasn't just the explicit violence of the words. It was the dead-center truth behind them. If not for Quick's presumed criminality, he wouldn't be here.

Quick tilted his head as though slightly puzzled. Cheskis had never seen him afraid, and he wasn't sure if that's what he was seeing as he turned to address Johnny. "Mr. Carson, I know this is a talk show, but sometimes talk is cheap."

"I love being a fighter," Qawi said. "I get to beat people up and not go to jail for it."

That's when they cut to a commercial. At the end of the break, Quick and Qawi were nowhere to be seen. "Well folks," Johnny said, "don't let anyone tell you our conversations are scripted." The studio crowd applauded and Johnny called his next guest.

Cheskis left yet another message on Lorraine's answering machine and received a call five minutes later, but it was Castro, who'd just spoken with the prosecutor. "This fucker's not right," Castro said. "He called me at home just to tell me it's too late for a deal."

"What did you say?"

"I don't want to make it personal. It just adds to Quick's problems. Besides, when the case gets sent up to Oregon, we'll be rid of the guy. But I did ask how his making calls to Quick's promoter served justice."

"What'd he say?"

"I didn't know Yale men could swear like that. Incidentally, I watched the show. That Qawi is one scary dude. Glad *I* don't have to fight him."

Cheskis called Lorraine every twenty minutes until midnight. Unable to sleep, he tried again at 2 A.M., already mid-morning in London. No answer. His luck was running bad. What if she'd changed her mind again? Why wasn't she sleeping in her own bed?

CHAPTER 24

COMMON COLD

The Lorraine mystery cleared up the next afternoon when she rang Cheskis's bell. He was just leaving for the pizzeria. She was in summery white shorts and a simple pink blouse, longer hair, a new perfume, and perhaps a little makeup. "Damn, you look good," he said. She threw both arms around his neck and he pulled her inside. They stood inside the door making out like teenagers until Cheskis stepped back. "I gotta go," he said.

"What?"

He pulled her out to his car and explained his fiduciary pizza duties on the way over. They spoke of small matters—London weather, where she stayed, when she got back. Mostly he just absorbed her presence, hoping she felt the same. Lucretia paid her the supreme compliment of turning down the TV for the introductions. Helping Cheskis lug pies out to the car, Lorraine absently walked directly into the path of an aging hippie on a bicycle even though he frantically rang his little ringer. He screeched his brakes and his rear tire skidded into a parked car. Nothing but apologies from both of them. If you're going to get into an accident, Cheskis decided, get into one with a hippie or a Buddhist.

After racing through the deliveries like an ambulance driver, Cheskis whisked her back to his place. "I didn't make any big decisions over there," she said, stepping out of her panties. "But crossing an ocean didn't help at all. I still missed you every day."

"I missed you every day all day," he said, sliding into bed.

An hour later he returned to the pizzeria while she stayed at his place and put together a tuna casserole. Lucretia immediately kicked him back out the door. She'd called her brother to take the rest of his shift. "Don't screw up," she said. "You don't want to lose that one."

Lorraine paid no attention to sports stories and knew nothing about Quick's arrest or his upcoming fight. Throughout her absence, Cheskis had resisted the urge to point out to her that if Quick, his only fighter, went to prison, her objections to his role in the fight business would be a moot point.

As Las Vegas muscled more big fights away from New York and L.A., Benny Diamond's gym a couple miles east of the Strip had grown in importance. It was deep inside a sandy horizontal wasteland sprinkled with pawnshops, junkyards, fast-fooderies, and gas stations. Stubborn sage and detritus from moving vehicles studded the sandy earth. With no actual humans to be seen, the neighborhood could pass for a lost civilization whose builders had moved on or perhaps been murdered by the vehicles that now controlled the streets. Pulling up to the door with luggage in his trunk, Cheskis opened the car door to a fierce wave of heat. Inside, the gym was in good repair, much bigger than Eddie's, with two standard-sized rings. Benny always hired a fighter to watch the door and keep out kibitzers. If you didn't have business inside, you didn't get three feet. A prominent yellow sign with black lettering informed everybody not to spit on the floor, smoke, litter, or get behind in their dues. "Do Not Talk to Another Trainer's or Manager's Fighter!" was its final decree.

Quick was suited up in the corner of a ring in his headgear, gloves, and foul protector. Valaitas spoke to him as a sparring opponent in the opposite corner conferred with Caddy. Eddie was nowhere around. Both fighters were soaked in sweat. When the bell rang to resume their session, they circled and traded, each man trying to startle the other. Lots of feints. The other guy had skills—good balance, fast hands, and he anticipated well. But Quick's combinations were crisp, and he moved his head out of trouble.

"Keep moving your feet!" Valaitas yelled up to him. "Smaller steps!"

Cheskis went over to Caddington, who turned, smiled, and said. "Stanley, I remember you." His voice sounded like it came out of a blender running at half-speed.

"I remember you too, Caddy."

"Don't fall for that!" Caddy yelled to his fighter. "Double jab him! That's it!"

Benny sat behind the counter installing a new bladder inside a speed bag. "Where's Eddie? What's going on?" Cheskis asked him.

"That's no way to say hello. Ask me about my health."

"How's your health?"

"I piss every half hour. Haven't had a good hard-on since the Carter administration. Can I go on?"

"No. Where's Eddie?"

"He asked Valaitas to take over."

"Why?"

"I'm not sure. He's a temperamental guy, Eddie, but lots a trainers are like that. Like prom queens."

"Was he pissed off?"

"Hard to say."

Valaitas and Quick weren't sure what had transpired either. Eddie had walked out an hour earlier. Cheskis waited for Quick to finish his workout and the two of them set off for Valaitas's house. Quick and Eddie had been staying there nearly a month. Cheskis hated staying in other people's homes, but the Valaitases had insisted.

The sparring partner, Quick said, was an amateur Valaitas would turn pro by the end of the year. All the commissions forbade amateurs and pros from sparring together, but there were no inspectors in the gyms. "Valaitas has a bunch of good fighters," Quick said. "I spar with his middleweight, too. A tricky dude. You'll be hearing about him."

"You looked good in there. Really good."

"Don't tell me that, man. I'll get lazy."

"But you're not throwing enough combinations."

"That's what I want to hear."

With the fight scheduled in only two weeks, Quick's manager of record and the terms remained a mystery. When Castro protested to the commission, they just laughed at him. After the fight Powell would count all the nickels and figure out the optimum strategy to maximize his profit and minimize theirs. By now Quick was also concerned. He wanted to make enough to help out his aunt. His worrying about it could only help Qawi, which was no doubt part of Powell's plan.

"Don't try fooling yourself," Cheskis told Quick.

"What do you mean?"

"You're thinking maybe you can somehow win a big purse, beat the rap, and live happily ever after. It's not going to work that way. You knew it going in."

Valaitas lived not far from Wayne Newton in a two-story home with rooms all over the place. Two giggly little kids and a big dog with a giant wet tongue greeted them at the door, Natalie not far behind. She was on the short side, barefoot, and twenty pounds overweight, with a look in her eyes that said she knew your faults and didn't care.

Eddie showed up a little later and casually announced he was going back to L.A. for awhile. Quick looked thunderstruck. "What's this all about, Eddie?"

"I told Valaitas just now. I want him to take over while I go back and look after the gym."

"You're coming right back?" asked Quick, confused.

"Don't worry, mate. I'll be in the corner."

"I can't beat him without you, Eddie," Quick said.

"See what he can teach you. It's better this way, mate."

"Eddie, you don't have to go," Cheskis said. "If you want Valaitas to help, just let him work with you."

"It wouldn't work. Believe me, mate. This is best."

Eddie, a fine trainer, recognized a virtuoso, which is what Valaitas had become. He spotted little vulnerabilities in opponents no one else saw. More important, he spotted them in his own fighters and fixed them. In Qawi's corner would be Hall of Famer Davey Campbell, who'd trained dozens of world champions all the way back to Marciano. But the prospect of Eddie's absence struck like a malevolent wind. He was a spiritual compound of belief and hope, expectation and possibilities. Without him the future looked unknowable and more frightening.

"What about my vitamins?" Quick said, pleading.

"You're the one that reminds me, mate. You can handle the vitamins."

"But we'll lose," Quick pleaded. Eddie wouldn't budge. He wanted his fighter to learn from Valaitas, but his ego wouldn't let him watch.

Quick knew of trainers who didn't trust fighters with the truth. They told nervous ones they were ahead and lazy ones they were behind. "Don't ever bullshit me in the corner," he told Valaitas. "Or in the gym either."

"That goes both ways," Valaitas replied.

"He's quicker, isn't he?"

"Yeah, but not on every punch. No one throws everything at the same speed. So what I want from you is intensity. I know you're dedicated, but I'm talking about absolute concentration. What we're going to do is kill his confidence. He fights so sweet, he's never known real adversity in there. He beats everyone to the punch, and eventually they either back up, which is like serving him lemon pie, or they come to him, which is maybe worse. You've got the conditioning to circle him all night. Both directions. He'll get tired following you around. Meanwhile, you stay in your envelope. When he gets close, hurt him. Never throw just one. A combination, then move. Got it?"

"Yeah."

"Another thing. He thinks he owns the inside. We have to show him different, make it a torture pit. Outside, we'll take away his jab."

"How you do that?"

"Always counter it. Always. Lots of double jabs. If you can't make him pay, make him think, see? I can't tell you how important that is."

"Other guys tried that, Sam. I watched the tapes."

"The other guys weren't you. You got confidence in me, Quick?"

"Yeah."

"But you want Eddie here too, right?"

"Yeah."

"Quit whining."

Quick knew he'd been right to take this fight. But he loved fighting so much he was already mourning for it, and that's something he hadn't counted on. He loved running in the morning, he loved taping his hands and the feel of the gloves around his fists, the feel of a gym around him. Any gym. Inside the ring, he loved it when some other part of him took over while he just watched. A lot of the training felt that way, like he was cheating because a hidden somebody did all his work. Even though he hated it when a man caught him asleep, he also thrilled to survive those shots, to master all that power and talent conspiring against him. Because of his opponents, he was more alive than he ever suspected possible. No one was closer to his heart than another man enduring the same pain, mingling his sweat and blood with Quick's while they searched for God, to determine His will. And if another fighter killed him, what better way to die? He thanked God every day for allowing him the sweetness of these days, for making Marvin understand he had to make way for Quick.

He even forgave the officials who'd robbed him. He forgave Ches for talking him into holding back that night because Ches was God's instrument, his bridge to Eddie and Tommy and everyone else who helped him escape the darkness. The Lord brought them together and told Quick he must save Ches so Ches could save him. The Lord made them kings with full hearts. He prayed for Ray Powell, too, and that prick of a prosecutor, prayed they'd find Jesus.

"Jesus, kid, have you heard anything I said? Where the hell's your mind?"

"Sorry, Sam. Won't happen again."

Valaitas showed him plenty that day, and the next and the next. Caddy was a big help too. He seemed to know every one of Valaitas's tricks. It was everything else that Caddy forgot.

Valaitas showed Quick how to hide his chin behind his shoulder as he threw the right. He'd been forgetting that. "And stay off those ropes. I don't care what happens. You feel the ropes, turn him, grab him. He boxes beautifully, so don't let him. He likes to hit after the bell. It pumps him up. He does it maybe twice, no more, so he won't lose a point. So don't drop your hands when you hear the bell, and when he goes for it, you counter with something harder. He hits you again? You hit him again. Don't let this guy breathe, understand?"

Little by little Valaitas let Quick know that Qawi wasn't just quicker. He hit harder, too. "Now at some point he's gonna throw that monster right hand. But you're going to watch his shoulder and sense it. Slip it if you can. But even if you can't, let your hook go, maybe over his right, maybe under. Wherever the door's open. Get there first and his won't land. You'll murder him with that hook of yours, and follow with the right. Think speed, not power, but twist into it. And don't be trying to knock him out. Just fight. Your body will tell you when it's time to commit."

When her employer refused to extend her leave of absence Lorraine had quit. But she received two job offers shortly after deplaning from London. She accepted the one that allowed her to delay her start date. A few days before the fight she flew into Las Vegas. By then Eddie had shown up with Tommy and Stu. They took a couple rooms at Caesars Palace but spent much of their time at Valaitas's. Quick's workouts were over, but he still did light roadwork. The morning of the last press conference Cheskis dropped Lorraine off at the Valaitas house before running a couple errands. When he got back he found Natalie, Eddie, Caddy, and Quick meditating with Lorraine on the living room floor. Later Natalie told him to call back Gary Goldberg. "His number's next to the phone."

First Goldberg congratulated Cheskis.

"What'd I do?"

"You got so much damn publicity I had to postpone my show, is what you did."

Cheskis apologized.

"Listen, that's the game we play, and you played it well. A manager's got to get the right fights, but none of it means anything if no one watches. Getting all this sympathy for a crack dealer—it was just beautiful."

"Everybody who invested with me lost their money."

"The game's not over yet. Besides, everybody gets fucked by Powell. I've been fucked by Powell, and not just once. When a guy's out to swindle you from the get-go, and he's smart as Powell, hey, he swindles you. Once in a while, anyway. Look, the reason I called—I won't be at the fight, but I'd like you to stop by my office. You know I'm right here in town."

"I think someone's offering me a job," Cheskis told Lorraine.

"Don't be so surprised. Who's this Goldberg?"

"He doesn't get sued by fighters all the time, the way Powell does. That's a good sign. But the job's probably here in Vegas."

"So what do you think?" She tried to hide her concern, but duplicity was foreign to Lorraine's nature.

"It's probably not right to discuss this stuff with this jail thing hanging over us."

"Marvin wouldn't care. He thinks you were sent by God. Don't you ever talk to him?"

"Of course," Cheskis said.

"I mean *talk*. Men don't talk. Anyway, let's just say he appreciates you," she said.

"I appreciate him."

"Then tell him."

"Okay."

"Promise."

"Promise," he said.

"So, think you'll take Goldberg's job?"

"I'm not moving to Vegas. I wouldn't do that to you. You were already down on America. This town would make it worse. Buddha wouldn't make it here. He'd end up sitting at a slot machine smoking Luckies."

"Bullshit. Besides, who said I'd be with you?"

"Me." He took her in his arms.

"I won't live in your nasty little garage."

"I won't live in your stupid mansion on the hill."

"That's okay. I've got some rental property near the beach. It's small enough so you won't be embarrassed."

"I was thinking about maybe getting off the beach, moving up to the West Side. It's more like a real city. Hey, you never mentioned property on the beach. What else're you hiding?"

"Money's not important enough to hide," she said. "I'll think about the West Side. You're going to take that offer from Sam? Manage his fighters?"

"I don't know, probably. I can do it from L.A. How'd you know about that?"

"He tells Natalie everything."

"Your disciple."

She threw a bunny punch at his arm.

"I might help manage Eddie's fighters, too, when he gets some. If I can handle it. It's no good to have too many."

"Everybody wants you, don't they?"

"When I manage, they go broke slower. How come you don't hate boxing anymore?"

"Because there's so much love in it," she said. "But you do know it's insane, don't you?"

"I know," said Cheskis.

Press conferences were an anachronism left over from the days when reporters wore ties and hats and boxing was the Number Two sport behind baseball. Now most of the media people who showed up were from tiny radio stations and throwaway boxing newsletters with barely a pulse. They'd already cleaned out the buffet, and perhaps forty or fifty people milled around waiting for something to happen. Out on the street it was 108 degrees Fahrenheit. The ballroom felt like 67. Qawi showed up twenty minutes late accompanied by an entourage that included his trainer Davey Campbell; his manager, a Harvard law grad who used to promote rock concerts; a physical trainer; and several individuals with vague or indefinable duties that included keeping the fighter amused.

241

The key figures from both camps sat on the dais. Cheskis had planned to sit in the audience, but Quick and Eddie insisted he join them on stage. The revered little Campbell, speaking slowly and precisely, pronounced Quick an excellent prizefighter. "But without that amateur background, he lacks some skills. He's a nice young man and I wish him well, but he's going to have his hands full with Leopold."

"Qawi is a great fighter," Eddie said. "But he won't make it to the closing bell."

A reporter asked Eddie if he was still the trainer. "I hear Sam Valaitas has taken over."

"I'll answer that!" Valaitas yelled from the audience. "It's bullshit. I've been helping Eddie with physical training, but he's the fight trainer. Always was."

Cheskis took the microphone for one sentence: "Eddie runs the camp, and he runs the corner."

Qawi thanked God and Powell for this opportunity, but not in that order. He advised Quick "to run like pantyhose"—a quote snapped up by the reporters.

Said Quick: "I told Leopold a while ago that talk is cheap, so I don't want to make any predictions. Just that I'm well pre-pared, and I know he is too, like always. I'd also like to say a few words about Mr. Powell. I'm very grateful to him for putting all this together. He's a great promoter. But we want to get paid when this is over and we don't know how much is in the purse. We've never seen a contract."

"That is absolutely untrue!" Powell thundered from a dis-tance of eight feet. He looked like he'd just been injected with crazy anger juice.

When a reporter asked Quick about the court case, he replied, "To tell you the truth, I don't even think about it. But the way Mr. Powell here runs his business, we could wind up playing pinochle in the joint together. If we do, I can tell you right now, we won't be using his deck."

Powell stepped up to the microphone. He'd already under-gone a mood makeover. "Let 'em blame me," he said sadly. "The Johnstown Flood, World War II, the Lindbergh kidnapping, they all blame me."

Later the network's Ryan Upchurch pulled Cheskis into a corner and promised if there were no answers on the contract by fight night he'd drag Powell over the coals on camera. "You should also know we have a clip of the prosecutor. I don't know if we'll use it," he said, "but we were afraid if we didn't put a camera on him he'd try to perform lewd acts on us."

"He's full of shit," Cheskis said.

"And you and me aren't?"

"Well, this is boxing," Cheskis said.

"Quick seems like an awfully nice kid," Upchurch said. "Is that genuine? I won't quote you."

"He's probably a lot nicer than both of us. Me for sure."

"You know, I remember you from *The Times*," Upchurch said. "Someday you'll have to tell me how you got from there to here."

"Didn't take any planning. I remember you too," Cheskis lied.

"We were both pompous sonsabitches, weren't we? Don't say it. I still am and I know it. Try to work around it."

Next day Quick woke with a sore throat and a bronchial infection that made his breathing sound like a babbling brook. While everyone else ran around Valaitas's house like they had a date with the executioner, Eddie had Quick stand under a hot shower for several minutes. He passed him several layers of sweat clothes, called him into the kitchen, and handed him a tall glass of steaming reddish brown liquid with lemon slices.

"Man, this is hot," Quick said without enthusiasm. "What is it?"

"It's good. Drink it fast."

"What was that?" Quick said afterward.

"Red wine, honey, brandy, cloves, and lemon slices."

"It wasn't bad."

"Sweat," Eddie told him.

"Huh?"

"Sweat. I want you to sweat out your cold, just like you're doing. Stay bundled up. Watch TV for awhile, then go to bed."

Next morning, Quick said he felt pretty good.

243

CHAPTER 25

QUICK O'BRIEN

What's that they're playing? James Brown? Quick would have preferred Miles or Coltrane, but Caddy and Cheskis had pleaded with him. Okay, cool. Ches looked like a coach down forty points. Worried about money, too. They'd all put down serious cash on those 3-1 odds. And somebody'd been calling Ches's hotel room, leaving strange messages late at night. But Quick wasn't supposed to know. Lately they treated him like he was pregnant. Eddie taped his hands like always, but it felt different, even though he tried not to feel different. Big fight, big casino, big TV. And probably the last fight, too. *No, don't go down that road.*

Caddy led the prayer, talking to God in his mumbly, damaged, heart-breaking voice. "Lord, give strength to Your servant Quick," he said. "Let him hurt this guy just enough." Hard not to laugh at that. "Forgive us all for our imperfections and help us tonight. Help us all. Amen."

"There's a lot more people I could name," Quick added, "but if the Lord would give a hand to Felix Oliveira, pull him up into His light and His mercy, we'd sure appreciate it."

"Amen," Eddie said.

Valaitas stepped close and grabbed Quick's upper arms with both hands. "Listen, he's all alone in there with a fucking monster, you understand? You're a monster with no pity and there's no one to help him. That's what your face shows him."

"There *is* no one to help him," Cheskis said.

"No pity," Caddy said.

"No pity," Quick repeated.

They raised their index fingers in a Number One signal. Caddy tapped him on the gloves. "Stanley," he said, "rearrange the man."

Stanley? Did he just call me Stanley?

Cheskis: "Tomorrow you can go to church. Tonight you're the prince of fucking darkness." Then Eddie gave him the hug, and they went trooping out, Benny carrying the bucket, Tommy looking so innocent. That little reporter, Grantz, so proud to tag along. Up in the ring everything felt like a dream, moving fast. *Awful lot of people in those seats.*

"Forget the judges," Eddie said. "They belong to Powell. This guy's gonna go. I promise." Eddie kissed him on the cheek, and there was no more ducking it. It wasn't his night. He didn't feel it. One of those times it wasn't there, the spirit. When they touched gloves, even though he hadn't planned to go along with it, he *did* look at Qawi as though there were no help for him. Because if God wouldn't help, he'd ask the devil. The purse, the penitentiary, he didn't care about any of that. Everything that mattered was here in this ring. *Go ahead and abandon me. I'm still going to fuck this guy up.*

But he shuffled around flat-footed, clumsy, had a tough time seeing the punches. Qawi's jab came from some hidden place, was so hard to counter. But finally he remembered to feint, and it worked, followed with a hook to the body. Sank in like a pickaxe. That had to hurt. *This ain't over yet, motherfucker.* Heard the ten-second bell and jumped forward like a damn amateur. And a bus rolled over him. Felt it everywhere, even in his toes. Sitting on the canvas while Qawi strolled away, another day in his office. *Get up fast.* Referee counting, looking like his head would pop. These guys get excited too.

"You okay?"

"Never better."

"Look at me. Step forward." Referee wiping his gloves, but the bell must have rung. Back in the corner, it's Eddie's face. Valaitas, Benny, Tommy all leaning in. Benny gave him water. "How you feel?" Valaitas said, talking gentle, like nothing much going on at all.

"A lot better now. I think I'm seeing him better."

"Keep your hands up," Eddie said.

But that jab was hard to deal with. And inside he was getting smacked everywhere. Guy's so good, but maybe a little too good,

245

too cocky. Everybody's got to be open sometime. Stepping back, landed a right that maybe changed this fucker's mind a little. But damn it, there's that big bus, came through again. Both knees on the canvas. Referee counting. Up. Gloves wiped again and stayed back, trying to focus.

Back in the corner. "What round is it?"

"Seventh round coming up," Eddie said.

Valaitas: "He's getting away with murder on the inside."

Benny: "Powell owns this ref."

Valaitas: "Give him some back. Lean your head in, and hit low. You have to slow this guy down. But watch for the uppercut."

Out there again, it felt better, but at a distance, not inside, like Valaitas wanted it. Stepping left, stepping right, pumping out jabs and hooks. And for just a little while, he felt like he was watching himself again, like it's supposed to be, but it didn't last, and now he had to think about everything first. *It's okay, Jesus. I love You if I die right now. Love this man in front of me, too.* And caught him with a hook just before the bell. *But he's tough as nails this guy.* Who now stuck out both gloves, friendly. Quick gladly touched them with his own. *He feels it, too, the love.*

Eleventh round. *His eye's a mess. Musta been that right hand, the one that put him down. But he's not falling for it anymore. Not this man. Got to be like Miles, like Monk and Mingus. Improvise. Do the unexpected. Be the invisible man.*

Qawi didn't bet it all on the right hand, the way Valaitas figured. It was a left hook. Cheskis saw it come out of nowhere, a rocket. But Quick sensed it and came underneath with an uppercut, swinging his legs into it—he had to pack his whole life into this punch—and in that frozen, wondrously terrifying moment, Cheskis knew Quick was outside himself, watching, maybe even dreaming he'd stay free long enough to give Qawi another chance on another night as Cheskis marveled at all the brave possibilities a man can squeeze into this tainted, magnificent life.

04161	DATE		